I0689676

Changeling Press. LLC

ChangelingPress.com

Plain Brown Wrapper (*C.H.A.S.E.*)
Deep Cover - in a Human Trafficking Ring
Shelby Morgen

Plain Brown Wrapper (*C.H.A.S.E.*)
Deep Cover - in a Human Trafficking Ring
Shelby Morgen

ISBN: 978-1-60521-940-0

Publisher:
Changeling Press LLC
315 N. Centre St.
Martinsburg, WV 25404
ChangelingPress.com

Printed in the U.S.A.

Editor: Maryam Salim
Cover Artist: Bryan Keller

The individual stories in this anthology have been previously released in E-Book format.

Table of Contents

Dedication

In remembrance of the 4th AFDS and the men who tried to change history one night in a small bar somewhere in the Southeast Asia... and for my father, who never forgot.

Although this is a fictional story, debt bondage and slavery around the world are still all too real.

All I Want For Christmas (*C.H.A.S.E.* 1)
Deep Cover - in a Human Trafficking Ring
Shelby Morgen

The wrong place.
Candy Nelson has wandered into a nightmare -- a slave auction in Southeast Asia.

The wrong time.
Things like this don't happen -- not in the twenty-first century.

One wrong move could get her killed.
One woman. Alone. She isn't supposed to be here. She needs to get out. Now.

But from across the room, a man raises his head, and his eyes meet hers. And Candy knows she'll do whatever it takes buy this stranger his freedom.

Though setting him free is the farthest thought from her mind...

2:45 PM Friday, 17 December 2004
A Dilapidated Warehouse
Somewhere In Malaysia

The gavel hung in midair while the auctioneer waited. Nothing. At last the German turned away, his nostrils flaring in anger as he shook his head.

"Sold!" The gavel banged on the rickety wooden podium, echoing through the room. All other sound ceased. "To the lady in the white suit."

Candy finally remembered to breathe. The auction workers brought her purchase to her, and Candy handed over a stack of American dollars.

Now what?

She turned to face the incredible hunk standing before her.

Good Lord. What had she done?

1:15 PM Friday, 17 December 2004
Singapore Changi Airport

Candy ran for the cab pulling up in the loading area, but before she could flag the driver down, he was gone. "I hate Christmas!"

She dropped the handle of her rather unwieldy luggage cart. Predictably, it collapsed, raining suitcases across the sidewalk. She jammed the toe of her black leather pump into the nearest bag. Ouch. Shit. That was stupid.

Lord, she was tired. Airport security was so tight now it had taken her over an hour to get through customs.

She was going to be late.

Candy hated being late.

Goddamnit. She watched yet another taxi drive away. *I shouldn't even be here.* Any of the junior attorneys could have handled the job, but not even an all-expense-paid trip to Singapore could get anyone else to take an out-of-the-country assignment over the holidays.

Well, she would have been just as alone back in New York. No matter how you looked at it, the holidays sucked.

It wasn't just Christmas. Her birthday fell on December 25th. The worst part was her parents had wanted a Christmas baby. But now they were gone, and there was no one around who would even remember it was her birthday, let alone go out of their way to make the day special for her.

Time, as Richard would say, to move on.

Asshole.

The thought of Richard gave her enough energy to pick up her suitcases and search for a cab.

Funny how *Richard* and *asshole* just naturally went together.

She'd bet a hundred dollars it was Richard-the-Asshole who'd screwed with her flight schedule. She should have landed last night, just before midnight. Instead she'd ended up on the later flight with a plane change at LAX. Twenty-nine nerve-wracking hours after taking off from BWI she was finally in Singapore. It wasn't even about the money, though he'd probably saved a grand on the tickets. No, it was about keeping her under his thumb.

Screw you, you sanctimonious bastard. I will not miss this auction, damn you.

A cab pulled up to disgorge a touristy looking couple overburdened with packages. "Taxi!" Candy screamed. Jerking hard on the handle of her luggage cart, she raced for the cab, waving madly at the driver. "Taxi!"

This driver actually came around to help her with her bags. Maybe her luck was changing. While the driver piled her luggage into the trunk, Candy poured herself into the back of the cab, ready to pass out. She'd dressed for winter in New York, not the warmth of Singapore. "The Mandarin Oriental, please."

"*Shiok, lah?*"

He didn't speak English? Well, that was just great. *Lah* she was pretty sure meant *yes* in Malay, but *shiok* she didn't have a clue about. She held out her confirmation email and pointed to the address.

"*Lah,*" the driver agreed. At least she hoped he was agreeing to take her to the hotel. He wasn't her idea of a hot date. Once he got started, he chattered non-stop, waving his hand at various buildings as they wound their way across town. *Blah, blah, blah, blah…*

Candy closed her eyes and drew in a deep

breath. The light breeze brought the smell of the ocean in with it. The Mandarin Oriental, Singapore, sat right on the bay. She'd have breakfast tomorrow on her balcony, overlooking the Keppel Harbour, in an opulent and exclusive hotel, newly remodeled.

The Mandarin Oriental was one of the few luxuries she permitted herself. After all, it was… appropriate. It fit the corporate image. The concierge knew her by name. There would be stationery in the drawer with her name printed on it. Room service would have a double espresso sent up precisely at 7:00 AM, with the *New York Times*, delivered in English.

All that luxury came with a price, and Richard-the-Asshole was picking up the tab. She reminded herself to order room service more often. Would serve him right if *she'd* brought along an "assistant" and charged the entire trip for two off to her expense account.

She would have, too, if she had an *assistant*. But that was his department. Bastard.

The driver pulled to a stop in front of the Mandarin Oriental. Candy gave him a twenty-dollar tip to wait while she checked in. She'd put that on her expense account too. It was Richard's fault she was late.

This was *her* time now. Visions of crisp silk and aging bisque brought a smile to her lips. She didn't bother to follow her bags up to the suite. They'd be unpacked by the time she returned. If the driver hauled ass and it wasn't too far away she could still make the most important part of the auction -- a dozen late 1800's vintage *Bru Bebes*, all from the same collection, all pristine, with their original boxes. Too bad she couldn't afford all of them, but even she didn't have that kind of money. At least not on her, in cash.

Unless they went very, very reasonably, she'd be doing well to manage one…

The cabdriver shook his head adamantly when she showed him the Web page she'd printed out. "*Sotong!* No woman! No go! *Terok! Ulu, kayu, lah*?"

No woman? What the hell did that mean? The auction had started over twenty minutes ago. She didn't have time for this. She waved the printouts at him. "Auction," she explained. She pointed to the picture of a little girl holding an antique china doll. "Auction. Antique auction. This address."

The man shook his head. "No go. *Terok, ulu*. No woman. No go."

Sweat trickled down her shoulders in an irritating and unbecoming fashion. Candy searched her phrase book impatiently. "*Auction*," she attempted in Malay. Assuming he spoke Malay. "Where I come from women go to auctions all the time. Alone." She tapped the face of her watch. "I'm late." She held out two more Singapore twenties.

Finally the man snatched the money from her hands, still muttering in a curious mix of Malaysian and broken English as he turned the key in the ignition. Candy smiled smugly as the cab lurched forward with a cough and a sputter.

After all, it was Brasden-Marten's expense account. She was here on company business. The American fifties stowed in her purse were her own, to be spent however she wished, and he couldn't say a thing. Not anymore. Her "ridiculous hobby" was an asset he despised too much to even bother to get appraised.

Moron.

She tried to focus on the joy of the hunt, the impending victory. Maybe if she closed her eyes, just

for a moment while the cab took her across town...
Maybe a tiny, short little power nap and she'd regain
her equilibrium. Maybe...

2:15 PM Friday, 17 December 2004
Chinatown

A dreadful lurch brought Candy back to consciousness. The driver must have hit a pothole. Candy looked around in bewilderment. Gone was the dense mass of glittering high-rise hotels and office buildings. They appeared to be in Chinatown. Which Chinatown she couldn't be sure. This certainly wasn't the modern, beautiful Singapore she knew.

Gaudy red painted dragons adorned the rundown buildings, flashing fierce teeth at her. Glittering gold leaf signs adorned the fronts of tawdry little shops. Street venders waved their products at the windows as the ancient cab crept down the narrow streets. The smells of food steaming in bamboo containers mixed with other, less pleasant smells to give the place an air of the disreputable.

This couldn't be Singapore. Singapore was always spotlessly clean. There were well enforced ordinances against this kind of -- litter.

Wherever they were, she didn't belong here. Candy gripped the edge of the seat, her purse trapped tightly to her side. "*No woman!*" the cabdriver had tried to warn her.

She should have listened. She never listened. Wasn't that one of the things Richard was always bitching about? What was she doing here? Where the hell was here? Candy fingered the rat-tailed comb she always carried in her purse for protection. It wasn't much of a weapon, but airport security never noticed the hard plastic handle ended in a sharp point.

The driver pulled up behind a long, low hovel of a warehouse, chattering away. She didn't need to speak Malay to know he expected her to follow him, and apparently stay close to his side. That wasn't a problem.

She could do this. She'd flown halfway around the world, primarily to go to this auction. She wasn't going to be held at bay by a rundown old building.

It wasn't as if she were here alone. There were several limousines parked behind the building, a few Mercedes, and even a couple of small vans. By the look of the license plates it would seem this auction had drawn diplomats from around the world.

Surely with that kind of clientele the auction house could have found a building more suitable than a seedy deathtrap in the slums. The place didn't feel right. Unless… She gulped. Unless some of the items had been smuggled in. She should have known these dolls were too rare to be on the market legally. She closed her eyes for a moment, her determination wavering.

No. She hadn't flown halfway around the world to turn back now.

These weren't just any dolls. Twelve -- twelve! -- original 1880's vintage *Bru Bebes*. One would suffice. She wasn't greedy. Just let her win one. It would be the pinnacle of her collection. Someone was going to buy them. It might as well be her. She would pack it in her carryon luggage. Not one customs agent in a thousand would know what it was. What was it anyway? Just a doll…

The door opened immediately when the driver beat on it with the flat of his hand. Candy followed him in, her grip tight on her hard plastic comb. She found herself in a crowded, smoke filled, dimly lit hall. A dozen men turned to stare at her, their gazes making her skin crawl. She clung to the cabdriver's arm.

As her vision adjusted she focused on the raised platform in the center of the building, set up like a stage. Gradually the noises broke through her trance and the setting began to make sense. Numbers. Men calling out numbers. The gavel banging. Merchandise being offered for sale. All familiar. Yet all terribly, terribly wrong.

Her pulse slammed in her temples like the beat of a bass drum. This was an auction, all right. But they weren't selling antiques.

There were *people* on the platform. Dozens of people.

Candy just stared. This was the twenty-first century, for the love of God. You couldn't buy people. Things like this didn't happen. Not in her world.

The cabdriver had brought her to the wrong place. She had to leave. Now.

The lawyer in her stayed, rooted in morbid curiosity. If she got out of this alive, she needed to tell someone. Report... Report what? To whom?

Richard called her naïve, and for once he might have a point. Things like this probably happened all over the world.

There were men and women and children here. They looked Southeast Asian, much like her cabdriver, and they were all nearly naked. They stood with their eyes downcast, even the children, their expressions vacant. As if no matter what happened to them, it would be no worse than what they'd already lived through.

There had been a time, once, a long time ago, when she'd thought being a lawyer meant helping people. If anyone ever needed her help...

Who was she kidding? She was one woman. One very alone woman in a room full of wealthy, powerful men with enough influence to keep a system like this alive half a century after such things had been outlawed most of the world over. She'd be lucky to get out alive.

What the hell had she gotten herself into?

The men around her quit staring, their attention focusing on the auctioneer's new offering.

Time to go, to get out while the crowd was distracted.

Something pulled her attention back to the stage, rooting her feet in place. Someone was watching her, staring at her. The force of the man's gaze made her skin prickle, like a small electrical shock. Who? Where?

There. In the center of the platform, standing a little apart from the others, his head thrown back in defiance, his eyes scorching holes in her flesh. He had a large tattoo, like an upside-down Y, on his chest. One of those oriental things. A kanji. And the chest under it was smooth and solid and hard, like a wall of muscle. A tentative smile pulled at one side of his mouth as he caught her staring at it.

Oh. My. God. *I'll take that one. Wrap him up for me, please.*

A wave of pure sexual heat swept over her, stirring a tight, cramping need in her gut. For a moment she thought her knees would buckle under her. He had to be the most gorgeous man she'd ever seen.

Was he *flirting* with her?

What the hell was he doing here? Was he one of the bidders?

She couldn't see all of him, but he stood with the others, the ones being auctioned, and what she could see of him was nearly naked.

The man didn't exactly blend in. Long, lean,

broad-shouldered, narrow-waisted, his body sculptured like a Greek Adonis, skin darkly tanned, he stood nearly a head taller than the other laborers around him. Long, straight, almost black hair hung down well past his shoulders, streaked with gold where it had been lightened by the sun.

The room was so dark and dingy she couldn't be sure what nationality he was, but his height and build assured her he wasn't native to this part of the world.

Wave after wave of hot burning lust, so strong, so visceral it made her body tremble, shot through her. It had been years since a man had stirred her like that.

And all he had done was stare at her from across the room. If he touched her...

He turned now, standing with his head down, his hair thrown over one shoulder, looking up at her from under dark, thick lashes, as if he'd been posed by a photographer. *There. Hold that pose. Perfect.*

Everything about him screamed sex.

What was she thinking? A man like that? He might be cover model material, but she knew better. He was definitely not her type. She went for men with brains, like Richard.

Yeah. That worked out well, didn't it?

What the hell is wrong with you? What does it matter what he looks like? You're going to get yourself killed. Get the hell out of here while you can.

She wanted to head for the door. That was the sensible thing to do. She tried to turn away, but his eyes held her. Why was he staring at her? She stared back, as if they might form some sort of telepathic link.

God, he was gorgeous.

Maybe gorgeous wasn't the right word. He was lean and hard, rippling with the kind of muscles a man got from demanding physical labor. She'd seen construction workers with bodies like his -- hard-bodied men with hot, knowing eyes that understood just why she was looking.

Not that she'd ever done anything more than look. Naturally she'd never dated someone so -- so inappropriate. No. She stuck with sensible men, men like Richard.

Why did her mind always come back to Richard? The thought of him made her angry enough to do something rash. She spoke little Malay, but she understood money. The bidding seemed to be mixed -- she heard Euros, yen, and dollars so far. As the bidding closed on a smaller Asian man, she realized she could have won him for five thousand yen -- about five hundred dollars.

She chewed her bottom lip. This was crazy.

A man with a cattle prod in his hands shoved her construction worker toward the auctioneer. Candy gasped as he stumbled, disappearing from sight for a moment. Anger flared. Had they hurt him?

He resurfaced, like a drowning man pulling his head above water, immediately scanning the crowd, his eyes searching.

He was looking for her. She could feel the heat of his gaze twist something down deep in her gut, and lower. It had been years since she'd wanted a man this badly.

Their gazes met and locked. He wasn't smiling now. The only reason Candy didn't flee the room like her life depended on her escape -- which for all she knew it might -- was the expression in the man's eyes.

It wasn't raw sexual need she saw there. It was fear.

She was his last hope.

No, mister. Don't look at me like that. I can't save

you. I don't save people. Not anymore.

She'd given up on saving the world years ago. Lengthy corporate battles had taught her, it wasn't about what was right. It was about winning.

A large man in a rumpled business suit moved forward to inspect the merchandise before he shouted his bid in a thick German accent. "Four thousand yen."

Candy didn't like the looks of the bidder. He was short and bald and ugly. Two young women stood behind him, their eyes downcast. They were barely more than girls.

She didn't like the way the German grinned when he bid on her giant. His initial bid was too high. She knew that trick. Bid high, then dare the other bidders to go against you. She didn't know whether he could back up the threat in his eyes. Didn't want to know.

This was all wrong. So wrong.

She glanced back toward the platform. Her Adonis still focused on her, as if trying to hold her attention, his expression all too easy to read. He didn't want the German to win, but no one else was bidding. He knew what the German was doing. She read the desperation in his eyes.

Candy didn't want to know what the German would do with his purchases. This wasn't her fight. There were hundreds of reasons not to do something so foolish, she told herself as her hand reached into the air, countering the German's bid. "Five hundred dollars."

"Six thousand yen." The German again. He scowled a warning at her from across the room, his eyes narrowed into two slits. Whoever the hell he was, he obviously thought he could intimidate her, the way he had the other buyers.

Compared to Richard, he didn't know a thing about intimidation. Richard would be furious if he ever found out she'd been in a place like this. She was probably breaking a dozen international laws just being here. "Seven hundred fifty dollars."

"Eight thousand yen." Another, more threatening glare.

The auctioneer pointed at her.

They might not be together anymore, but Richard still expected her to maintain a certain image for the sake of Brasden-Marten. If he found out he would try to force her out of the company. Or have her committed.

Fuck Richard.

"One thousand dollars."

"Eleven thousand yen."

Fuck Brasden-Marten.

"Twelve hundred dollars."

"Fifteen thousand yen."

Fuck images.

"Seventeen hundred fifty dollars."

"Twenty thousand yen." The German's eyes glimmered with rage.

It was a mission of mercy. She had to save this man. The crowd went silent. Candy swallowed hard. It wasn't about the man -- her man -- and she knew it.

It was about the win.

It was about not letting the German have what he wanted.

It was about not letting any man get the better of her ever again.

"Twenty-five hundred dollars." Her voice rang strong and clear, easy to hear above the subdued sounds of a hundred bodies holding their breath.

The gavel hung in midair while the auctioneer

waited. Nothing. At last the German turned away, his nostrils flaring in anger as he shook his head.

"Sold!" The gavel banged on the rickety wooden podium, echoing through the room. All other sound ceased. "To the lady in the white dress."

The dark haired giant stared at her. He didn't move when the auctioneer's assistant prodded him. Another assistant shoved him, hard. He stumbled, nearly falling, catching himself as they threatened him with the cattle prod. She could hear the electricity crackle off it, smell the hair singe.

No! She'd won. No one could touch him now. He was hers.

Candy wanted to scream at the auction workers, but the crowd was frenzied again, the noise overwhelming.

Her man came back into sight, following obediently now. He didn't look too badly hurt. Only a bit subdued. Candy finally remembered to breathe. The crowd parted to let him through, and she could see what the press of bodies had hidden before. His hands were bound together with a piece of stout rope.

She'd seen some of the others tied this way. The bigger, stronger men. The ones who might cause trouble.

The guards kept away from him, as if a little afraid of the man's size and strength. They had reason to be afraid. Surely he wouldn't hurt her. She'd -- she'd saved him. Yes. That was what she'd done. Saved him, from whatever fate the German had in mind. That ought to be worth something.

She wouldn't let herself be afraid.

The auction workers brought the man to stand in front of her, keeping a safe distance from him while Candy handed over a stack of American dollars.

"*Terok! Kayu, lah*?" The attendant laughed as he took her money.

Terok she recognized from the cabdriver when he'd warned her not to come here. As if she needed a man with a cattle prod telling her the man was dangerous. "*Lah*," she agreed. *Especially if you're telling me I'm an idiot.*

Now what?

Up close, a faintly metallic smell like old sweat and blood clung to the man. He was badly in need of a shower. He looked huge. Not a pretty boy Adonis at all -- more a Titan. A huge, muscular giant, towering over her.

She would treat him like a client, maybe one she'd just bailed out of jail. A gorgeous, nearly naked client, with a strange symbol on his chest -- a chest she really, really wanted to touch.

No. Client!

She was just doing her job. Not exactly the first time she'd gotten a client out of trouble. A rock star, that was it. He was probably used to having women stare at him like he was sex personified. All she had to do was act professional.

Professional. Right. With a man whose leash she now held in her hands.

Well, she couldn't just stand there. She had to do something. At the very least the rope had to go. She'd have to find out who he was, where he came from, and get him back where he belonged as soon as possible. Before she did something they'd both regret.

She pulled his hands to her. They were broad and long fingered, the nails broken and dirty. Why was she imagining those hands running over her skin? What would he do if she traced his tattoo with the tip of her tongue?

He flinched at her touch, then steadied while she fumbled at the knot in the thick hemp. Maybe she wasn't supposed to take the rope off? To hell with that. She used the point of her comb to help pry the knot loose. It finally gave way under her relentless attack. Her heart was thudding like she'd just run a marathon. She turned his wrist over gently, noting the abrasions on his skin. Either the rope had been there too long, or he'd tried to fight.

"*Toi la nguoi My. Ong noi tiong Anh khong?*"

Candy looked up into huge silver-gray eyes, their gaze fastened on hers, waiting, as if expecting something from her. "I'm sorry, I don't speak -- whatever that was."

"American? You're an American?" He spoke slowly, his English sounding sort of rusty, but the relief in his voice clearly audible.

"Yes. I'm Candy. Candy -- Nelson. From New York."

He blinked, a kind of dazed, shocked look in his eyes. "Brook. Brook Harper."

She wanted to wrap her arms around him, tell him whatever had happened to land him here, she'd help him get home. Hell, she was looking for any excuse to touch him, but she wouldn't. It wasn't professional. She could have her fantasies, though, couldn't she?

Brook glanced at the crowd, rubbing his injured wrists. The German was still watching them, his glare openly hostile, even though he was already bidding on another young Malaysian woman. No one else besides the cabdriver was paying any attention to them. "I can't believe they sent a woman in here alone."

Candy felt herself flush. "The cabdriver brought me."

"The cabdriver." He ran his gaze over her again, assessing her deliberately. A slow, hesitant smile formed on his lips. Oh God. When he smiled like that she nearly melted at his feet. "Thank you, Candy Nelson. You are either very brave or very foolish."

She shook her head. "I hope I'm not foolish, but I'm not all that brave. The cabdriver brought me here by mistake. Wherever here is. A bit of a communication problem." For some reason it was important to her that he understand she didn't do this sort of thing every day. It was an accident. A fluke. A --

"A communication problem? What do you mean, a communication problem?"

"The cabdriver brought me here by mistake," she repeated. "It was the wrong auction."

He just stared at her, all expression washing out of his face, his body going completely still, one hand frozen on the opposing wrist. The moment was over as fast as it had happened, but in that moment he changed. The hint of laughter disappeared. Something died in his eyes, leaving them flat and wary. Everything about him was suddenly distant and formal. Reserved. "A tourist," he sighed. "I apologize, Ms. Nelson. I thought you were someone else. I didn't realize I was just a souvenir you'd picked up. I shall do my best not to disappoint you."

He smiled, his lips taking a cynical twist. "I suppose there are worse fates that could befall a man. If I had to be arrested and sold into slavery, I'd rather belong to an attractive American woman than the German mob. I'd have ended up in one of the Japanese whorehouses. Not a pleasant fate, I assure you."

It was Candy's turn to feel dazed. Her worst fear, the gut feeling she'd had congealing in the pit of her stomach throughout the entire auction, was just confirmed.

Arrested? Slavery? German mob? Japanese whorehouses?

Oh God. What had she gotten herself into?

3:15 PM Friday, 17 December 2004
Singapore Immigration Authority Checkpoint

As the cab slowed again, Candy fought the overwhelming sense of having drifted off into the Twilight Zone. She glanced about uneasily. There was some sort of a roadblock ahead. Her nerves worked into a tight bundle as they moved toward the uniformed officers.

Ordinarily she wouldn't have cared about anything but the delay.

Ordinarily she wouldn't have had a nearly naked man sitting as far away from her as possible in the back seat of a cab. A man who, incidentally, she now *owned*.

There was no way this man looked like a tourist. One look at him and they'd know what she'd done. Slavery was illegal even here, wasn't it? She was going to be arrested.

The cabdriver didn't seem too concerned. As they joined the line waiting to move through the checkpoint, the driver turned and spoke rapidly in his odd mixture of Malay and English.

Brook glanced over at her, then looked away again. The muscles along the edge of his jaw knotted. "*Sotong! No! Pai seh, lah?*" he argued.

The cabdriver repeated his instructions, waving his hands erratically. Candy had no idea what either of them was saying, but she was almost sure she didn't like it. However, the guards were getting closer, and she liked them even less. "What does he want? I have enough cash on me to cover a -- an import duty." She'd spent enough time in this part of the world to know that fees paid in cash, especially American dollars, tended to solve a good many problems.

"He wants me," Brook explained, his words short and clipped, "to kiss you."

Oh, yeah, well, she could see how *that* might be quite an imposition. "How's that going to help?"

She felt the heat in her face as Brook picked her up. He pulled her across his lap, sliding her thighs over his, guiding her to straddle his legs. Oh, God. They wouldn't look like they were kissing. They would look like they were having sex. She was about to be arrested.

Before she could protest, his hands tangled in her hair, pulling her into an embrace that assaulted her senses. His lips paused, close enough to touch. She tried to focus -- he was saying something. "Apparently your cabdriver carries spare ID."

Oh. They were trying to *hide* as much of him as possible. So he'd pass for whoever was on the photo ID. Well then. Candy raised her arms to wrap them around Brook's shoulders, concealing as much of his body as she could from view. After all, it was for a good cause. Keeping them both out of some foreign jail.

Yeah. Right. And it was for a good cause when her lips opened in a soft sigh of delight, the tip of her tongue touching his, too. The cause deepened when he crushed her to his chest, no longer playacting as he kissed her in earnest.

Oh God. There was no uncertainty about him now. The man knew how to kiss. She could feel the heat of his cock rising up through his shorts. His erection where it pressed against her felt long, and thick, and aching to escape his scanty clothing. If he was acting, this was a stellar performance with great props.

She heard laughter in the background. "*Terok,*

lah?"

"Lah," the driver agreed. The cab lurched forward again, but Brook didn't let go. When the kiss finally ended neither one of them moved.

"Wow," Candy managed, her voice still breathy. "It's been a long time since anyone kissed me like that." It had been a long time. Maybe never. But she wasn't ready to admit that. Not just yet.

Brook just stared at her, something cynical clouding his expression. "That's what you paid for, isn't it?"

So much for her mission of mercy. "No!"

"What? No string of brothels to ship me off to? What are you planning to do with me, then, Candy? You own a factory somewhere? Mexico maybe?"

"No!" she squeaked. "I was just -- I just wanted to help you."

"Help me. Riiiight…"

Just great. He had been staring at her back there. She hadn't imagined that. It wasn't her fault she wasn't whoever he expected her to be. She could live without the attitude.

Well, fuck that. The sooner she was rid of this man the better.

3:45 PM Friday, 17 December 2004
Mandarin Oriental, Singapore

This wasn't the sort of souvenir most tourists brought home. She couldn't just tuck him away in her luggage to get him through customs. How the hell could she get him back to her hotel room wearing nothing but a pair of dirty cutoff shorts? She might be a preferred customer, but this was over the line, even for the Mandarin Oriental.

First things first. Candy shut down her emotions as she turned her attention to details. Richard had always counted on her for organization. She was good at details.

The hotel's huge open atrium would present their first major obstacle. Brook didn't look like one of the guests. She didn't want people thinking --

Screw what people would think. Why should she be embarrassed? Brasden-Marten didn't pay her enough to own her personal life. She didn't have to answer to Richard anymore.

Besides. No man would need to hide a scantily dressed woman following him back to *his* suite. Whose business was it, anyway? She didn't have to answer to anyone. Still…

"Ms. Nelson. Good to see you, ma'am."

"We need -- ah, my friend lost his shirt -- at the beach…" Damn. She sounded like an idiot.

"Of course, madam."

Candy swallowed a sigh of relief as the doorman signaled to the bellhop and a short pool robe mysteriously appeared, apparently conjured out of thin air. Considering some of her clients' drunken escapades, she didn't need to ask why the front desk kept such things handy. Trust the Mandarin to be discreet. One paid well for the privilege of having such services available.

Brook slipped silently into the robe. The fabric clung to his broad shoulders, falling open across his smooth upper chest, where the tattoo just peeked out. The fabric molded itself to his narrow hips as he knotted the belt, the hem ending low on sculpted thighs dusted with thick, dark hair. He had great legs. Even his calves looked sexy, playing with muscles that bunched and rippled as he shifted his weight.

Images of the two of them in the hot tub together crowded her imagination. Candy tried to push them out of her mind. Pool robe or not, Brook didn't exactly look like he'd just climbed out of the water, but at least he would be a little less conspicuous. Heads turned as he followed her across the large open atrium, but somehow she didn't think the women whose eyes followed him were paying attention to what he was wearing.

Candy looked too, thinking the same things, but she had to get her thoughts back under control. Fine time for her missing libido to reappear. She kept a careful distance from Brook, avoiding even accidental contact. They rode up in the elevator together in uneasy silence. Once she'd entertained fantasies about what she might do with the right man in an elevator, but now was not the time. No matter how well he kissed, Brook had made it perfectly clear what he thought of her.

"This isn't really happening," Candy mumbled as she swiped her key card through the electronic lock on the door to her suite.

Brook shrugged as he surveyed the opulent room. He skimmed out of the robe and dropped it over the back of the brightly colored couch, seemingly oblivious to the latent sensuality of his moves. "Then maybe you're not really out twenty-five hundred dollars." The sexy, catlike grace of his movements stood in contrast to the sharp, clipped tone of his words.

She felt like running back down the hallway screaming.

Enough.

"Look. You're missing the point here, Brook. I'd be lying if I said I didn't find you attractive. But I did *not* buy you for sex. I'll do whatever I can to help you, but I can't own anyone. Slavery is illegal."

"Sure it is."

"It's the twenty-first century for God's sake!" Candy tossed her purse on the coffee table on her way to the wet bar. Lord she needed a drink.

"Funny. Seemed real enough to me. Don't recall anyone asking whether it was legal or not." His voice dropped lower, tinged with bitterness. "Listen, Ms. Nelson, whatever you had in mind, this isn't going to work. Send me back with the cabdriver before he gets another fare."

"Send you back?" Damn it, he'd been asking for her help back in that hellhole. Candy spun to confront Brook, reaching out to grab his arm as he turned away. She moved too fast, held on too tight.

Brook flinched, his whole body going rigid. Anger snapped in his eyes.

She loosened her grip, letting her fingers rest lightly against his skin. She hadn't looked past the surface. Almost hidden beneath the bronze of his deeply tanned skin she could see the fading outline of a large purplish bruise. She inspected him carefully now, taking the time to really look. There were others.

Bruises and scars, some fresh, some older and fading. Not offensive wounds. He hadn't been in a fight.

These were defensive marks.

He'd been beaten. Fairly often, from the looks of things, by someone who knew how to do it without permanently disfiguring the merchandise.

The reality of it all came crashing in on her. She outlined the purple ring with her fingertips. "Oh my God. I'm so sorry, Brook."

The spell broken, Brook looked away, the hard muscles in his arm bunching under her touch. He inhaled in long, deep pulls that made his chest ripple, as if he'd forgotten to breathe. He seemed intent on studying the heavy brocade drapes that obscured their vision of the harbor.

She hadn't noticed. The maid should have opened the drapes.

Her hand lingered on his arm, her touch feather light now. "How did this happen?"

A muscle worked in his jaw, bunching into an angry knot. "You waved a handful of American dollars at an auctioneer."

Candy closed her eyes, trying to rein in a quick flash of temper. "How did you end up in that auction?"

He shook off her hand. "What difference does it make? Have the cabdriver take me back and send me through again. At least you'll get some of your money back. You can go back to your safe little world. I'll be somebody else's problem."

Candy kept her voice pitched low, but firm. "I am not going to send you back to the auction house, Brook. The money isn't important to me. I'm just trying to figure this all out. In my *little* world people don't own people. And they sure as hell don't beat them into submission."

He didn't even try to keep the sarcasm out of his voice. "Look, lady. If you don't want me, you have to send me back. I have nowhere else to go. I don't have a work permit or a visa or any sort of ID. I can't work anywhere legally. How long do you think I'll last on the streets before they arrest me again? I didn't make it two days last time I escaped. And let me assure you, there are a lot worse places to end up than back in that auction house. At least the bidders feel the need to protect their investment."

Want him? She'd never wanted a man so badly in her life. But wanting didn't make it right. With the sort of precision she was known for in business Candy snapped open her briefcase and took out a steno pad. "I'm not going to take you back to the auction house, Brook. I know you don't think very highly of me right now, but you're wrong. Just because I'm not willing to *own* you doesn't mean I'm going to turn you out on the street. I got you here. I'm willing to take responsibility for getting you out of this mess. I do have a conscience, and at least some sense of common decency left."

Brook shrugged, his face stoic again, as if he didn't care in the least about what she'd said. "Do they charge you for the crackers?"

Crackers? She was trying to help him put his life back together and he was worried about crackers? "Help yourself." She found the local phone book and began organizing a list of contacts.

"Is there anyone --" She looked up just as Brook was stuffing the last of several packages of hotel crackers into his mouth, hardly even bothering to chew them. "Oh my God."

His face turned a dark crimson as he spun toward her. He swiped a hand hastily across his mouth. "What? You said they were free."

A knot of anger twisted itself in her stomach. She laid her Cartier pen down perpendicular to the spine of the legal pad. "When's the last time you ate, Brook?"

He shrugged, his eyes going distant again. "They fed us last night."

Last night. Twenty-four hours ago at best. Probably longer. Some of the others had looked thin, gaunt even, but Brook had looked too good to be hungry.

Well, sympathy was getting her nowhere. Candy crossed to the bedroom to find her shampoo and conditioner and a fresh disposable razor. She held them out to him. "Go get a shower. I'll call room service and have them send up dinner. In the meantime I'm going to have to get you something to wear. Do you have any preferences?"

He shrugged, his gaze focused on the things she'd shoved into his hands. "I could use a pair of jeans and a T-shirt. Forty-four thirty-four jeans, 2X T-shirt. Tall if they have it."

Forty-four? He'd been a size forty-four? Candy tried not to laugh. "Brook."

There was that flash of temper again. "What?"

"Have you looked in a mirror lately?"

"Oh, yeah. I keep one in my hip pocket, with my passport."

"Just look." She tugged him over to the dressing mirror. "Size forty-four jeans wouldn't even stay on you. They'd be way too big."

Brook squared his shoulders as he turned reluctantly to frown into the mirror. He stared for a moment, finally turning sideways, looking more critical than conceited. "Guess I've lost some weight." He tugged at the shorts that hung almost obscenely low on his hips. "You're right. Bet I'm down to forty jeans by now." That thought, at least, seemed to please him.

Candy arched an eyebrow at the thought of buying him jeans and T-shirts, though he'd undoubtedly look great in them. "Shoe size?" was all she said out loud.

He frowned at his filthy feet. "Fourteen. Good luck."

Candy smiled. "Nothing is all that hard for a concierge to find."

She didn't wait to see whether he headed for the shower before she picked up the phone. "Concierge, please. Thank you. Candy Nelson, room eighteen-fifteen. Yes. My companion has arrived without his luggage. I'll need a tailor in the morning. For tonight I need a few ready-made items sent up…"

The sound of water running brought a smile of relief to her lips. Brook was stubborn, but not impossible, especially when what she wanted was for his own good. She'd dealt with more difficult clients. It might take her some time, but she'd chip away at his attitude.

"American sizes. A forty-eight long dinner jacket, dark, maybe charcoal, eighteen thirty-six white dress shirt, thirty-six thirty-four dress slacks, and a pair of Italian loafers, size fourteen. I'll need a man's travel kit and a garment bag too." She thought briefly of the way those ragged shorts had hung on his hips as she answered the last question. "Boxers. Silk. Size… large."

She made her first check mark on the list on the yellow legal pad.

5:00 PM Friday, 17 December 2004
Mandarin Oriental, Singapore

Brook sat across from her at the round glass table, dressed now in a dark charcoal suit. His white dress shirt hung open casually at the neck. His damp hair fanned out over the crisp, clean fabric. Everything fit well enough, though tailoring would be an improvement. Room service had spread a small feast over her table.

So rather than eating, why was he staring out the window? She couldn't tell where he'd wandered off to, but she'd never felt more alone with a man, not even with Richard at the end. She felt the tension knotting in her shoulders. This wasn't going as well as she'd hoped. He'd barely touched the shrimp *Pad Thai*.

"What's wrong?" she asked, not really sure she wanted to hear the answer.

"Ms. Nelson, I --"

"Candy."

"Candy," he repeated. "I'm sorry. I just can't eat this."

Candy chewed on her bottom lip. "I love Thai food. I should have asked."

His gray eyes shimmered with warring emotions. "There's nothing wrong with the food. It's just too much. There's enough here to feed a family of six. I guess I'm just not used to eating like this anymore."

The food wasn't all that was wrong, but at least he was talking to her. Taking a chance, she reached out to lay a hand over his. "Eat what you want, Brook. Whenever you want. Call room service. They'll bill it to my account."

"I've already wasted enough of your money."

Was this about money? "I get paid well to be here. I don't mind spending money if there's a reason. Right now making sure you're not hungry seems like a pretty good reason."

He looked down at her hand where it rested on his. "Why were you at that auction, Candy? You weren't there looking for me."

She laughed a little at that. "No. I wasn't looking for you. It really was an accident. I wanted to buy an antique China doll at an auction I found on the Internet. But the cabdriver didn't speak much English. I guess he misunderstood where I wanted to go... and there you were."

"You didn't have to go in once you realized you were in the wrong place. Do you have any idea how much danger you put yourself in? You could just as easily have ended up on the block yourself. Without your cabdriver standing guard over you the whole time you probably would have."

Candy felt the flush rising up her cheeks. "I didn't know what the place was until we were inside."

Brook pinned her hand down as she started to pull away. A slight pressure of his fingers conveyed his message. He could be dangerous if he chose to be. His voice conveyed the same message. "Once you went in, once you knew what the place was, why didn't you run? *Why did you bid on me?*"

That was the real question, wasn't it? She looked up, needed him to see the truth in her eyes. "I couldn't leave once I'd seen you."

Desperation tinged the anger in his voice. "*Why?*"

He was looking for more, for some answer she just didn't seem to be able to put into words. What was it he needed to hear from her? "You looked… You didn't belong there."

"Yeah. I've heard *that* a lot the last two years."

"You're very handsome. Any woman would have noticed you. Still, I was going to leave. But then you looked at me, and I --"

His voice softened. "What?"

There were so many truths, working on so many levels. "I didn't like the looks of the German. I thought you -- I thought you wanted my help. I thought you were asking me to bid on you, so I did."

Brook picked up her hand and turned it over, running his calloused fingertips over her palm. The silence in the room became as troubling as his scrutiny of her palm. He raised her fingers, pressing his lips to the base of her thumb. "What exactly do you want from me, Candy?"

The question caught her by surprise. "I -- nothing."

"Everybody wants something." He glanced down at the suit. "People right across the border live for a year on less money than you spent tonight. Why are you doing this? What's all this for?"

He was upset about the clothes? "You can't run around naked."

He just stared. "There's someplace you have to go that you can't afford to show up without an escort, isn't there?"

She blinked at the intensity of his gaze. "Maybe I just wanted to help you."

A little piece of the truth.

He just kept staring at her, her hand still held captive in his.

Candy felt the heat rise in her face. "Maybe I was just after sex."

And a little more.

He offered a self-deprecating laugh. "Right. Sex. With a man like me."

She swallowed hard. Honesty… "A man like you? You're very handsome, Brook. No, don't laugh. I'm not the only woman who thinks so. Did you see the women staring at you when we came through the lobby? Every single one of them was wishing they were me."

He pulled her hand closer, raising it to his lips once again. Slowly, giving her time to anticipate every subtle nuance of the move, he drew her index finger into his mouth, running the tip of his tongue over the whorls of her fingerprint, teasing, stroking, promising.

Moisture flooded her pussy, but it wasn't enough to squelch the long forgotten fires of lust bringing her blood to a boil. Oh, Lord. If he could get her wet just tasting her finger, there was no telling what he could do to the rest of her body.

He tugged gently on her wrist. Candy hesitated, then eased out of her chair, letting him pull her closer. He curled his head against her, wrapping both arms around her waist. "You're right. I did want you to bid on me, Candy. And it wasn't just because I didn't want to end up in a whorehouse in Japan. I don't want to belong to anyone. Not because they paid for me. But if I was leaving there with someone, I wanted that someone to be you."

She draped her free arm over his shoulder, combing her fingers through his damp hair. "I don't expect anything from you for that money. I don't *expect* anything at all from you."

His arms tightened around her, pulling her down into his lap, crushing her against his chest. Something in his tough façade gave way. "No one could be as innocent as you appear."

"I'm not all that innocent. I'm not totally selfless or altruistic either," Candy confessed.

"What did you want from me, Candy?" he asked again, gentler this time.

"I -- nothing." She blushed. "It doesn't matter."

"It matters to me."

Candy swallowed another denial. "I -- I didn't want to spend Christmas alone."

"Christmas. I've lost track… when is Christmas?"

"Next Saturday."

His gaze fixed on hers, though his arms still held her captive. "That's it? You don't want to be alone over Christmas. That was worth twenty-five hundred dollars to you?"

It sounded so petty when he put it that way. She tried not to let her voice crack the way it did when she was going to cry. "Getting you out of whatever trouble you were in was worth twenty-five hundred dollars. Isn't that enough?"

He didn't say *Yeah, right* again -- he didn't have to.

"Tell me."

"Saturday is my birthday."

She knew even before he moved he was going to kiss her. It was there in his eyes. He framed her face with his hands, moving slowly.

Oh Lord. *Why* didn't matter. His lips brushed over hers, soft and gentle. His tongue teased hers with the hesitant trip of a butterfly's wing, then danced away, only to return stronger and more demanding. He let his hands drift down over her shoulders until they rested on her waist. "Just you."

His voice jarred her back to reality. "What?"

"There's just you? No friends flying in to join us

for the week?"

Friends? She remembered the look on the German's face. A knot rose in her stomach. "Just me," she promised.

"I can think of a lot worse jobs than keeping a beautiful woman entertained on her birthday." His voice sounded slightly amused now.

A job.

Right.

Well, what do you expect? You weren't exactly looking for a date. You bought the man.

Yes.

She was going to have to get rid of him, and fast. She wanted all the things his kisses seemed to promise. She wanted fire, passion that threatened to sweep her away from her safe, ordinary existence. He could give her all that -- at least for now. Like hiring an escort for the week. She was the client. That was *all* she was to him, and all she'd ever be.

Just a job.

She slid slowly off of his lap. "It's been a really long day... I'm exhausted. I'm going to get a shower." She looked over at the king-sized bed. "I wasn't planning for two when I made the reservations."

"I can sleep on the couch if you want, Candy."

That would be safer. A reminder to keep their relationship purely professional.

"No." To hell with professional. She brushed her lips over his in a light caress.

Nothing would happen between them tonight, anyway. They were both exhausted. He looked sexy as hell, but there were lines of strain around his eyes. Well, she'd had a pretty long day herself, and no one had sold her to the highest bidder. "It's been a while since I've looked at my life and thought about how

Shelby Morgen   Plain Brown Wrapper

lucky I am. People tend to take things like freedom for granted."

He captured her face, pulling her down for a kiss that made promises she couldn't afford to let him keep. She had to remind herself he was just doing his job. Still, she closed her eyes for a moment and tried to imagine a future where a man kissed her like this on a regular basis. Wouldn't work. She'd never get anything done.

"Candy?" He had the most incredible voice. Low and deep and oozing with sex.

"Yeah?" Eloquent. Truly eloquent.

"We've got all weekend. No need to rush anything. You're falling asleep on your feet. Why don't you go take that shower?"

"Will -- will you be here when I get back?"

He laughed softly. "I'm not an idiot, Candy. I'll choose keeping a beautiful woman company over hiding in dark alleys any day. I'm not going anywhere."

She should protest. Somehow, she should… "All right." She dragged her body off toward the promise of steam that could never approach the heat of his kisses.

The door to the bathroom had barely clicked shut before Brook Harper picked up the phone. His hand shaking, he dialed the number from memory. "*Mot-mot-ba-nam-bay… Xin chao. Toi manh gioi. Mau len. Troi dat oi! Da khong. Khong dau! Xin loi… Da khong. Lam on ran chiu.*"

Xin loi… forgive me, he whispered as he hung up the phone.

4:45 AM Saturday, 18 December 2004
Mandarin Oriental, Singapore

A thin cry broke the stillness of the night. Candy sat up with a start.

"*Khong dau! Mac toi!* Leave me alone!" A man's voice, the words sobbed out in panic.

Who…

Yesterday came flooding back. Candy reached out, but the bed beside her was empty. The warmth of the body cuddled around her was gone. She nearly tumbled out of the bed trying to untangle herself from the sheets.

Brook.

"*Toi khong biet! Di di!* Go away! *Di di!*"

She didn't have to know what the words meant to understand the terror haunting his dreams. She stumbled blindly toward his voice, finding him huddled in a ball on the floor near the foot of the bed.

"*Khong dau! Dung lai!* Stop! *Toi khong biet! Xin loi, xin loi!*"

She kept her voice pitched low, as non-threatening as she could manage. "It's all right, Brook. It's Candy. You're safe here."

Despite the warmth of the tropical night, the nightmare had left his skin cold. He shivered beneath her touch. Candy pulled the trailing bedspread down over them, holding her body jackknifed around him, trying to give him as much of her warmth as she could. She half expected him to fight her, but he curled up even tighter, shrinking in on himself. She held on, trying to reach him. "It was a dream. Just a dream. You're safe now."

Gradually the knotted muscles beneath her

stroking hands began to feel warm and alive again. The hard fought breath of panic lowered itself to a more even rate. Candy relaxed a little too, laying her cheek on his back.

"I'm sorry I woke you up." His voice sounded stiff with embarrassment. "I'm all right. Go back to bed."

Her hands stilled, but she didn't let go. "Come back to bed with me."

She felt as much as heard the sharp intake of his breath. "In a minute."

"All right." She should leave him alone, but she couldn't seem to quit touching.

He twisted in her arms to face her, his voice strained. "Go back to bed, Candy. *Now.*"

"Not without you." Her hand slid over the hard planes of his chest, outlining the spot where she knew the tattoo sat, then lower, across his abs, tracing the soft V of hair pointing downward like a roadmap.

Brook captured her hand in a grip like a steel clamp, dragging her hand down to the heat of his cock where he tented the silk of the boxers he'd slept in. Rather than pull away, she wrapped her hand around the long, thick, rigid length of his dick, smiling when he danced under her touch.

"Don't tease me, Candy." There was more than a hint of warning in his voice.

Idiot, she screamed at herself. She pulled back like a child too close to the fire, her cheeks flaming crimson. "I'm sorry. I -- I'm not very good at this." It was true. A flaw Richard had pointed out often enough. She rolled away, climbing back to her feet.

He caught her, his fingers digging into her hips, jerking her back against the scorching length of his cock. His voice turned bitter as he ran his rough hands over the soft silk of her nightgown, his fingers dipping to curve around her mons. "Don't play games with me, Candy. It's not safe."

"I -- I'm not playing games. I'm just not very good at -- at --"

"At what?"

Candy stared out at the waves rolling gently along the harbor. "Sex. Seduction."

His hands stilled, one cupping her mons, the other curled around her waist, holding her trapped against his chest. "You're not good at sex."

"I'm sorry. I didn't mean to…"

"To what, Candy?" He ground his hips against her in slow, sensuous sweeps. "To get me harder than I've been in years? To make my cock ache like a horny teenager's, just because you say my name? To make me want to tell you it was worth it -- two years in hell, and worth every minute, if you'll just fuck me? Well, I'm glad you're not good at sex, Candy Nelson, because I'd hate to see what would happen if you were *trying* to seduce me. If you were any fucking better at it you might kill me."

"Brook, I --"

"Make up your mind, Candy. No more games. Don't touch me unless you mean it." He let her go, shoving her back toward the bed.

Candy watched him as he turned to face the huge plate glass window. "What do you want from me, Brook?"

"Want?" He spun back to face her. "I want *you*, Candy. I want to devour you. I want to fuck you until you collapse on me, until my name is your last conscious thought."

She closed the distance between them. All he had to do was breathe deeply, and their chests would touch. "So what's stopping you?"

She leaned closer, covering his mouth with hers. As if she'd unlocked some hidden restraint, his lips jumped to meet hers, more than willing, aggressive now, his arms tangling around her. She could feel his cock pressing into her, hot and demanding.

His fingers found her breasts through the slippery silk, and she groaned at his touch. "God, that feels good."

"Candy…" He breathed her name like a benediction.

She traced the long, dark tattoo with the tip of her tongue. His skin jumped beneath her touch, his breath coming in a ragged gasp. Good. She wanted to touch him the way his very presence affected her, sending her senses reeling, turning her world upside down. Raising her head, she nipped gently on his bottom lip.

He bit back, and there was nothing gentle about it. His hands were everywhere, touching, exploring, stroking. "You can't be real. This is just another nightmare. I know it. When I wake up and you're gone again it's going to take what's left of my sanity."

Candy rolled her head, exposing more of her neck to his probing tongue. "I'm real, Brook, and I'm not going anywhere."

His hands were busy, one holding her head while his fingers stroked through her hair, the other hand teasing her left nipple into a state of almost painful awareness. "You even smell different. Everywhere. You smell like home." Apparently everywhere included the back of her ear.

She giggled. "I use apple pie for a perfume."

His hands stilled. "Apple pie. I bet room service would deliver apple pie."

"Um-hmmm. And ice cream too."

"You're making me hungry."

"Good." She let her hands slide down his waist and over his ass, cupping his buns to pull him closer. "You make me so hungry I want to devour you." She rolled her mons back and forth over the length of his thick, rigid cock, loving the way he responded to her touch, jerking helplessly against her.

His breath hissed out in a thick gasp for air. "Oh Christ Jesus, woman. I thought you said you weren't good at this?"

"I'm not."

"Whoever told you that lied." He kissed her again, his tongue battling with hers for supremacy. His fingers stroked down her sides to find the hem of her thin silk nightgown, pulling it up and over her head in one fast, sure stroke. He stood there, studying her in the faint moonlight, until she thought she would combust. "God, you're beautiful."

Beautiful? Her? Candy would have argued with him, but she needed to feel beautiful, just this once. "I want you, Brook. I want to feel you inside me. Now."

"Now is good." Scooping her up as if she weighed nothing, he carried her back to the king-sized bed, trailing the bedspread with them. Moments later he was kneeling between her thighs while her hands found the waist of his new silk boxers, tugging them down until she could stroke him with both hands.

He groaned, capturing her wrists and pinning them beside her shoulders on the bed. "Candy."

He picked the strangest times to want to talk. She refused to remember this was a mistake. "What?" she demanded.

"This is a lousy time to remember, but I don't have anything. Protection."

Candy wanted to scream. She could already feel the first drips of wetness from his cock sliding along the lips of her pussy. How could she have taken a chance like that? Knowing where he'd been the last two years? And he knew nothing of her... "I -- I had a physical. Last month. And I gave blood back in September. They test you for everything. There hasn't been anyone since then. For almost a year before, actually. I'm clean."

"I had all the standard tests before I came over here three years ago. There hasn't been anyone since. For a long time before that, either."

She had a perfect way out. She should take it. But damn it, she didn't want out. "I think I saw hotel condoms, in the drawer there, beside the bed."

Still he hesitated, just standing there, staring down at her naked body. "What?"

"Are you sure this is what you want, Candy? No regrets in the morning?"

She strained to reach him, to pull him inside her waiting body. "I'm sure," she managed. "I've never been more sure of anything in my life."

Cold air hit her, peaking her nipples and strumming over her pussy like an icy finger. Her body wanted to cry out at the loss. In the early morning quiet, the ripping foil package sounded loud, harsh.

He pulled her toward the edge of the bed where he stood, condom in hand. Candy propped herself up on her elbows, watching him slowly unroll the ribbed latex sheath over his glistening cock. His head flung back, his expression tense and strained, he could have been posing for a porn shot. Naked Hunks of the Month, Mr. December...

You won't need any lubrication. I'm already wet enough for both of us, babe.

The condom in place, he slid his arms under her knees, spreading her wide, lifting her onto his waiting cock. They both watched in fascination as he disappeared into her.

"Christ. You're so tight, Candy."

"Practically a born-again virgin."

"Candy…" He held her there a moment, his length a burning heat melting her from the inside, then he withdrew, only to thrust in again slowly, so slowly, laughing as she fought to hold him in place with the strength of her pussy gripping his cock. "Candy. And your birthday is on Christmas Day. Peppermint Candy."

She couldn't be serious. Not while he was teasing her. "No. Worse." She rose up to meet him, pulling him in with her heels hooked behind his back.

"Christmas Candy." Down and in with a nice hot thrust.

"No." She tried to pull his head down to the tips of her straining nipples.

He drove into her harder, meeting her thrusting hips. She clenched her legs around him, grinning at the sound of their sweat-dampened bodies slapping together. "Candy Cane."

"No," she protested feebly.

"Don't try to lie to me, Candy. You're not very good at it." The words came out in short pants now.

"Swear you won't tell anyone. Ever."

"I won't tell anyone. Ever." He leaned forward as far as he could, swiping his tongue over her breast on each down stroke.

Yes. Yes! That was what she wanted. Her nipples reached for him, wanting so much more than the brief swipe of his tongue. She rolled the damp tips between her fingers, offering them to him like candies.

This time was going to be different. She was so ready. So close. She threw herself against him, her hips bucking up off the bed.

Faster. Harder! The muscles in his chest and shoulders tightened, straining with each thrust.

She knew what would happen next. There was only one possibility when a man moved like this. Candy felt herself tighten, the tension building until her muscles ached. She clenched hard around him, trying frantically to throw herself over the edge. Desperation drove her to work harder. She wanted to scream in frustration. So close this time. She'd almost made it. If she just had a little more time...

"Candy?"

The shock of his voice, lucid and even, was almost as great as the shock of his body, stilling within her, though she could feel his cock still pulsing fiercely. Why had he stopped? Surely she'd have known if he came, even with a condom.

"Candy."

"What?" She almost wailed in disappointment.

"You're supposed to be enjoying this. Not looking like your world is about to end."

The unfulfilled ache made her want to cry. "I'm sorry. I told you I wasn't very good at this."

"Candy. Look at me."

His voice was so gentle. She opened her eyes to scan his features in the soft light of first dawn. The ache faded. She let it go with a sigh.

At least he didn't look angry.

"Look around the room, Candy. Tell me who you see here."

What? What the hell... "There's no one else here. Just us."

"Exactly. There's just the two of us here now. No

matter what happened before, this is going to be different, okay?"

Different. Right. She swallowed her regret. "Okay."

"We're going to try this again. I want you to enjoy yourself."

She blinked in confusion, feeling like an idiot as she parroted his words. "Again?"

"Why not? You have something better to do?"

She laughed at that, her voice a little shaky. "I can't think of *anything* I'd rather do."

He pulled out of her, leaving her feeling empty and cheated, taking a step back from the bed.

"What are you doing?"

"You need to know, don't you? You need to know what to expect, so nothing surprises you."

Oh, hell. He knew her too well, and it had been less than a day. "Yes."

His slow smile looked dangerous. "I'm going to worship your body, Candy. I'm going to lick you and kiss you and touch you places you've never been touched before. I'm going to make you come until you forget who you are, forget who I am, forget where you found me. I'm going to lick your pussy and fuck you with my tongue until you beg me to ram my cock into you."

Oh my God. She was going to combust just from the sound of his voice. "Then what?"

His smile widened. "Then? You mean after I fuck you till you can barely remember your own name? We're going to order breakfast from room service. Or maybe it'll be lunch. Do you know what I could do to you with a jar of honey? Later we'll get a shower and go downstairs to dinner, just so you can show me off to those women you were talking about. You can make them jealous. We'll come back here and order dessert. Apple pie and ice cream, and I'm going to use you for a serving dish."

"All day?" she whispered, more than a little impressed.

"All day. All night. Maybe all weekend. We'll see how good your stamina is."

"But we need to…"

"It's Saturday. There's nothing on your calendar till Monday morning. Do you want to check your planner?"

She knew what Kelly had written across the pages in bright red ink. *Relax.* "I don't think --"

He pulled a pillow off the bed and dropped it under his knees, sliding her legs up to his shoulders as he knelt on the floor. "Don't think, Candy. Anyone who has to pencil in a walk on the beach thinks entirely too much."

She might have argued, if he hadn't been right. If he hadn't nipped the inside of her thigh, causing just enough pain to have her jumping, twisting in secret pleasure, her pussy crying, weeping for his touch.

He spread her labia wide, just looking at her.

A flush of embarrassment spread over her face. "Brook, you don't have to…"

"Shhh. You're thinking again."

She was feeling, too. Feeling helpless and out of control and -- and -- *open*. She squirmed, trying to close her thighs. "I don't…"

"Do you know how beautiful you are? Have you ever really looked at yourself, Candy? Stood in front of a full length mirror, naked, and spread yourself open?"

"No." Her voice was so low she could barely hear it.

"You look like a flower. An orchid. Dark,

mysterious, twisted petals all folded in on themselves. A man might spend half his life searching the jungles for a flower so rare." He ran his tongue slowly up her thigh toward the flower his hands held open.

A shudder ran through her as her resistance crumbled. "You were a poet in your last life, weren't you?"

"I was a man who worked too hard, and didn't spend enough time appreciating what I had."

She wanted to ask him what he'd lost, who he'd been, but then again, she didn't want to know. Not tonight. The world outside the door ceased to exist.

"What are you thinking?"

"I -- I was hoping I don't -- you know -- smell bad."

He laughed. Under his scrutiny, a thin trickle of fluid escaped her pussy and started to roll down her hot, pulsing skin. His tongue caught it and followed the trail it had traveled, licking her thoroughly, igniting nerve endings she hadn't even known she possessed. His tongue traced a course from her perineum over her inner lips, outlining her opening, licking, sucking, all the way to her clit in long, slow, lazy patterns, getting close, so close, but never actually touching.

She reached for him, spreading herself open further, her clit crying out for his attention. She was close. So close. Every nerve in her body screamed for release. If he would just...

"What do you want, Candy? Say it. You can tell me."

Her thighs quivered in helpless anticipation. "Suck me," she begged. "Please."

"There. Was that so hard?"

She couldn't answer. Couldn't form a coherent

thought. His tongue licked higher, closer, taking a wide, lazy swipe across her clit, bringing her hips up off the bed. Spread soft and flat, it bathed, rather than prodding. She could feel each bump of its rough surface, like a cat licking her sensitive skin. He circled closer, tighter, teasing, to outline the entrance to her hungry pussy, then zeroing in on his target. She shrieked at the electrical charge that went through her when he sucked the small hood between his lips.

Soft, gentle, yet relentless, he licked and sucked, fluttering his tongue over the tiny organ, slowly urging the hood open to reveal the trophy within. Wave after wave of sensation washed over her, building like a tide, threatening to pull her under.

"Come for me, baby," he breathed over her dampened skin. He thrust his fingers deep into her, stroking the top of her vaginal wall, looking for that elusive G-spot. She was about to tell him it didn't exist, she didn't have one, when her hips shot up off the bed as though he'd stabbed her.

She screamed. She never screamed during sex. Ever.

Damn it, why the hell had he stopped? She reached out blindly, finding his head and pulling him back to her target.

"That's right, baby. Show me what you want."

Her voice came out a low moan. She thrust her wet, aching pussy toward his face. Want? She wanted everything, all at once. She wanted…

He worked her clit with his lips and tongue, licking, sucking, teasing, while he plunged his fingers into her, reaching, stroking, demanding. Oh, yeah. Nice, slow, steady strokes that had her building to a fever pitch. Was that her, thrashing wildly on the bed, moaning with need as he fucked her with his tongue?

Surely that wasn't her voice crying out in pleasure bordering on pain as her pussy contracted around his fingers, pulling, squirming, reaching for him with every lick, with every thrust? That couldn't be her body rising up off the bed as he stroked harder, faster, filling her, pushing her, demanding more, while he sucked her clit back into his mouth.

That definitely wasn't her cry of release as she broke around him, shattering like so much glass, the pieces falling in gentle arches to litter the ground like rose petals. And those weren't her tears, rolling uncontrollably down her cheeks to stain the fine linen sheets as she sobbed out her pain and her anger and all the things she no longer needed.

He left her empty for a moment, the cool air assaulting her sensitized skin, while he slid onto the bed next to her, taking her in his arms to hold her, rocking her, her head cradled against his chest. "Shhh. It's all right, baby. I'm here."

"I'm --"

"No. I don't want to hear you say 'I'm sorry' again, Candy. You don't have anything to be sorry for. Let it go."

Some other woman lay there, lifting her empty pussy toward him, stroking over his skin, wrapping her legs around his waist, guiding his cock to where she wanted it. He was so hard, so loaded she was sure he would burst the moment he entered her wet, hungry slit. She shuddered as the last of the contractions wrapped around him, but he held, buried within her, unmoving.

He leaned in to kiss her, his face still wet with her juices, her smell clinging to him, and the two halves of herself collided. She rubbed her skin against him, absorbing the smell and the taste of what he'd done to her. "More," she pleaded. "Don't stop."

"I'm not going anywhere, baby."

She hated being called baby -- except by him. She pushed her breasts up toward his mouth, hovering just out of reach. "Please…"

He rose up on his knees, her legs wrapped around his waist, his hands stroking over her skin in long, sensuous sweeps. "You have a beautiful body, Candy."

He knelt over her, studying her like an artist might. She choked back a desire to cry again. "No one's told me that in a long time. I thought… well, you know, things -- change -- as a woman gets older."

A slow smile settled on his lips. "I don't know how old you are, Candy. I don't care. When I saw you in that crowd the first thing I thought was you were the most beautiful woman I'd ever laid eyes on. You're perfect."

"Perfect. Me." She let herself really look at him. All of him. His bronze skin reflected the early morning light. He had the face of a model. If anyone should know, she should. And he had the body to go with it. He was hard and fit and sculpted like a Greek god. She needed to tell him. "So are you," was the best she could manage.

He grinned down at her. "Nobody's ever told me that before. I'm glad you like my body. Maybe these last two years were good for something. Touch it, Candy. Touch me. Anywhere."

Her hands rose to stroke over his magnificent skin, gathering courage as she touched.

"Just relax. Enjoy yourself. Sex is supposed to be fun."

She was ready this time as he began to move inside her again, rocking slowly, his hands on her hips guiding her in this new rhythm.

Her fingers brushed over his lips, and he sucked them in, worshiping each one in turn. He laid his thumbs on either side of her clit, stroking with each long, slow, lazy thrust. "Let go," he whispered. "Ride the wave."

Surprise had her laughing as the orgasm built, sweeping over her easily this time.

"Come for me, Candy," he murmured.

The next one came faster, harder, and he picked up the pace.

He was the one who looked strained now, building back to a fevered frenzy, pulling her hard against him, driving deeper into her wet, waiting flesh. "Is this what you wanted?"

Her muscles tightened around him as an even stronger orgasm threatened to rip the breath from her lungs. "Yes," she moaned, her fingers digging into his hips.

As if what he'd done before had been only a tease, he pistoning into her, hot and heavy, pulsing with need. Her legs locked around his waist, tilting her pelvis so he could push more of his length into her. Candy could feel the weight of his balls slamming against her with every thrust. The hotel bed frame creaked with the strain of their efforts. He bared his teeth, growling like a feral animal as he shattered at last, spilling into her in a searing gush. She shattered like glass as he screamed out her name.

Brook's arms buckled. He would have fallen to her side, but she pulled him down flat, keeping him locked inside her until his last final spurt filled the condom. Still she held him, enjoying the feel of his weight, his cock going slack as the aftershocks milked him of his last resistance.

He propped himself up on one elbow, moving his free hand to brush the hair from her face. Candy thought he would speak, would say something to shatter the mood, but instead he brushed his lips across hers in a tender kiss too perfect for words. He slid his arms around her, rolling them so that they lay with her head on his chest. He stroked gently over her skin with one hand while with the other he carefully removed the condom, dropping it into the wastebasket beside the bed.

Cradling her body against his, Brook held her until her eyes fell closed and she drifted off to sleep in his arms.

9:05 AM Saturday, 18 December 2004
Mandarin Oriental, Singapore

The concierge buzzed the room promptly at 9:00 AM. By 9:05, Candy was dressed in her freshly pressed white business suit, sans jacket, and reading the *New York Times* over coffee, black, no sugar. Brook stood nearly naked, first extending his arms, then suffered the indignity of having his crotch probed by a set of small, male hands and a tape measure. "*Di di,*" he hissed at the smaller man.

"*Xin loi, xin loi,*" the tailor responded, looking surprised.

"*Mau len.*"

Candy lowered her paper to survey the two, her eyebrow raised a notch.

Brook glowered back at her. "Is this really necessary?"

"Yes."

"You already spent a small fortune on clothes. And as soon as I put them on you'll want to take them back off."

"It's like unwrapping Christmas presents. The wrapping paper is important. It reflects the quality of the gift inside."

"Well, if anyone's going to have their hands on my crotch, I would much rather it be you."

She motioned to the tailor, who was apparently done with his measurements and was now producing swatch books. "Why don't you go work on the wrapping paper, Brook? I'll order breakfast as soon as I'm done here."

A slow smile spread over his lips. "Why don't we just start with dessert?"

Candy touched the point of her tongue to her upper lip. The thought of what he might do made her wet, and oh-so-ready. "I'll try not to take too long."

She closed her eyes and ran her fingers over the fabric samples, imagining what each one would feel like when she ran her hands over Brook.

Except he wouldn't be here.

Come Monday she would take him to the US Embassy. There would be forms, and paperwork, and records from the US, but with her personal assistant, Kelly, working on the list back home, they could have it all together in a couple of days.

By this time next week Brook would be gone.

At least wherever he went he'd not be mistaken for a construction worker again. She tried to concentrate on the fabrics, and not the hollow, lonely ache his leaving would bring. Getting him home was the right thing to do.

She'd lived half her lifetime and come halfway around the world to find a man who was exactly what she wanted, and now she would have to give him up. Sometimes morality was damn inconvenient.

He *wasn't* perfect for her. He wasn't *anything* for her. He was a man she'd paid for, pretending to be just what she wanted him to be. She didn't know anything about him. Who he was. Where he'd come from. How he'd ended up in that auction. She hadn't even had a real conversation with him. He could be a criminal, for all she knew. An -- an…

An intelligent, caring man who'd taken the time to get to know her body, and given her the best sex of her life.

Well, that wasn't a basis for a relationship, was it?

He wouldn't want to stay with her anyway. She

was old enough to be… well, maybe not his mother, but too old for him. Judging a guy's age was always harder, but she'd bet he'd been in grade school when she graduated law school.

And even if he'd been the *perfect* age for her, the *perfect* man for her, that didn't make it right. She'd *bought* him. At an auction. If rescuing him from the mess he'd been in came with a price --"I'll get you home if you'll just spend the week giving me multiple orgasms" -- then it wasn't much of a rescue.

Candy signed the tailor's bill and firmed her resolve. No matter how handsome Brook was, no matter…

"Hey, beautiful. What are you frowning over?"

Candy looked up with a start. He stood in the doorway, white dress shirt unbuttoned, charcoal suit jacket falling open to reveal the broad expanse of his chest, long, dark hair flung back over his shoulders, a questioning smile on his lips.

How the hell was she supposed to remember this was temporary, just a romantic interlude they'd shared, when he looked at her like that?

Oh, God. She was so fucked.

"What's wrong, Candy?"

He stalked closer, a predatory cat about to pounce. Every nerve ending in her skin responded to him, crying out for his touch. "Nothing. I was just -- I downloaded a list of things we need to do from the US Embassy Web site. I thought you'd want to know…"

He stopped behind her, his hands on her shoulders, kneading gently. "I'm alone in a luxury hotel with a beautiful woman. Monday will be here soon enough, Candy. I don't want to think right now." He leaned down to trace the curve of her ear with his tongue. "I'm hungry."

She stood, turning in his arms to drag his body closer. "I ordered room service."

"Yeah?" He sucked her bottom lip between his, nibbling on it.

"Blueberry crêpes with whipped cream on top. And sausage. Links. It comes with blueberry syrup."

"Christ," he whispered, his breath ragged as he pulled her body hard against his raging erection. "Do you know what you do to me, woman?"

She stroked over the length of his pulsing cock. "Do I make you want to forget there's a world out there full of people and responsibilities and just stay here forever? Because that's what you do to me."

"When I see you looking like that, your expression so serious, I want to pull you into my arms and distract you from whatever makes you think so hard."

"Distract me, Brook. I need distracting."

He lowered his head to bite her nipple through the fabric of her sheer silk shirt. She pushed against him, already dripping with need. Pulling the skirt up around her hips, he explored the backs of her thighs and the smooth curve of her ass.

She mewled in protest as he let go of her, stepping back to skim her panties down her legs, then fishing into his back pocket for one of the hotel condoms.

"Let me do that."

He handed it over wordlessly, his face a tight mask of concentration as she ripped the foil packet open and unzipped his fly. She pulled the boxers down, hooking them under his engorged shaft. Her hands were shaking, with need or excitement she wasn't sure which. Maybe both.

"Nervous?" His hands covered hers, helping her

roll the condom down his cock.

"Yeah."

They stood, foreheads just touching, staring down at their hands, linked over his cock. "Me too."

"Really?"

"No one's ever made me feel like you do, Candy."

She brushed her thumb across the head of his cock, watching him surge into her hands. "How do I make you feel? Besides hard?"

"Sexy," he whispered. "Desirable. Attractive."

"You are sexy," she assured him. "And I find you very, very attractive and desirable. All I can think about when I'm around you is sex. I've never felt like this before."

He pushed his cock into their joined fingers, his movement slow and controlled, before he lifted his hands to caress her, sliding slowly up and down her sides and over her ass. "Kiss me, Candy. Touch me. I love the feel of your hands on me."

His shirt was in the way. Nudging it aside with her nose, Candy leaned in to run feather light kisses along the length of the large, dark Kangi. His skin shivered under her touch. Inspired, she ran her kisses lower, swirling her tongue over his nipple. He jumped, pulling her hard against his cock. She tried it again, sucking the tiny, hard bud this time.

He jerked back, thrusting his pelvis toward her. "Jesus, Candy. I can't take much more of that. I'll embarrass myself."

Laughing, she swiped the nipple again, this time attacking with her whole mouth. Her laughter faded when he picked her up, pulling her legs around his waist, his cock so hard, so close to her pussy she could feel the scorching heat of him on her sensitive skin as she rocked her hips, trying to pull him even closer.

Where was he *going?* The bed wasn't…

He set her on the floor behind the nearest living room chair. Turning her in his arms, he caressed her body and kissed her shoulder blades through the silk blouse, finding erogenous zones she didn't know she had, awakening every nerve in her body with the long, slow, sensuous sweeps of his hands. Still, she was almost shocked when he pushed her forward, bending her over the back of the chair.

Surely he didn't mean… her muscles tightened involuntarily. He was too big. She'd never…

"Relax, Candy. I won't hurt you. Ever."

It was a lie, and they both knew it. He'd be going home, back to whatever life he'd had before.

He stroked between her legs, finding her pussy flooded and ready. His cock eased in where his fingers had been, the heat of him startling her even now. *Yes. Oh, yes.* This was what she wanted. His kisses sent shivers down her neck. "Oh God," she managed. "You feel so good in me."

"Yes," he agreed, chuckling. "I do." He slid in and out once, twice, slowly, as if to get the feel of her in this position.

"Fuck me."

He slammed in all the way to his balls, laughing now. "That what you want?"

"Yes!" she screeched. "Oh, God, yes!"

Long and hard, deep and fast, he pumped into her, his thrusts knocking her forward. She braced her hands on the chair's deep, overstuffed arms, her hair cascading down around her face like a curtain.

She wanted more. "Fuck me," she begged. "Oh, Jesus, Brook, fuck me!"

His fingers slipped around to caress her clit as he

rode her, pushing her higher, higher, rocking her back even as he pushed her forward. She wanted to help him, to touch him, to touch herself, but she couldn't. She clung to the chair helplessly, slamming back as hard against him as she could. He used both of his hands to work her mons and clit now, stroking, teasing, demanding. "Come for me, baby. Come for me."

As if all she'd needed was his demand, his breath hot and fierce across her sweat dampened skin, she exploded, bursting around him. "Oh God," she screamed, her words lost in a tumbling moan.

"That's it, baby. That's it." One hand, wet with her come, slid between them to circle her anus. She came again, the room going dim, as he slipped one finger into her tight opening. He played her body like a guitar as she writhed beneath him. On every stroke something filled her. She didn't know which she wanted more, his cock or his fingers. His balls slapped against her, their coarse fur rough against her smooth, sensitive skin, one more assault on her senses. Harder, deeper, the pressure of his fingers within her and the tight clenching of her orgasms urged him to join her. "Come for me, baby," she echoed. "Now!"

With a groan he shuddered against her, his hips pistoning in their final flurry of frenzied need, his seed spurting long and deep, filling the condom until its burden stretched her, a hot liquid barrier, caressing and soothing, and binding them together.

He lay over her, his cheek plastered to the damp silk clinging to her back, his breath coming in long, slow, ragged gasps.

A low knock sounded at the door. "Room service," the voice announced.

2:55 PM Saturday, 18 December 2004
Mandarin Oriental, Singapore

"The maids will hate us."

Brook dove after a dripping stream of blueberry syrup, licking his way to the tip of her nipple. "Put an extravagant tip on your expense account."

Candy laughed. Lord, she couldn't remember when she'd last laughed. Then she shrieked as he bit her, shoving playfully at his shoulder. "I should."

Brook collapsed beside her, beyond caring whether the sheets would stick to him or not. "Do you want to talk about him?"

"What?"

"The man you're angry with. The reason you don't mind running up huge bills on the company credit card."

Candy shook her head. "Richard? No, I don't want to talk about Richard."

"Okay."

"A client asked for an audit of his expense account. One of Richard's personal clients. Seems his expenses included a week's worth of dinner for two at places like *Hôtel Plaza Athénée*, in Paris. When I confronted Richard, he reminded me I'd refused the trip. He took his personal assistant instead. He said it was unprofessional of me to question his business and personal ethics in front of a client."

"Bastard." Brook pulled her head against his shoulder, massaging her scalp with his fingertips. "What did you do?"

"I apologized to the client and walked out."

Brook's fingers kept up their lazy pattern in her hair while he waited. The man had an unnerving capacity for pregnant silences.

"I kept walking. Out of the conference room, out of the office. Out of the building. I packed two suitcases, cleaned out the checking account, and moved out of our apartment."

He laughed. "Kick 'em in the balls, Candy. Underneath your pristine business exterior you're a real scrapper."

"Thanks." She licked slowly over the outline of the tattoo on his chest. "What does this mean?"

Brook glanced down at the nearly black Kangi. "It's the symbol for *Human Being*. I'm half Cherokee. Most Native Americans call themselves the *Human Beings*. An ancient Laotian man did the tattoo for me."

Candy traced the tattoo with her finger, waiting.

"My grandmother used to tell stories, Cherokee prophecies. In all the stories, the Cherokee were the *Human Beings*, the people responsible for overseeing the earth, and maintaining balance in the world. If we did not fulfill our destiny, to warn people they were bringing the Earth out of balance, bad things would happen."

"And how is one man supposed to change the course of the world?"

"Grandma would say, as the world speeds up, you have to slow down. You teach by example, showing people how to appreciate the balance of the world, how to see the good balances out the bad."

Candy closed her eyes, trying to find the good in the world. All she could find was Brook, patiently showing her how to slow down. "Who are you, Brook? Who were you? Before?"

His fingers stilled on her skin. He waited so long to answer she almost thought he wouldn't. "Three years ago I was a grad student at the University of

Michigan. History of Southeast Asia. I was working on my doctorate, and I had a chance to do my fellowship at Hanoi University."

"Fellowship? You're a college professor?"

"Yeah. I was. Assistant professor, at least."

She almost laughed. "When I first saw you I thought you looked like a construction worker. I was afraid anyone as good looking as you are would be dumb as two rocks."

One heavy black eyebrow arched. "I suppose only women are capable of intelligent thought."

"No, of course not, but --"

"Can *you* read a blueprint?"

Candy blushed. "No."

"Can you measure an inverted right angle cut?"

"All right. I get your point. There could be one or two brain cells floating around in all that prime beefcake."

"I've done construction work. It's not all that easy." He still sounded a little peeved.

Candy captured his hand. "So how the hell did you end up here, Professor?"

He snorted softly. "Typical college fuck-up. I was doing fieldwork at a site in Laos between semesters. Went into a local bar one night and ordered a Lao-Lao. A kind of local whiskey, but stronger than I ever expected. Tasted like dirt. That's the last thing I remember. I think I got rolled. Next morning I woke up in the local jail. No wallet. No cash. No passport. No ID. No way to prove who I am. That one phone call thing? That's not Laos."

He pushed a hand through his thick, dark hair. "Three days later this man I've never seen before pays my bond. I owe him for my bond, so I have to work at his factory until I can pay him back. But I wasn't very good at the work. Pretty soon I owed more for food and the roof over my head than the wages I've earned. The longer I worked there the more money I owed him."

A hundred questions came to mind, but she waited for him to continue, hardly daring to breathe.

"It was like being caught in a nightmare, with no way out. I kept expecting to wake up back in Michigan. Instead there's a man with a cane ready to beat me if I don't do what I'm told. We were in a really remote rural area in Xam Nua province at that point. I keep thinking if I can just find a phone, let someone know I'm still alive -- but there aren't any phones there. Every time I escaped the village authorities would catch me and sell me back.

"I didn't learn very fast. Kept thinking I could get away, somehow get back to the life I had before. Instead I just kept getting farther in debt. The bosses don't want to be bothered with guys like me who cost them money, so when the next trader came through, I was one of the first to go. Ended up at a brickyard outside Vientiane, the capital of Laos. Vientiane's a big city, modern, even if it is one of the last communist strongholds. I figured in a city that size there has to be a working phone. It's near the border to Thailand. At the worst I figured I could slip across the border, get help in Thailand.

"But the guards here have guns. The monsoons hit and it's raining so hard you can't see three feet in front of your face. I have to search the gutters near the bars for change for a pay phone, and then the phones don't work in the rain. Two days of shivering in doorways soaked to the skin before the local cops arrest me and sell me back to the brickyard. By this time I'm so far in debt I could never work my way out.

Next slave trader comes through, I'm on my way here."

Candy swallowed hard, trying to find her voice. "What -- what will happen to the other people who were sold there yesterday?"

He shrugged. "It's either slave labor or forced prostitution."

She'd known. Hadn't wanted to voice the unspoken truth, but she'd known... that was the fear she'd seen in his eyes. "Oh, God."

"Human trafficking. Debt bondage. It happens all over the world. Most people don't want to know."

Was what she'd done any different? She'd wanted her doll badly enough to look the other way at a few minor technicalities. Where was the line? If you broke one law, then another...

Brook's hand skimmed up over her shoulder to brush back the hair from her face. His hand played over the curve of her hip. "I want this world. Your world. I want to believe. I don't think I can go back again, Candy."

"I won't let anyone take you back again, Brook. No matter what."

His fingers teased the outline of her nipple. "You really don't own a factory, do you?"

Her answer came out sounding like a sob. "No."

The tip of his tongue swiped over the hollow of her throat. "Or a brothel."

She shivered, caught off guard as much by the question as by the sensation of his tongue on her skin. "No, I don't own a brothel. But I --" She was as guilty as the German. "I *bought* you, Brook. What makes me any better than anyone else at that auction?"

"In the first place, you're a woman."

She nearly choked. "You mean --"

He kissed the place where her pulse shivered at the base of her neck, his breath hot against her moist skin. "What did you think? Women would pay to have me fuck them?"

"That's what I did, didn't I?" She swallowed hard, trying not to cry. "You don't owe me anything, Brook. Not sex. Not anything else."

His breath played over her ear, sweetly seductive even now. "Candy, I owe you everything. My sanity. Probably my life. But I'm not trying to pay you back with sex. This is just for me." He placed her hand over his randy cock, which jumped at her touch. "I want to be here, Candy. I don't think a man could fake that."

Her eyes closed as she explored the feel of him, fine, smooth, silky skin over heat that promised so much. His mouth was doing the most erotic things to her breasts.

He stilled. "What happens to me after Christmas?"

There wasn't much of her thought process still functioning, but perhaps it was for the best, because she finally managed to ask the question she should have started with. "What do you want to happen, Brook?"

Beautiful gray eyes fastened on hers. "Nobody's asked me that in a very long time."

She took advantage of the space between them to run her hands across his chest. "Well, I'm asking you now."

She could feel the effort it cost him to share that part of himself. "I just want to go home."

"I think I can probably manage that. I'll do everything I can to help you."

His eyes searched hers, looking for something she didn't know how to give him. "Candy, do you know what it would take to get me out of here?"

"A passport and a plane ticket."

"You make it sound so simple…"

"It's just paperwork. The kind of paperwork I do for a living." She traced the outline of the tattoo once again. "What about once you're home? What do you want to do once you're back in the States?"

He took his time thinking it over, but she was getting used to that by now. "I don't know. Go back to school I guess. Try to put my life back together."

She shouldn't say it. He was a client. Just a client. When this was all over, he'd be going home. She had no right to ask for anything else. But the words wouldn't stay down. "Have you ever thought about modeling, Brook? With looks like yours, you're a natural. Come back to New York with me. Follow me around for a week and I'll land a dozen contracts on your doorstep."

She could feel his heart thudding beneath her hand. "Follow you around? What do you do for a living, Candy?"

"I negotiate contracts. Booking agents, advertising agencies, bands, models, actors. I'm an Intellectual Property Rights attorney."

"An attorney." He closed his eyes. "Intellectual Property Rights. You deal with celebrities. It really *isn't* a big deal for you, is it? You've done this before, for clients, haven't you?"

"More times than I care to think about."

"You really think you can get me out of this mess, Candy? I don't have anything. No ID of any kind. I can't prove any of what I've told you is the truth."

She tried to keep her tone hopeful without making things sound too easy. "I think the consulate at the US Embassy here can help us."

He swallowed hard. "God, I want to believe you. I want this all to be a nightmare I can wake up from." He bent his head to suck on the tip of one tight, swollen nipple. "Except you. I don't want to wake up from you."

They lay together, naked and tangled around each other, Monday looming over them.

"Candy?"

"Brook?"

"If I tried to walk out the door right now would you try to stop me?"

"Yeah," she answered honestly. "I don't want to send you home Monday, Brook. I want to help you get your life back, but I don't want to have to let you go."

"But would you use force to try to keep me here?"

She pulled back a little, remembering the bruise on his arm. "No! Never."

He ran his hand up her hip and along the curve of her waist, pulling her closer, into a long, lingering kiss that explored the possibilities between them. "You haven't forced me to do anything, Candy. This wasn't coercion."

She closed her eyes and swallowed the tears that threatened. "Coercion doesn't have to be physical. I brought you here. I spent enough money to make you feel obligated. I'm a lawyer. I'm supposed to know better. What I did was wrong."

"I escaped from armed guards, remember? More than once. I could have escaped from you too. I could have overpowered you or just walked out the door while you were asleep. I'm here, right now, because I want you. We can talk all afternoon or we can fuck. Which do you want, Candy?"

She found herself laughing as she rolled over him to straddle his hips. "I want to fuck."

4:10 PM Saturday, 18 December 2004
Mandarin Oriental, Singapore

He rolled with her, wrestling until she let him win, then just poised there, his aching cock inches from where they both wanted it.

No. Not like this. Not in a hurry. He wanted more.

He stared down at her, the naked beauty who held him captive more effectively by the force of her passion than any owner's chains ever had. She wanted him. The wonder of it washed over him. Right now there was only here, only Candy, and a fire burning within him in a part of his soul he'd thought long dead.

Monday would raise its ugly head soon enough. Today needed to be something special. Memories stirred. They were in Singapore, after all... what could be more appropriate. He pulled the sheet over her to keep her from getting chilled. "Shhh. Wait here just a minute. I promise I won't leave you alone for long."

She smiled up at him, her eyes trusting. "I'll miss you."

The pang hit him low in the gut, a dull ache. There was nothing even vaguely similar about her. Nothing. And yet sometimes...

He rolled to his feet, bending back over the bed to kiss her quickly and escape before she could see the memory in his eyes. She was here. She was now. She was real. And he needed this. Lord, how he needed this. It was time to let go of the past. He'd done his penance, and then some.

A smile quirked his lips as he gathered the candles from the living room into the crook of his arm. There were roses in the vase on the table, still fresh despite the tropical heat. But then, the room was climate controlled. His nipples hardened as a blast of refrigerated air hit him.

Matches. Naturally there were matches to go with the candles. He remembered seeing them somewhere… next to the minibar. He'd seen them next to the crackers, a lifetime ago.

The hotel staff might almost have been planning this, he thought as he arranged the candles in front of the vanity mirror. The size and depth of the huge heart-shaped tub had annoyed him with its extravagance when he first saw it. In his other life, whole families had lived in huts smaller than this hotel's bathroom.

Now he appreciated its opulence.

Perfect.

This had to be perfect.

If there was one gift he could give her, it was patience.

The water pressure was good. The tub wouldn't take too long to fill. He pulled the petals off of the roses, dropping them into the steaming water, then carefully broke open the fruity rose hips, dropping those into the water as well. Last came a handful of bath oil beads, from a bowl arranged decoratively on the vanity. He wondered briefly if they were supposed to be merely ornamental.

Not tonight.

Some inner sense alerted him to her presence. It was as if his body had become so attuned to her he could feel her, sense her. He looked up to find her standing in the doorway, transfixed, like a moth caught in the candle's flame. Aphrodite wrapped in a hotel sheet.

He was nervous at being caught in the act. If she

laughed...

She wasn't laughing. She was trying not to cry. Unreasonable anger toward a man he'd never met washed over him, but he let it go. There was no room for that here between them. Another day, perhaps. If they had other days.

He held out his hands to her, palms up, and she let go of the sheet as she crossed the room to him. Candlelight reflected off the mirrors to play over her skin, soft, pale, luminescent. He gathered her close to kiss her, marveling at the taste of her lips, the feel of her, so soft and acquiescent in his arms.

The water was perfect, hot and steamy and fragrant with the roses. Hands still interlaced, they stepped into the water together. He slid down to rest against the gentle curve of the heart's bow, guiding her to lay her head under his chin when she would have taken the opposite side. She settled slowly between his thighs, his knees on either side of her, as she relaxed enough to find the curves where they fit together, her head barely above the water level.

"This is nice," she whispered, as if surprised. "This is... I like this."

He leaned forward to caress her ear with his lips. "You inspire the romantic in me."

She loosened slowly, trusting him to keep her head above the water, as the steam penetrated her tight, tired muscles. He ran his hands over her arms, massaging gently at the knots where she stored the tension in her shoulders.

"Mmmm."

He loved the way she purred when he stroked her. She leaned into him when he slid his hands lower, over her shoulders, down along her sides, over the curve of her hips, and back up over the soft swell of her belly, outlining her breasts. He wanted to touch her there, but he didn't. Not yet.

As if she'd suddenly remembered her own hands, she began to trace the outline of his legs wrapped around her. She brushed backwards against the hair, sending tiny shivers over his skin. "No fair," he whispered.

"You mean I'm not allowed to touch?"

"No. I get to do all the work this time. This is all for your pleasure."

"Mmm. But touching you pleases me."

A little pang of warning hit him down low, but he ignored it. He lifted her hands and placed them over her own breasts. "Show me what you like."

Her hands stilled, then moved, hesitantly at first, shy beneath his. She lifted her breasts slightly, so he could feel the weight of them, then circled the nipples with her thumbs, barely brushing the tight, taut tips. A shudder passed through him, surprising him with its intensity, and he bent his head to bite gently on her shoulder. Heat surged like molten fire through him as his erection turned painfully hard.

He stilled for a moment, letting things calm down, then tightened his hands over hers just a little, massaging her fingers into her breasts. He felt her respond, her breasts thrusting out to meet him just a little.

Patience. This was about taking things slow.

Straightening her legs against the bottom of the tub, she slid up his wet, bath-oil slicked chest until they were more closely aligned, then tucked her legs over his, spreading herself open for him, like inviting a hungry man to a feast. His ravenous cock approved.

But his mind was in control here. Yeah. Right. As if maintaining control was ever an option around this woman. Still, he had a plan. He slid his right hand down lower, tracing her belly, sliding across the soft skin of her inner thigh, the water lapping his arm with a sound like the gentle waves of a low tide receding.

She practically jumped out of the water when his fingers brushed over the soft wet tendrils of hair at her mons. He rested his fingers there, just touching, not demanding, until she settled back against him. "So soft," he whispered as he stroked over her, nothing more, really, than a wisp of a touch. "So perfect." He let one finger drift between her lower lips, teasing, testing, though he already knew what he'd find. She was slick and ready for him, ready and impatient. He stroked gently, outlining her labia, feathering her soft folds of skin until they bloomed beneath his touch. She bucked against his hand, refusing to be calmed.

"You said we were going to fuck. Now you're torturing me. Not fair."

"No. *You* said you wanted to fuck. I decided I wanted to make love to you instead. We can fuck later."

She groaned, throwing her head back as she raised her hips toward his fingers. "I want you now."

"Patience, kitten. Patience."

Very slowly she relaxed, submitting to his long, careful exploration of her body, mewing in contentment as his hand replaced hers on her breast. Slow was good. Yes, slow was good. Except...

What was she doing with her hands?

A groan tore from his lips. She'd spread her cheeks, enveloping him between the soft mounds and then let go, clenching against him with all of her small strength. "Do you not understand *slow*, woman? You're bad for my concentration."

"Good," she agreed. "Because I haven't had any

since I met you." She tightened around him, then released, the feeling almost like being inside her, her skin wet and slick, her muscles toned and --

No.

She was not going to break his control. Not this time.

He lifted her, setting her once again where he wanted her, telling his randy cock to quit trying to run the show. Slow. This was going to be slow. She whimpered in protest as he pulled her back against his chest, her body weight pressing his cock between them. That would be good enough. For now.

"Behave." He nipped her ear as he issued the order. He stilled his hands, letting her cool down a little as he waited patiently for her to relax. Finally she settled back, the water and the steam working their magic, her muscles melting into his until their bodies seemed to be joined at the nerve endings.

You couldn't exactly call this relaxed. Her body hummed like the vibrato of an opera singer under his hands. Hell. His cock wasn't all that relaxed either. If she moved at all…

He brushed his hands down her waist and over her thighs, back to where they had been, and she moved. She pressed against him as she opened her thighs wider, inviting him to touch wherever he wanted to. He reached deep inside of himself for control, for patience.

He was just going to touch her, to tease, but somehow his fingers were inside her, her body demanding as she moaned, surging up toward his touch. Maybe if he --

She cried out, straining against the heel of his hand as he buried his fingers deep in her pussy. Lord. She was coming already, her body so taut he could have strummed her like a guitar. He closed his left hand over her nipple, pinching hard, and she screamed, climaxing in wave after shattering wave.

He held her until she calmed, listening to her breathing slow. Then he let his fingers go back to work. Her body felt lethargic beneath his touch.

Perfect.

Raising her up just a little he slipped inside her, letting her own body weight impale her over his tortured cock. "Mmm," she murmured as she slid down over him.

The angle was awkward, but it didn't matter much. He felt at home.

They lay together, joined but not moving, as he reached over to turn the hot water back on. The running water had a soothing effect, calming his shattered nerves. This was just sex, damn it. Great sex, but sex. Nothing more. Monday he would…

"I like the feel of you inside me. I could get used to this."

Oh, yeah, that helped a lot. "Me too." And that was as close to the truth as he was going to let himself get tonight.

He lifted her breasts, loving the feel of their weight in his hands. Her slick sheath tightened around him convulsively as he flicked his thumbs over the sensitive buds of her outthrust nipples. He pinched gently, rolling them between his fingers like little gummy bear toys. She rose up on his cock, surging into his hands, only to slam back down, trying to take more of him inside her.

That was more than he could stand. The hell with slow. The water lapped fiercely at the sides of the tub. "Ride me," he groaned, throbbing desperately within her.

Her laughter promised retribution as she arched her back, sliding up his pulsing length before she settled back again. "Slow, remember?"

He pinched at her nipples, demanding. Her shuddering gasp was reward enough. "Bastard."

"Yeah." He slid his fingers over her clit, riding her with his palm, his fingertips just out of reach. She surged up to meet him, her strength impressive as she clamped onto him, pulling him into her.

Now it was his turn to groan. He found her hands and placed one on her own breast, the other with her fingers against the soft curls of her mons. "Your turn," he instructed as he scooped her hips into his hands. That was better. Now he could thrust up into her, slamming her all the way down against his balls. Watching her stroke her clit only made his balls ache harder.

He could just see her in the bathroom mirror, her image blurred by the water and the steam, her face a mask of concentration as she massaged her breasts, first the left, then the right. His fingers bit into her hips, driving her down harder, while his teeth closed over her shoulder, alternately biting and licking whatever skin he could reach.

"Fuck me," she pleaded, her voice hoarse as she strained against him, pushing with her heels as she rode him hard now.

"What happened to slow?" he teased, laughing against her ear.

"This is slow, Goddamnit!"

All semblance of control snapped as she tightened around him, her body jerking in frenzied release as her fingers stabbed at her clit. He heard a voice that sounded like his screaming her name. The waves washed over him, drowning him in sweet release. "*Pom rak khun,*" he breathed. *I love you...I love you.*

Oh, shit. Where the hell had that come from?

10:15 AM Monday, 20 December 2004
United States Embassy, Singapore

"This is a mistake, Candy. I shouldn't be here."

Candy watched Brook pace, trying to figure out what he wasn't telling her.

"I can't just walk up to the U.S. ambassador and say 'Here I am, send me home'."

"Why not?"

"It's not that simple. You have to have documents. Identification."

Patiently Candy pointed to the printout the receptionist had handed them. "Yes, I can see that. Your birth certificate and seven forms of secondary ID. We have a whole list to choose from. Some of these things must be available. I've e-mailed Kelly. She'll start on the list Monday morning, their time. It's going to take a couple of days to get all this together, but if anyone can do it, Kelly can."

"Where would she even find any of that? I've never had a union card."

"Your high school yearbook should be on file in the public library. School transcripts from high school and college are no problem. She gets those for employment purposes all the time. Copies of your diplomas will take longer, but they can be had. And the college can produce a W-2 and a copy of your insurance card from their records, I'm sure. If not you must have had some medical bill somewhere at some time. Kelly will take care of it, whatever it is. She'll send a courier to pick everything up, then expedite it all to us. We should have your ID in hand by Friday morning."

Brook paced the room, looking more and more

agitated. "It's not that simple. It can't be that simple."

Candy laid down her pen, trying to read between the lines. "What aren't you telling me, Brook?"

"It's just too easy."

"It's easy because I have Kelly back in the States to do the legwork. Kelly's the best. If anyone can find what we need, she can."

Somehow her explanation didn't seem to help all that much. He stopped, turning to stare out the window.

"The Secretary will see you now."

* * *

The embassy was almost anticlimactic. Paperwork. Everything revolved around paperwork. Forms to fill out. Backgrounds to be checked. A few small fees to be paid. And always, with the government, there was waiting.

They visited the tailor's shop, staggering out under the weight of newly acquired purchases. Candy dragged Brook to the hairdresser, who took extra care to restore order to his mass of sun bleached hair, leaving Brook looking even darker, more stylish, and devastatingly handsome. The manicurist worked her own miracles while he grumbled about unnecessary expenses. No more broken, work-scarred nails.

Candy sensed Brook had had as much of civilization and polite society as he could handle for one day. He seemed relieved when she suggested they head back to their suite.

"I'm starving," he assured her. "I might even let you order room service for me."

Candy laughed as he kissed her, demanding more when he would have pulled away with a quick touch of his lips. "Why do I think you're talking about something more than *Pad Thai*?"

"You can see right through me, woman," he whispered as he cupped her hand around his throbbing cock. "Let me show you what I mean by room service."

"We're going to have to behave until we get back to the room. Too bad."

Brook slid his hand up the inside of her thigh, shielding her body from the cabdriver's view in the mirror with his bulk. "Who says?"

Candy tried to look scandalized, instead of exhilarated. "Brook, we're in *public*."

"We're in Singapore. The birth rate here is so low they've passed laws making it legal to make out almost anywhere. Including in a car." His fingers paused as they found the naked triangle of fur pressing against his hand. "Forget something?"

She blushed as he slipped a finger inside her, trying not to moan in delight. "No…"

"No what?"

"I didn't forget -- I was planning to surprise you."

"I'm surprised," he agreed, sliding her hand over the length of his scalding erection. "If this cabdriver doesn't hurry up I'm going to find out whether cabs count as cars or not."

He kissed her, swallowing her cry as she drenched his hand with the first flood of her delight.

* * *

Except for the air of sultry defiance that shimmered in his eyes, Brook could have been any other hotel guest. That, and of course, he was far too handsome to escape notice. Women turned to stare at him as they passed through the atrium on the way back to the elevator. It wasn't the same stare they'd given him the first time she'd brought him up to her room. Candy knew what they saw. He looked like the kind of man who'd have something more exciting than her on his arm.

Well, men walked out of here escorted by beautiful women all the time. Candy held her head up high as Brook led her back through the atrium to the main elevator.

Shopping bags filled his arms. "Tell me you're done spending money for a while," he whispered against her ear as he waited for the elevator. "I'm beginning to feel like a gigolo."

Candy laughed as the elevator doors swept open. "Darling, if you were a gigolo, you'd already have a wardrobe like this. Probably much more expensive. If you're going to model, you have to look the part."

"Model." Brook shook his head, sending the carefully groomed sable curls spinning. "Why on earth would anyone ever want to pay me to dress in their clothes?"

Candy felt the heat in her veins as he shifted the open neck of his dress shirt. She leaned forward to lick the hollow at the base of his throat with the tip of her tongue. "I'm sure you could make as much or more money taking those clothes back off," she ventured.

"You're insane, woman." Still, he pulled her lower body against the erection that seemed to be constantly ready to greet her. His hips ground slowly against her, teasing, heating her blood past endurance.

Candy slipped her hands between them to unfasten the waist of the pleated dress pants, straining now to contain him. In moments her questing fingers had captured her prize. His low gasp of surprise and appreciation had her fingers drawing over the length of him as she bunched her skirt up higher on her hips.

"Candy, anyone could -- Oh, Christ!" His

protests died as she slid over him, impaling herself on the length of his steel-hard shaft. He pulled her higher, lifting one leg to wrap it around his waist as he struggled with the logistics of maintaining his hold on her, his protests already forgotten. He reached out past her shoulder to stab at the elevator's emergency button.

The lights went out. The elevator lurched to a stop.

"Someone will notice the elevator's quit moving. They'll call hotel security."

"It'll take 'em a while to get here," Brook assured her. "We won't be long."

She hitched her leg higher around his waist, allowing him better access as he thrust into her, but it wasn't enough. Supporting her with her back pressed to the elevator wall, he cupped the curve of her hips, raising her completely off the floor, tilting her pelvis for better access. The red light began to blink on the elevator panel, lending an eerie glow to his face.

Candy rocked against him as hard as she could with the limited movement allowed her, clenching tightly with her legs wrapped around his waist. "You think this is covered under that public sex act you were talking about?" she whispered.

His breath tickled her ear. "I don't know, Counselor. You tell me."

"Hello?" A man's voice, faintly accented, called out in the dark. "Is everything all right up there?"

"The lights are out," Brook answered, his voice incredibly calm and poised. "And the elevator quit moving. What's wrong?"

"We're not sure, sir. We'll try to get it fixed as quickly as possible."

Candy fastened her teeth over his shirt collar,

trying to swallow a moan.

"Please do. My wife is getting a little hysterical."

"I'm sorry, sir. We've got our best team on it."

"Oh, yes," Candy agreed. "Please hurry."

"Shh," Brook laughed against her ear. "They've left the speaker on."

"Oh my God." She wasn't sure whether it was the sizzling pace of his frantic thrusting, or the feel of his lips nuzzling her ear, or the very real possibility of getting caught, but the orgasm ripped through her like the pain of a shattering blow. Brook's mouth covered hers, helping to swallow her cries.

"Can you get this thing moving?" Brook asked the speaker grill that showed intermittently in the blaze of the flashing red light. "My wife is afraid of small places. I'm afraid she's coming a bit unglued."

Candy bit his ear, daring him to protest.

"Why do you want to hurt me?" he demanded, his voice sounding amused.

For torturing her right now, for earlier, for --"Do you know what it was like, watching the tailor's little apprentice running her hands all over you?" she snarled. "I wanted to punch her."

"Vicious wench, aren't you?" His pace increased to a mindless frenzy as he slammed into her, his thrusts urgent and demanding now. "Are you going to get jealous and possessive on me?"

"Yes!" she cried, hiding the truth of her answer in her scream as she shattered around him.

"Good," he agreed as he rocketed into her. "Because I won't share you either."

Tears streamed down her face as she dug her fingers into his shoulders, clenching around him helplessly as she came again and again.

He wanted her. For however long this lasted, it

was she who was his slave. She'd done the one thing she'd promised herself she would not do. She'd lost her heart. To a man she was going to send off to another life within the week.

Candy woke up with a start. It took her a moment to figure out where she was. She heard water running. She brushed her hand over the still warm place in the bed next to her, and everything came crashing back. She was the proud owner of the most beautiful man her fantasies could ever have devised. By the end of the week he'd be gone and she'd never see him again.

And why would a man like him hang around once he didn't need her anymore? She couldn't keep a man her own age interested, and Richard hadn't been anywhere near that handsome.

Well, Brook was certainly interested. Maybe he *was* only doing his job, but if so, he did it damn well. Candy ran her hands over her breasts, remembering the feel of his teeth raking over her nipples. God. Just the thought of him got her wet and aching all over again.

* * *

Brook braced his hands on the tile shower wall, letting the water beat down on his head. The nightmare wouldn't go away, even with his eyes open. He might be in a luxury hotel suite at the moment, but the reality of his life was just outside the window, down some squalid back alley where tourists weren't allowed.

The hot water felt reassuring -- the strongest proof he had this was all real. You couldn't dream hot water up, could you? Not this hot, for this long. For the first time in two years he wasn't hungry. He'd eaten most of the leftovers from the tiny fridge before it occurred to him Candy really wouldn't mind if he called room service to order up breakfast.

Not that he would take a chance on calling room service. Too many people had already seen him with her. She'd had him all up and down Orchard Road, for Christ's sake. She'd spent a small fortune on him. Money wasn't all that important to her. Hell. If he had been her client, Candy wouldn't have minded spending twenty-five hundred dollars to get him out of trouble. Couldn't an ordinary civilian get involved, just because it was the right thing to do? If she had been his contact, would she have done anything different?

He wouldn't have fucked his contact.

He wouldn't have let his contact get to him like this.

He could just walk away. If she really could get him out of the country, he could just go home.

Like hell he could. He had an assignment to complete. These last two years had to have been for something. People had died. Someone had to pay. He had to pass along what he knew.

There was only one problem.

He'd violated the first rule of undercover work. Never get involved personally. He cared what happened to Candy. She was more than just a handy fuck. She mattered to him.

But she'd still broken the law. She was a lawyer, for Christ's sake. She'd known what was going on in that auction was illegal, but she'd bid on him anyway. She'd wanted him, and she'd been willing to pay his price, legal or not.

That wasn't fair, not really. He wanted to believe she'd really been trying to help him. There was no reason for her to have turned to trafficking in slavery and prostitution. A woman like Candy could have any man she wanted.

What the hell had happened to the people who were supposed to get him the fuck out of there months ago? He hadn't had any illusions standing there on that auction block. No one was coming for him. If it hadn't been for Candy…

He'd asked for her help, damn it. Maybe not with words, but he'd been desperate when he saw her in that crowd. He knew instinctively she didn't belong there. She was too innocent. Too willing to make eye contact. No one else had done that. He'd asked her to bid on him, the only way he knew how. The alternative had been trusting his contacts to find him in Japan… eventually.

He'd subjected himself to grueling physical labor and beatings and everything else the job had demanded of him. But he knew where he would draw the line. The first time some man tried to use him, he'd have killed him, and it would have been all over. She'd saved him from that. Ultimately, she'd saved his life.

He'd never had to sort out feelings like this before. Things had always been black and white. Right or wrong. This gray area in the middle was enough to drive him crazy.

If he turned her in now, no matter what happened, it would be over between them. She'd never trust him again. Not that he blamed her. Christ. Why couldn't he have met her three years ago?

Maybe it should be enough that, for whatever reasons, she'd wanted him to make love to her.

She'd wanted him enough to pay twenty-five hundred dollars for him, and that was a crime.

She hadn't exactly forced him into her bed. Coercion? No. She'd encouraged him, but you couldn't call that coercion. Not that she'd had to try very hard. It had been so long -- a lifetime had passed since he'd held a woman in his arms.

He closed his eyes, remembering the feel of her hands on his body, her lips touching his. He got hard just remembering how good her skin felt when he touched her.

Thinking about her didn't make things any easier.

He heard the bathroom door open and then click quietly, as if she'd kept her hand on the handle and turned the knob rather than just letting it catch as she pushed the door shut. For several long moments the only sound in the room was the water beating against the tile shower stall. Then cool air sent a shiver up his spine as the shower door slid open.

His cock jumped to rigid attention. He didn't dare turn around -- there was no way to hide what he'd been thinking. Still, Candy didn't say anything. Just stood there, staring. Or at least he could imagine her staring. He hated being watched. Always had. And the silence was getting to him.

"Morning," he managed.

"Good morning." Her voice had a soft, sexy purr to it. "You've been in here long enough I got a little worried."

He hadn't thought… She was a lawyer. Contract law. She was here on business, after all. He'd probably made her late for a meeting. "I'll be right out," he mumbled, trying to regulate his breathing.

"Brook, I --" There was a catch in her voice. "I was thinking I could come in, instead. If you don't mind sharing."

She didn't make him feel like her slave. If he had a lifetime he doubted he'd ever get used to the idea this woman really wanted him. Of course if he'd misunderstood somehow…

He turned to look over his shoulder, still a little embarrassed at the way her eyes swept over him. She was standing in the shower doorway, wrapped in a towel, looking more than a little uncertain herself. That helped. He turned slowly so she could see what he'd been trying to hide. "I was just thinking about you."

The uncertainty left her face as her eyes swept over him. Her smile turned brilliant as her towel dropped to the bathroom floor. Brook drew his breath in sharply, trying not to stare. Then he remembered he was allowed to stare. Or at least admire.

The hell with not looking. He wanted to devour her.

He pulled her into his arms and kissed her. Her lips parted instantly under his. In a hurry. She was always in a hurry. Well, someone had taught her that. He would teach her to slow down. Saturday was five days away. He could put off making any decision until after her birthday. He owed her that. A great many things could change in five days.

Slow would have been easier if he hadn't already been so hard from just thinking about her. Slow was not what his body wanted. Still, some finesse was required. He couldn't just grab her and…

"I woke up thinking about you." She ran her hands over his body. "You were gone."

"I won't let that happen again," he promised as she kissed her way down his chest, stopping to run her tongue over his nipples in a way that threatened to unman him. Still, he wasn't prepared when she dropped to her knees to take him in her mouth. His hands fisted in her hair. "Sweet Jesus," he managed. Her hands framed his throbbing cock, pushing him hard against the shower wall as she slid her mouth over the length of him, somehow managing to massage his cock with her tongue as she slid her lips over him.

His world took on a narrow focus. His assignment meant nothing. The last two years meant nothing. His life before meant nothing. His entire existence had had only one purpose -- to bring him to this place at this time. He couldn't remember ever having been so focused on his own sensations before. He ought to say something. Let her know how good...

His legs were going to give out. He was sure of it. She'd moved her hands, stroking his tight balls as if knowing how they ached for release. She stroked his cock as she drew her mouth back down, concentrating her attentions now on the painfully sensitive head. He bucked into her helplessly as she stroked with her tongue.

Gradually sound penetrated through the haze to the small remaining functional part of his brain. Someone was knocking on the door. God. If she quit now...

She urged him on, demanding he come for her now. She raked him deliberately with her teeth. That was more than he could stand. Thrusting into her, completely out of control, he shattered, pumping into her in wild desperation. She massaged his scrotum as if trying to milk him of everything he had.

Moments later he was empty and she was gone. He was dimly aware she'd turned the water off and wrapped herself back in her towel as she headed for the door.

He came back to his senses slowly. Voices. He could hear voices.

"... *foolish of you to bid against me, voman. Turn him over to me now.*"

"He's not here I tell you. I woke up and he was gone."

Shit. Schumacher had tracked him down already.

Candy was trying to cover for him, give him time to escape, but he couldn't do that. He couldn't leave her alone to face Schumacher and his goons. Brook pulled his filthy cut-off shorts out of the trashcan. Thank God Candy had hung up the Do Not Disturb sign. He'd be damned if he'd die naked. Maybe if he went peacefully Schumacher would leave Candy out of this. It was worth a try.

Brook armed himself with one of the huge hotel towels and shoved open the bathroom door.

There were only two of them. Lukas and his brother Otto. "I didn't go very far. Hello, Lukas. Otto. How's your pop?" If Candy hadn't been in the room... What was she doing, anyway? She was wrapped in a towel. What the hell did she need with her purse?

Lukas laughed, his voice amiable, as if this were just a social call. Overconfident, as always. "Brook. Ve missed you."

"Leck' mich," Brook replied with a sneer. *"Bierficker."*

Candy chose just that moment to drop her towel -- all the distraction Brook needed.

"Hurensohn!"

Damn. She'd stabbed Schumacher with something. Brook didn't take the time to look. His first left knocked Otto out cold. "Glass jaw," Brook noted in surprise as he looked back at Candy's victim. Blood ran down Lukas's hand. He was yanking Candy's weapon -- a comb? Candy had stabbed him with a comb? -- out of his forearm.

Brook laughed softly. "Here, Lukas, looks like you need this."

Schumacher spun to catch the towel, turning his

back on Candy. Mistake. A hotel lamp crashed into his skull. "Nice work." Brook ripped the cord out of the shattered lamp remains and used it to tie Schumacher's hands behind his back. Otto hadn't recovered yet. Still naked, Candy tossed Brook the belt from the robe the doorman had dressed him in. It didn't take long to get Otto tied at the wrists. Brook stripped off their belts and used those to bind their feet together, looping the cord for the wrists through the belts as well.

By the time he had the goons trussed up, Candy was dressed and throwing clothes in a suitcase. Damn, the woman was calm. Too calm. He crossed the room to her and rested his hands on her upper arms. "You got any duct tape?"

She whirled to face him, searching the floor behind him where the goons were sprawled. "Duct tape?"

"Yeah. You can fix anything with duct tape."

Her shoulders shook. He gathered her into her arms as she tried to figure out whether to laugh or to cry.

"Who are they?" she managed. "I'm not an idiot, Brook. I may be a little naïve, but even I can put the pieces together when they're pointing a gun at me. This was more than just a lost bid at an auction. It was from the beginning, wasn't it? Why did the man want you badly enough to come hunting for you? What's going on, Brook?"

"I'm sorry I got you into this, Candy. I don't know how they found me, but Schumacher does own whorehouses, all over the world. He really is part of the German mob. He wants me bad. He'd have killed me. Eventually. You just saved my life. Again. We gotta get out of here. If I can get you to the embassy I think you'll be safe. We gotta go. Now."

Candy just stared at him. Her silence was unnerving. He waited twenty seconds, thirty, but nothing. "Damn it, Candy, say something. Argue with me. Scream at me, but say something."

Candy crossed the room, throwing her damp towel at him with enough force to suggest she wished it were something larger, heavier. "You better put some pants on. Your cock's about to jump out of those shorts."

* * *

"I should have killed them."

Candy restrained herself from strangling the man only because his body was physically stronger than hers. "Oh, yeah. That would work just fine. We'd escape notice real well with the Singapore police looking for us as well as your German mob friends. How about this? How about you tell me what the hell's going on here before I terminate you myself. All I need is a female judge. The phrase justifiable homicide comes to mind…"

The elevator stopped at the fifteenth floor. Without warning Brook pulled her into his arms, slanting his head so his hair cascaded over them as he kissed her. Candy heard a woman gasp, then laugh nervously as she walked away from the door. Lord, it was hard to stay angry with a man who could kiss like that, even if he was only trying to keep her hidden. She was pretty sure he forgot why he was kissing her long before the elevator doors slid shut.

"I'm sorry. I forgot. Why are you angry with me?"

Candy pulled back enough to look up at him, noting the laughter in his eyes. "Calculating bastard, aren't you? You think I can't stay mad at you just because you kiss like a satyr?"

He shrugged. "I don't know. We could experiment."

"Brook, start talking."

Brook kissed her again, his lips no longer soft, but demanding now, stopping her questions more by the force of his agitation than by the strength with which his arms closed around her. "I'm sorry," he whispered finally, ending the kiss but still holding her. "Whatever happens, Candy, I want you to know you're the best thing that's happened to me in a long, long time."

"Bullshit." Candy stomped her foot on the floor for emphasis, ignoring Brook's wounded look. "I'm a lawyer, remember? Don't feed me that fucking crap. Men with guns just tried to kill us. You can't change the Goddamned subject and think I'm just going to buy it. What the fuck is going on here?"

He leaned back against the elevator wall and ran a hand through his thick mane of hair. "I'm sorry, Candy. I really am. You deserve more of an answer than I can give you. I promise I'll get you to the US Embassy and get the hell out of your life, all right? It may take some time, but I'll see you get reimbursed for your expenses."

"No."

This time his surprise looked genuine. "No, what?"

"I'm not letting you ditch me at the embassy. I'm not leaving you to get out of this on your own."

He looked up at the floor lights, five now, then four. "You're one tough lady, Candy. I wish I'd met you under different circumstances."

She kept her voice calm, the anger and fear neatly filed away. "Who do you work for? CIA? Covert ops? Military intelligence?"

He laughed, though the sound conveyed little humor. "Nothing that well organized. I'm just a civilian who got caught up in something bigger than me. All I wanted to do was help people. I never expected anything like this. And then I was too far in, I knew too much, and I couldn't get out."

Candy just stared at him, trying to understand what he wasn't saying. "Let me help you. We go to the embassy together. Within twenty-four hours we're on a plane headed for home."

His eyes focused on the floor, anywhere but her. He shook his head, swiping at his hair as it fell in his face. "If I walk away now, it was all for nothing."

Candy reached out to lay a hand on his cheek, tilting his head up. "If these men kill you, what will you have accomplished?"

Their eyes met, his filled with uncertainty and regret. "I'm not a hero, Candy. I'm not sure how to get out of this mess and I don't want to drag you under with me."

The elevator door opened into the lobby. Candy hooked her free arm through Brook's, trying to look casual as they headed for the taxi lane, bags in hand. "I'm not asking you to be a hero, Brook. Let's start with the basics. What would you do if I weren't with you? Where would you go? Who would you contact?"

"I have a number to call… I checked in every time I escaped."

"Have you called it?"

"I -- yes."

"And?"

"And I let them know I was alive. That was it."

"Why?"

Brook looked away, in an odd way he had that said he felt more than he was willing to voice. "What do you think I was investigating, Candy? Brickyards? It's my job to get people who buy and sell other people arrested."

Her step faltered. "You shit."

He stopped, still not looking at her. "Yeah."

"You'd let those goons kill you rather than take a chance I might get arrested? You don't think I might just be a good enough lawyer to get myself out of trouble?"

His head snapped around, the worry in his face easier to read now. "Do you know what you're saying? You could end up in prison, Candy!"

"I could tell the truth and end up with some sort of a Goddamned award too, but my guess is it'll be something somewhere in the middle." Candy motioned to the attendant to find her a taxi. She barely glanced at the cab as they slid into the backseat. "Where were you supposed to end up, Brook? What was supposed to happen Friday?"

He ran a hand through his hair, shoving it back out of his eyes. "I don't know. I was under too long. I lost contact."

"You could have ended up in Japan then, with no way out."

"I was hoping you were my contact, there to pull me out, but by the time we got back to the hotel I knew things had gone wrong."

Candy wound her arms around him, laying her head on his chest. His arms closed tightly around her, and she felt his lips press against the top of her head. "You'd have gone back anyway, not knowing whether anyone still knew where you were."

"I had a job to do, Candy."

The cab lurched and he steadied her, his legs braced tightly against the floor.

"Why, Brook? How did you get into this in the first place?"

He turned to look out the window. "There was a girl -- one of my students back in Michigan. She went home over break. They took her. She -- her body turned up outside a whorehouse in Japan. She killed herself rather than live with the shame."

"And you gave up your life for her." Candy swallowed hard. "You're wrong, Brook. You are a hero."

He kissed the top of her head, burying his face in the soft mass of her hair. "I --" Brook's grip on her changed subtly. Something tense, something indefinable that brought her focus out of the past and immediately into the present surroundings. His voice whispered close to her ear. "Did you tell the cabdriver where to go?"

Candy fought back the rising panic. "No. I thought you did."

"Afraid not," Brook admitted, his lips still close to her ear. "Don't look now, Cat Woman, but I think Batman's in trouble. This driver looks real familiar."

Candy sat up slowly, snuggling against him casually as she turned to face the back of the driver's head. The man was small and dark and Malaysian from the looks of him. The face in the plastic ID case clipped to the visor looked remarkably familiar. He was the man who'd taken her to the auction in the first place.

"What was it you stabbed Schumacher with anyway? A comb?"

"Yeah. Pretty corny, huh? Cat Woman comes armed with a plastic comb."

"Got it handy?"

Candy shuffled her purse around to her lap.

Something electric passed between them as she guided his hand to the slightly used weapon. Brook slipped it into his hand as he turned, covering her body with his in an embrace that quickly moved beyond mere camouflage. Damn, the man made her feel way too much at the most inappropriate times. "Oh, yeah. That won't cause any suspicions," Candy hissed as she ran her tongue over his earlobe in punishment.

"Sex in cars is permissible, remember?" Brook explained as he shifted closer to the driver. "Want to try it?"

"Yeah," Candy agreed. "But not while I'm being kidnapped, if you don't mind."

"All right. Later."

For a big man, he moved fast. One moment he was wrapped around her like a lover, and the next he had the comb pressed firmly against the back of the cabdriver's neck, his other arm pinning the driver to the back of his seat. "*Sotong* -- this doesn't make sense. Where are you taking us and why? *Kayu* -- not very smart -- *lah*?"

The cabdriver shrugged. "I could just let Schumacher kill you, I suppose."

Candy stared at the man who now spoke perfect English.

"Fuck." Brook slowly dropped his arm from around the cabdriver's neck, slumping back against his seat. "You were my contact?"

"Not exactly. I was tracking Schumacher's movements. Our sources reported you as dead. But Schumacher knew better. He's pretty determined to see you don't testify."

"Once you knew where Brook was, why didn't you pull him out?" Candy demanded.

The driver shrugged. "Seemed like he'd be safe

enough with you. Somehow we figured the two of you could stay out of trouble for at least a couple of days. Instead you're out flashing his face all over town and running up the national debt on your credit card. Why not just put up a sign that says 'Look here'?"

"How does Candy fit into all of this?" Brook demanded. "Why did you use her to get me out in the first place?"

"Judgment call. We didn't have time to get an operative in. Even if I'd had the money I couldn't very well have bought you myself. Would have blown my cover. I saw Ms. Nelson's cash roll when she paid me for the hotel fare. When she asked me to take her to the auction, I did."

"That isn't exactly the auction I asked for."

The driver shook his head. "Of course it is. You handed me the ad off the Internet and you asked me to take you there."

"I had an ad for an *antique* auction."

The driver sat back, stretching his arms against the steering wheel. "You mean you really didn't know… you're just a civilian?"

It was Brook who answered, his voice tight and more than a little angry. "No. No, she's *not* a civilian. Not *just* a civilian. She's a citizen *you* recruited to help get me out. She's working with us, do you understand me?"

The driver stared at Brook's tense face in the mirror for a moment, then shifted his gaze back to the city traffic. "Right. That's just the way I remember it."

9:05 AM Wednesday, 22 December 2004
Somewhere in Singapore...

Candy paced the length of the small apartment, her arms wrapped around her for warmth. The air conditioning was on too high. Or else reality was just too close. She hadn't been able to sleep. Hadn't even bothered to undress. They'd whisked Brook away almost as soon as the cab pulled into the underground parking lot of an older office building bearing a faded Oriental Trading Ltd. sign. She'd waited all night, expecting Brook to reappear at any moment, his slow smile telling her everything was all right and they'd be leaving together.

Shit. She was such a fool.

Where was he? Where had they taken him? She doubted Brook was even his real name. Would she ever see him again? Probably not until he testified against her in court. If she didn't end up in prison over this, she'd get disbarred at the least.

Well, she deserved whatever happened to her. She'd been such a fool. Richard was right. For an educated woman, she was so naïve.

A light knock sounded on the door. Candy sprang for it, her heart doing double time. Even if she'd never see him again, she needed to say goodbye. She had to tell him...

"Ms. Nelson. Are you ready to go?" *The cabdriver*.

Candy swallowed hard. "Of course. Just let me get my things." She had to pull herself together. She wasn't going to cry in front of this man. She wasn't.

She had to leave a note. Not that she'd even expect Brook to find it, but she had to try. She grabbed her lipstick out of her purse. The bathroom. The cabdriver wouldn't see what she wrote there.

Two minutes later she was ready to go. It was all over. "Get me out of here."

11:00 AM Friday, 24 December 2004
Brasden-Marten Agency
Singapore

"Thank you for rescheduling with me," Candy offered with her most professional smile as she rose to leave. "And I apologize for missing our appointment on Wednesday. The seafood must not have agreed with me."

Vincent Armani merely smiled as he kissed her hand. "I would not have missed meeting with you for the world, *cherié*. Thank you once again for your time, Ms. Marten. Brasden-Marten has quite a treasure in you. If Richard ever forgets that, leave him and come to work for me directly. I will treat you as such a delicate flower deserves."

Candy gave him her most brilliant and professional smile. "Thank you, Vince. You are a pleasure to work with, as always."

The manager of their local office showed Vincent out. Candy watched him go, staring blankly into space. There were other things she could do here, more paperwork. But someone else could do it just as easily. The manager called for a cab. Candy kept her façade in place until the doorman pushed the cab door gently closed behind her.

It all seemed so unreal.

So useless.

It would almost have been better if they'd arrested her. She wouldn't have had to step back into her life as if nothing had changed.

Everything had changed.

* * *

Back at the Mandarin Oriental, the hotel

doorman opened the cab door for her. "Good to see you again, Ms. Nelson."

"Thank you."

The concierge looked up, smiling as she walked by. "You're looking lovely today, Ms. Nelson."

"Thank you." Candy flashed him her standard professional smile.

She couldn't do this anymore. Couldn't keep smiling and laughing and flirting with clients while she accomplished nothing with her life. Halfway around the world and thousands of dollars and billable hours to get some coked-up asshole of an actor a contract paying him twice what he was worth as long as he wore the right suits everywhere he went. No. Twice what his competition would work for. He had no worth. Not to her.

Her work had no value beyond the salary she was paid.

The faces of the women the German had purchased kept flitting through her mind. She could almost remember a time when she'd been young and idealistic enough to think she could change the world. She'd wanted to help people. Instead, she'd settled for Richard and Brasden-Marten. It wasn't enough. It would never be enough. She would never settle again. The moment she got back to New York this was over.

She might never know who Brook had worked for. Maybe, someday, she would find Brook. And if she didn't, she would find someone who needed her. Something she could believe in.

Maybe she could help repay some of her debt.

She swiped her key through the lock with a little more force than was necessary. The staff had put the room back in order without a comment, of course. She didn't want to know what they thought might have happened to the lamp. Or the cord.

Apparently the people Brook worked with had managed to pluck the Schumacher brothers away and deposit them safely into custody without attracting any undue attention. There was certainly no sign they'd ever been in her room.

Or that Brook had ever been here.

Or that anything in her life had changed.

But it had. Nothing would ever be the same again.

The scent of cinnamon and spice hit her nose. Candy stopped in the doorway, her hand on her purse. Nothing looked out of place.

Except the table.

An apple pie sat steaming in the middle of the table, flanked by candles, two gold rimmed china plates, and two glasses of milk.

Candy swallowed hard. She dropped her purse on the chair, scanning the room with her heart in her throat. *The bedroom*. He'd be in the bedroom.

She stopped in the bedroom doorway, her hand flying to her mouth.

He was wearing a black leather jacket and form-fitting black leather pants, his hair windblown, as if he'd just gotten off the back of a chopper. He'd threaded a red ribbon through the zipper pull, knotted into a large silk bow.

Her legs were shaking so badly she couldn't move. She tried to hold back the hysterical sobs that were about to break loose. He crossed the room, slowly, as always, stopping before her to hold out his hands, palms up. Candy threw herself into his arms. Then he was holding her, comforting, stroking, caressing. And his lips were on her, kissing, nuzzling, soothing, arousing.

"I didn't find your message until this morning," he whispered. "I didn't think you'd want to see me again."

Her hands trembled as she held him. "I've been dying inside without you. I thought you wouldn't want to see me again."

"I've been going crazy without you. I told the coalition if they didn't let me know where they'd taken you I'd leave the organization."

Candy raised her gaze to study his eyes. They were darker gray now, and stormy with passion. She could feel the heat of him pressing against her. "I love you, Brook."

He couldn't keep from grinning. "Good. Because I'd hate to be here alone. Marry me."

Her heart turned over with a thud that surely should have been audible. "Brook, I -- there are a lot of things you don't know about me."

"No excuses. Marry me." His voice was husky.

"I'm already married."

Whatever she'd expected, she should have known better. His arms didn't loosen their hold on her. "Richard."

"Yes. We don't live together. Haven't for over a year. We filed the separation. We just never got divorced. He said it was better for the firm's image. I never bothered to argue."

"Do you still love him?"

"No." Something inside her let go with saying it out loud. "And I don't think he ever loved me. There's nothing left but the paperwork. But it'll take a while. Probably a year or more."

"That's all right. We don't need to be in a hurry."

No. He never hurried… "There's something else. I'm older than you think I am. I'm forty-one."

"So?"

"You might care when we're older."

"I'm not exactly a teenager, Candy. Not that you ever asked."

Candy took a deep breath. "How old are you, Brook?"

"Thirty-six."

She let that sink in a moment or two. "You're not a grad student."

"Part of my cover. I got my doctorate years ago, but people always said I looked younger."

"Your name isn't really Brook Harper either, is it? Kelly e-mailed me back this morning. You don't exist."

"David. David Ellis."

"David." She laughed. "I like that name. Always have."

He kissed her then, in the way that always made her knees tremble. "We'd make a great team, Candy."

"I plan to resign from Brasden-Marten when I get back to New York."

"That's good. But I wasn't talking about work."

She kissed the tip of his nose. "Tell me about the people you work for."

"The Coalition for Humanitarian Aid for the Subjugated and Exploited. *C.H.A.S.E.* We're not government sponsored, so we're not subject to the same laws government agencies are. We target international crime rings that traffic in human slavery."

"Vigilantes?"

"More like… private detectives. We do what governments can't. We get enough evidence to make sure people like the Schumachers are convicted when they're brought to trial."

"We'd make a good team, David."

She watched the emotions war on his face. "The coalition wants me to head up the New York office. I thought I'd take the assignment, so I could be closer to you. And yes, we could use you. But I haven't got the budget to come anywhere near what Brasden-Marten must pay."

Candy looked around the huge, opulent suite. "I can live without the expense account. I need you more than I'll ever need *things*. I want to be where you are, David. Whether that's New York or Baghdad, I want to be there with you."

"I want to hear you say what you wrote on the mirror."

Her body stilled. She willed herself not to cry. "I love you. No matter what the cost, I always will."

"I promised myself I'd never care enough about anyone to ever get hurt again, Candy. You've changed all the rules."

"Did you love her? The girl that died?"

It took him a while to answer, and when he did, his voice was barely audible. "She was my wife. She went home to visit her family over Christmas break. She wanted me to go... I didn't have time."

Candy held him, not knowing what to say. "I'm sorry seems like so little..."

"You made me *feel*, Candy. Made me realize there was something left inside me besides anger. You made me a *Human Being* again. I can't lose you. Not now."

"You've got me," Candy promised. She tilted her face up, offering her lips for a kiss to seal the promise. He didn't disappoint her. "I don't want to wait till tomorrow to open my Christmas present."

He laughed at that, his voice steadying. "You don't have to. In my family we open Christmas presents on Christmas Eve."

Candy smiled as she ran her hands over the broad expanse of black leather.

"Candy?"

She paused, her hands on his chest, as she looked up at him.

"Merry Christmas."

Her eyes glittered with a mixture of happiness and unshed tears. "Merry Christmas, my love."

Glossary of Foreign Words and Phrases

Shiok (Malay -- fantastic or marvelous -- a great place)

Lah (Singapore expression -- yes? Or yes! -- at the end of sentences for emphasis)

Sotong (Malay -- doesn't make sense)

Terok (Malay -- unsafe, or troublesome)

Ulu (Malay -- rural, or deserted place)

Kayu (Malay -- not very smart)

Pai seh (Malay -- embarrassing)

Pad Thai (Popular dish from Thailand -- rice noodles stir fried with prawns, chicken, bean sprouts, green onions, egg and Pad Thai sauce, topped with ground peanuts)

Toi la nguoi My. (Vietnamese -- I am an American)

Ong noi tiong Anh khong? (Vietnamese -- Do you speak English?)

Mot mot ba nam bay (Vietnamese -- 1-1-3-5-7)

Xin chao (Vietnamese -- hello)

Toi manh gioi (Vietnamese -- I am all right)

Mau len (Vietnamese -- fast, or speed it up)

Troi oi /Troi dat oi (Vietnamese -- An enigmatic exclamation similar to "What the hell!")

Khong, da khong (Vietnamese -- no)

Khong dau (Vietnamese -- emphatic no)

Xin loi (Vietnamese -- I'm sorry, forgive me)

Lam on ran chiu (Vietnamese -- please be patient)

Mac toi (Vietnamese -- leave me alone)

Toi khong biet (Vietnamese -- I don't know/I don't understand.)

Di di (Vietnamese -- get away from me)

Dung lai (Vietnamese -- STOP!)

Pom rak khun (Thai -- I love you)

Leck' mich (German -- kiss my ass)

Bierficker (German -- beer-fucker. Idiomatic)

Hurensohn! (German -- son-of-a-bitch)

Plain Brown Wrapper (*C.H.A.S.E.* 2)
Deep Cover - in a Human Trafficking Ring
Shelby Morgen

Terry Bradford
InternationalMaleEscorts.com

Male Escorts. Women paid men for sex?

Maybe women did this all the time. After all, men weren't the only ones who wanted uncomplicated sex. Kelly could afford to hire him, just for one night, to explore her fascination with bondage. The fact that she's paying Terry just adds to the rush -- he really does have to follow her orders! One night. A layover in Paris. It's just sex, right?

Terry needs money, fast. So he answers an ad on the internet. Six thousand Euros for a week's vacation in France, all expenses paid, entertaining Lady Elizabeth at her private villa. Sounds like the perfect plan, right? After all, it's just sex.

Then he meets a woman in the airport -- a woman who will make him question everything he knows about what is means to be a man. Just one night, but even though she's never heard from him again, Kelly can't seem to get Terry off her mind -- or out of her heart. Then the emails start. Referrals from other Dommes to a private resort -- Lady Elizabeth's l'Ecole de Dominatrix -- School of the Dominatrix.

Junk email? Or a cry for help... from the man she can't forget?

10:15 AM, Thursday, 5 January, 2006
Brasden-Marten Agency

"Hand that to the secretary on your way out."

The secretary.

Kelly offered a professional smile as the young man handed her his résumé. As soon as the door closed behind him, she filed it neatly in the wastebasket next to her printer.

The secretary. Fifteen years in this God-damned place and she was back to being *The Secretary*. Fifteen long fucking years. Fifteen --

"Martha! Coffee."

Kelly reached for the coffeepot. She'd wager her co-workers had started a betting pool on how long she could hold out the day Candy handed in her resignation.

Damn. Almost a year to the day.

A pair of gorgeous twin hunks offered her brilliantly flashing smiles and two thumbs up. Funny. She'd spent so many years around models that their otherwise extraordinary good looks didn't even flutter her pulse anymore.

They probably had a stake in the betting pool. Well, they weren't going to make any money off her today. She wouldn't give them the satisfaction. She wouldn't let Richard Marten get to her.

"Martha!"

The hell she wouldn't!

Kelly picked up the e-mail from her printer tray in her left hand and the nearly empty coffeepot in her right. The coffee smelled vaguely burnt. "This just came in for you, Mr. Marten. It's a memo from Hamilton & Smythe, the law firm representing your wife. You need to notify your accountant to prepare a statement of assets on the firm."

Richard looked annoyed. "Candy wouldn't be foolish enough to ask for a share of my company. She knows those are prenuptial assets."

"No, sir. According to this memo, she's asking for half the added value of the assets accumulated during her employment at Brasden-Marten, claiming you used her social connections to bring in new clients. Apparently she kept records."

Richard frowned up at her as if she were speaking a foreign language. "The coffee?"

"Yes, sir." Kelly reached forward with the coffeepot. "But I think you should know, Mr. Marten, Martha hasn't worked here for five years. My name is Kelly." Calmly, Kelly emptied the remains of the coffee into Richard Marten's lap.

11:00 AM, Saturday, 28 January, 2006
New York, NY

"You're dropping your sex discrimination suit against Brasden-Marten?"

Kelly sighed. "I'm settling out of court. It's a good offer. A letter of reference and a year's salary as severance pay, with full benefits."

"So once again Richard gets to buy his way out of trouble."

"I dumped a pot of coffee in his lap, Martha. It was a stupid thing to do. Now I'm not only out of a job, I'm out of a career. What am I gonna do now?"

Martha circled an ad in the paper. "How about this one? 'Office Manager. Knowledge of Office Suite and Office Books required. Top salary for the right person'."

"A trained monkey can use a computer. That's not what I want."

Martha set the newspaper aside. "What *do* you want?"

Kelly hugged her coffee cup to her lips. "I stayed at Brasden-Marten after you left because I loved working with Candy. I loved researching and planning trips and running background checks. I practically memorized the city map of Singapore last December. It's been hell since she quit. I don't want to be just a secretary again. I need… more."

"What you *need* is to get laid."

"No fucking way. Not unless I find me a nice quiet lesbian chick who follows orders. I'm through with men. The only thing men are good for is sex, and that's not worth the rest of the bullshit you have to go through to keep one around." She dropped onto the couch next to her sister. "Not that there's anyone of either sex interested. I'm feeling old, Martha. Old and plain and utterly forgettable."

"You're thirty-nine. That's not old. Look at you! You could lose a few pounds, but you're still a knockout. Now you've got a whole year paid vacation. Why are you feeling so sorry for yourself?"

"Look at *you*. You've got everything I always wanted -- a husband who worships you and perfect kids and a perfect life." She ignored Martha's derisive snort. "You do! I'm never going to have any of that. My own boss didn't even know my name!"

"Getting out of Brasden-Marten was the smartest thing you could have done for yourself. Richard Marten got exactly what he deserved. I'll tell you something else. You know that asshole had to be a lousy lay. Why else would Candy have run off to do some sort of humanitarian work with a college professor?"

"Don't knock the professor. You haven't met him. I'd walk away from everything to follow him, too. You can't buy what that man's got."

"Oh?" Martha perked up noticeably. "You've seen him? Is he hot?"

"Yeah." She'd seen him all right. So had Richard. "Candy stopped by the office to clean out her desk when she got back from Singapore last January. David came with her. *Dr.* David Ellis."

It wasn't that he'd done anything. It was the way he looked at Candy, as if she meant the world to him. And the way he watched Richard. Something almost primitive glittered in his eyes. Damn, but she wanted that. A man who'd stay at her side, who'd fight back to back with her if it came down to that.

Kelly swallowed hard. Right. Well, David was

taken. "Hot enough to melt chocolate in a snow storm. He could model for Brasden-Marten. He's got the looks. Tall. Broad shoulders. Narrow hips. Beautiful gray eyes. Long, dark hair down past his shoulders, with red-blond streaks. Tanned like he'd spent hours in the sun every day. There's something about him... something that could be dangerous. If I'd known college professors looked like that these days, I'd have gone back to school."

Martha laughed. "So do it."

"What?"

"Go back to school."

"Martha! That's absurd! That's --"

"You've got a year to do whatever you want. Nobody owns you anymore, Kelly. Finish your degree if that's what you want. Whatever you want to do, do it. It's time to live, girl! You're like a *Playboy* centerfold, all wrapped up in a plain brown wrapper. Get a facial, get your nails done, buy something sexy, and go see the world. Indulge your favorite fantasies for a while. The real world will still be here when you get back."

Kelly wanted to argue, but she couldn't think of a single sensible defense against her sister's logic. "Maybe I will. I always wanted to see the world. Maybe I could get a job where they pay me to travel."

9:30 PM, Saturday, 28 January, 2006
Hazlet, New Jersey

Frequently Asked Questions:
Q) What can I expect -- how difficult is it to become established as a Male Escort?
A) Like any other new business venture, you must build a clientele based on advertising and particularly word of mouth referrals. A great deal of your reputation depends upon how well you fulfill your clients' fantasies.

Q) What kind of women use an Escort service?
A) Most of your clients will be successful, independent, attractive career women, generally between 35 and 60.

Q) What would a usual "date" entail? Will all my clients expect sex?
A) Generally your client will offer a detailed scenario of her fantasy ahead of time. Often she will take you out to dinner, giving the two of you time to get to know each other and become physically comfortable with each other. All your clients will expect sex.

Q) How do I know I'm "right" for this business? What if she doesn't find me attractive or if I can't "perform?"
A) Are you tolerant and open-minded? Do you know how to listen without dominating a conversation? Are you comfortable with your body? Can you delay your own pleasure for hours while concentrating on your partner's fulfillment? Can you get excited again after only a short delay once you come? If the answer

to all of these questions is "Yes," you will have a successful -- and profitable -- career as a Male Escort. On the rare occasions when you can't get it up right away, simply improvise...

* * *

Terry crumpled his carefully memorized sheet of instructions and tossed it into the waste can. He hadn't had sex with anyone since Cleveland. What the hell would he do if he couldn't get it up?

Improvise. Oh, sure. *Of course that's my dick. It only feels like a carrot from the salad bar when I'm really excited.* He was a complete and total idiot. He was going to make a fool of himself. More to the point, he wouldn't get paid, and if he didn't get paid he'd end up in prison.

Any woman who could afford to fly him half-way around the world for a week of fun in the sun on her private yacht knew her way around enough to tell the difference between a carrot and a dick.

Terry sighed softly. This was self-defeatist thinking. He'd signed a contract with the agency. He'd accepted Lady Elizabeth's deposit. There was no turning back now. He'd agreed to be her slave for a week. Anything she wanted. The problem was, he didn't know what she wanted. What did he really know about BDSM, anyway? Just what he'd read in magazines and seen on the Internet.

How far could he go to earn this woman's money? What would it take to make a man submit? He wasn't sure where he'd be forced to draw the line. What would he -- could he -- allow? He'd read about safe words. He had a safe word, all right. *Get-me-the-fuck-out-of-here.* He wasn't into bondage and submission. Men didn't submit. Not in his world. He was the oldest. The responsible one. Submission wasn't an option.

He didn't have to get off on it, he reminded himself. It was her fantasy, not his. He squared his shoulders resolutely. For six thousand Euros he'd damn well better allow any Goddamned thing Lady Elizabeth wanted.

He was no prude -- nor was he a total neophyte. He'd prepared for this job, the way he would have for any major contract. He'd read every handbook and visited every kinky porn site he could find, to make sure he went in as well prepared as he could.

A job. That was all this was. He could be her slave for a week. Couldn't be any worse than basic training. Besides, it was only for a week, and this was a woman, after all. One woman. If he ended up in prison, odds were worse things would happen than whatever this nice society lady could come up with. He was prepared for almost anything.

Almost anything. Some of the Internet sites were downright disgusting. No way he'd allow anyone to stick wires through his skin and electrocute him. He shuddered at the remembered image. Something else he was sure of after all that exposure -- other men weren't a turn-on for him. No children either. A man had to have some standards, even if he was going to rent his body out for sex. No piercings, no excrement, no children, no small fuzzy animals, and no dead things.

He'd never get the whole necrophilia thing. That was over the top.

Other than that, there wasn't much he wouldn't do -- or allow to be done to him. One person's hang-up was another person's fantasy. Who was he to judge, after all? It was just sex. As Cleveland had told him on more than one occasion, sex was about all he was good for. Whatever this woman's secret fantasies involved, he was going to do his best. In exchange, she was going to pay him six thousand Euros for a week of his time. Roughly seventy-five hundred dollars that Cleveland would never get her hands on.

Lady Elizabeth was going to keep him out of prison.

10:00 PM, Tuesday, 7 February, 2006
John F. Kennedy International Airport

Kelly's fantasies had never included spending three hours in airport security and baggage claims, or walking miles through the airport carrying her small carry-on bag with one change of clothes and that all-important portfolio. Nor had any of her fantasies particularly involved seven hours' flight time, or a twelve-hour layover in Paris.

Kelly gave herself a mental shake. She was getting to fly to Europe for free. She could deal with a few small inconveniences. Kelly clutched the small portfolio she'd picked up this morning. Documents. Corporate contracts. This was perfectly legal, just like the ad had said. Travel for free, expenses paid. All she had to do was deliver these contracts in Paris Wednesday morning, pick up the signed contracts Thursday morning, then fly those to Barcelona. She'd have the whole day Friday to spend in Spain before she picked up the second set of signatures at 5 PM and flew home.

She couldn't make a living at this -- it didn't pay anything but expenses -- but then, she didn't need to make a living. She was getting a free trip to Europe out of this. That was enough. Still, there had to be a cheaper way to deliver documents. Hadn't they ever heard of FedEx?

"Good evening, Miss Monroe."

Kelly jerked her head around like a wooden puppet. How did the man checking her bags known her name?

Oh. Of course. It was printed on her boarding pass. She was being paranoid. Perhaps there was a reason to be paranoid, if these documents were worth the price of a round trip ticket to Europe…

Nonsense. They were time sensitive. That was all. The agency had explained everything to her. So why did she feel like there had to be a catch? Why did she feel like everyone was staring at her?

Kelly glanced discreetly over her shoulder again. The man *was* staring at her. No doubt about it. She'd noticed him while she was standing in line to have her bags searched.

He was the kind of man a woman would notice. Handsome, although not the kind of poster-boy good looks Brasden-Marten usually dealt with. He looked strong, too, but it was all real, not that sculptured look the models got from working out at the gym. More the rugged, outdoors type. Darkly tanned skin. A few lines around his eyes from too much time in the sun. A tiny touch of gray at the temples streaking his otherwise dark hair.

Weathered. That was the word for him. Despite the business suit and the Italian loafers, something about him made her think of a cowboy. Or a military man. Yeah. He'd look good in a uniform.

He'd look good *out* of a uniform.

She'd have to stretch to kiss him. Unless he was kneeling in front of her. Oh, yeah. That was a pleasant thought. Better than wondering why he was staring at her. A few weeks ago she'd have killed to get a man who wasn't a model to look at her like that. At the moment, however, she didn't particularly want to attract attention.

Kelly tucked the portfolio into her carry-on bag. Picturing that man modeling some of the bondage gear from Brasden-Marten's client in Singapore did help ease her tension. Damn. She'd never had fantasies like this before she'd seen those modeling shots.

She'd seen the Singapore company's contraptions demonstrated at fetish club parties in New York, and she still didn't understand their appeal. Those rigs looked too complicated. She'd settle for handcuffs and hobbles and a plain leather riding crop.

Still, she'd found herself daydreaming about those catalog images of late. This couldn't be healthy. It was all right in the fetish clubs. Those people were professionals. She wasn't. She had to quit fantasizing about tying up every stranger she saw. After all, you couldn't walk up to a man in an airport and say "*Pardon me, but do you like to be disciplined*?"

Hardly the way to begin a conversation.

Still, after fifteen long years at Brasden-Marten, she wanted something new, something different. She wanted to be in control. She wanted more than the local clubs had to offer. She didn't want to watch. She wanted to participate. Maybe there were advanced classes -- somewhere she could go to learn more about bondage and discipline. Maybe she really would go back to school.

Right. That would look good on her résumé.

She'd promised herself she wasn't going to think about the future once this entire trip. Whatever it took, she was going to have a good time, damn it. She was going to meet people, have an adventure, and indulge in a few of those fantasies Martha was always talking about.

There was no time like the present.

* * *

Every time he turned to check the flight information on the electronic board behind the ticket counter, he caught the same woman staring at him. Terry straightened his tie self-consciously.

Under other circumstances he'd have welcomed her stare, perhaps even used it as an opportunity to introduce himself. After all, the woman was gorgeous. Tall. Legs that kept going till next Tuesday afternoon. Dark skin with a red-gold tone -- either a darkly tanned white woman or a light skinned black woman, perhaps with some Native American in the mix. It was hard to tell.

Exotic. That's what he'd call her. Like a cat. A full mane of thick, dark hair that hung in waves almost down to her ass. Like the rest of her, her ass had a nice, full, graceful curve that made him ache to slip his hands around her. She wasn't one of those starving model types. She'd be soft in all the right places, not like wrapping around a skeleton. And those breasts... he'd have loved to plant a few maraschino cherries in that cleavage and try to extract them using his tongue.

He could have forgotten his own problems just watching her pace back and forth across the waiting area. On her, that wired energy looked sexy, like a cat in heat.

Come pounce on me, baby. Whatever your problem is, I'll be glad to help you relieve some of that sexual tension. I bet I could make you relax...

Only one thing about her bothered him. Why was she staring at him? He wasn't exactly model material, but he didn't have a wart on the end of his nose either. He hadn't spilled coffee down the front of his shirt this morning, or worn white socks with a dark suit, or tennis shoes with dress slacks. There was nothing remarkable enough about him one way or the other to make a woman stare at him like that.

Especially not attractive single women.

She had to be single. She was waiting for the same plane he was, which meant she was about to board an overseas flight, and there was no one at the airport to see her off. If he had a woman like that -- and it wasn't just her looks -- everything about her turned him on, from the raw silk suit to the simple but elegant black leather carry-on -- he'd sure as hell have been at the airport with her.

Hell. He'd have put his life on hold to fly with her wherever she was going. She was more than beautiful. She looked tough, too. A she-cat who would defend her territory. No one came in -- or out -- unless she said so.

He'd been at the top. Money. Power. When that life dropped you over the edge till you were tumbling blindly with nothing to grab onto, you realized quickly enough that you needed a fighter to cover your back.

Maybe that was the whole problem with Cleveland. There'd never been anything more between them than sex -- and money. Hot, greedy, steamy, frantically wild sex, but when it all came down to it, she wasn't the kind who'd cover his back. He hadn't ever trusted her enough to tell her the truth about what he was doing financially, and she hadn't ever really cared enough to ask as long as the money was there. They were convenient for each other. Now he was conveniently financing her next relationship…

"Excuse me, but is there something wrong? Did I end up with cream cheese on the end of my nose or something?"

Terry looked back up with a start. "Wrong?"

"You keep staring at me."

He was staring at *her*? Well, maybe he was. He smiled to cover his embarrassment. "I apologize. I didn't mean to be rude. You're very beautiful. I was thinking I must have seen you somewhere before. A modeling shot, perhaps."

The woman laughed at that -- really laughed, not one of those polite little twitters society women hid behind their hands. "Not unless you're older than you look. It's been twenty years and thirty pounds since I did any modeling, and I never got beyond women's lingerie. But thanks. That was a sweet thing to say."

Sweet. Well, at least he hadn't offended her. "I hate waiting around like this. We've got another forty-five minutes till boarding. Starbucks is still open. May I buy you a cup of coffee?" he ventured, emboldened by his hint of success.

She glanced around the lounge area, then leaned toward him, lowering her voice conspiratorially. "If I let a stranger buy me coffee, will I be branded a loose woman?"

He tried to look worried as he surveyed the crowd. It would have been easier if she hadn't smelled so good. A hint of perfume, not something she'd tried to drown herself in, and another, headier fragrance that was the woman. "Probably," he whispered in return. "Your reputation may be ruined for life."

"Good." She headed for the Starbucks without waiting to see if he was following.

Damn. This was foolish. The man wasn't going to Europe for a holiday. The suit was too well cut and the carry-on too professional. He was probably a decade her junior, and much too good looking to be safe, but she was tired of playing things safe.

Kelly knew without even glancing back that he stood at her elbow as she perused the menu. She'd been trying to cut back on caffeine, but this was going to be a long, boring flight. Might as well indulge. "I'll have a Mocha Latte Grande with two extra shots of espresso, please."

"Make it two." Her stranger was still smiling in

that half-perplexed way that sent shivers down to her toes. If she didn't know better, she'd have sworn he had no idea how handsome he was. Something of a relief after years around models.

"Tell me you're not a model." She was glad the coffee hadn't been served yet. He looked so surprised she was sure he'd have choked.

"A model? Me?" He glanced over his shoulder, as if to be sure there was no one behind him she could have been referring to. "I'm a computer network consultant. Why?"

A computer geek? Looking like that? Damn. She almost forgot to answer his question. "I used to work for a law firm that dealt with entertainment law. Let's just say I don't have a very high opinion of models."

He did laugh at that. "Well in that case, I'm glad I'm not a model. I'd rather you had a somewhat better opinion of me."

She'd never met a computer geek who was that articulate either. What was a computer network consultant going to do in France anyway? "Business trip?"

He flushed slightly. Kind of cute, actually. "Yes. In a way. I've just started with a new company. Agency. Well, the agency's not new. I am." He hesitated, then took his hand out of his pocket, producing a business card.

She just stared.

Terry Bradford
InternationalMaleEscorts.com

Kelly read the card three times, to make sure.

"I've offended you, haven't I? I'm sorry. I'm not very good at this part."

"Offended? No. Not at all. I never would have guessed you were gay."

This time he did choke on his coffee. "Oh! No. Sorry. We cater to a female clientele."

Confounded, Kelly couldn't form a coherent sentence. "You mean…"

"Yes." Brilliant blue eyes laughed back at her.

"I didn't even know… I never thought…" *Oh my God.* "Women pay for sex?" *Damn.* "Sorry. That was crass. I didn't mean… I…"

"That's all right. This isn't exactly a normal conversation. We don't sell sex. That's illegal. Most places, anyway." He smiled that half-puzzled smile again. "Women pay for companionship."

Companionship. Right. Kelly blinked, still too rattled to trust sipping at her coffee yet. She looked him over carefully again. Sex. No strings. No emotional attachment. "So you fly to France, spend the evening with your client, and fly home again?"

"The week, actually. Valentine's Day special. I have a layover in Paris Wednesday between flights, then I fly to Lady Elizabeth's estate Thursday morning. And the client covers all my expenses."

Flying directly to her estate meant a charter or a private jet. Even Richard's wealthiest clients didn't spend that kind of money on personal entertainment. Kelly wished she had access to the Internet. She'd have checked InternationalMaleEscorts.com to see if their rates were listed, but she knew travel expenses. Even if the airline tickets and the hotel were half what his client was spending…

"You're not running screaming for the nearest airport security guard."

Kelly looked up from her quick math in surprise. "Should I?"

"I half expected you to. I'm new at this. The agency says to hand out cards, discreetly of course, but I'm still not very comfortable with the publicity end of things."

No. He wouldn't be. "From computer geek to gigolo. That's a long step. Why?"

That time he really laughed. "Nobody calls us *gigolos* anymore. That's not PC. I'm a *Male Escort*. Remember, I'm a companion. I'm not selling sex. As for the why, that's simple. I need money. Fast. The ex cleaned out the checking account. My signature is on a bounced check for seven thousand dollars made payable to the IRS. With AOL/Time Warner laying off hundreds of other 'computer geeks' again -- that's not the most PC term I've heard either, by the way -- it's not a good time to find a new consulting contract that'll pay me a forty-five hundred dollar sign-on bonus."

Seven thousand dollars? He could say whatever he wanted to -- whatever he was supposed to -- but for that kind of money there was no way he'd be spending a week at some rich woman's house and not having sex with her.

Sex for money. No strings. A hell of a lot of money, but you could have a week of fun -- or maybe one night if that was all you could afford? -- then move on. If you liked the man, you could hire him back again. And again.

Maybe women did this all the time. Maybe they'd done it for years. Centuries even. Men weren't the only ones who wanted uncomplicated sex, after all.

"Ummm." *Maybe you could pay him to act out your fantasies…* "So this is your first assignment?"

"Very first. Yes, Ma'am. Does it show that badly?"

"No. Well, you blushed a little when you handed me your card. It was kind of cute, actually." Hell. He was practically a virgin. In this profession at least.

"Cute. Yeah. That was what I was going for." His cheeks brightened up a little, but he wasn't blushing this time. Not really. "I'll work on that."

His cheeks weren't the only thing affected by the conversation. She tried not to stare at the front of his trousers. Oh, hell. Why not look? Maybe that was just advertising, too. "So, how does this work? Do you have to come up with ideas, or does the client tell you what she wants?"

"Ah, who did you say you work for again?"

That pensive frown really did things to her. Like a little boy caught with his hand in a cookie jar. Damn, but he was -- well -- cute. Kelly tried hard not to giggle. "I didn't. You didn't ask. At the moment I'm kind of between jobs, so I took an assignment with a courier service. By profession I'm an executive assistant and paralegal."

"What exactly is a paralegal?"

"You know all those forms and documents you pay a lawyer to prepare? They don't. The paralegal does. I also track down facts and figures to support cases and sometimes, if there's a court case involved, I track down witnesses or evidence, or even money or documents."

"And you do all that on computers."

"Yeah. Mostly. A lot of it, anyway."

"Which makes you another unemployed computer geek."

Kelly had to laugh at that. "That's not the PC term, you know."

Laughter did wonderful things for his face. She watched the tension ease out of his shoulders. "You ask a lot of questions, considering I don't even know your name."

She held out her hand. "Kelly. Kelly Monroe."

He kept the hand, raising it briefly to his lips with the kind of old-fashioned grace and elegance she'd mocked on TV. Now, with the warmth of his hand under hers, and the soft brush of his lips over her knuckles, she found herself trembling slightly, a warm breath of comfortable attraction stirring in her blood. Damn, but it had been a long time.

"Miss Monroe, please understand. The agency doesn't solicit clients for sex. I don't solicit clients for sex. I could get into a lot worse trouble than I'm already in if I got caught soliciting money for sex in the U.S."

His lips were too close to the back of her hand. That shiver melted into her bones as the words whispered over her skin. "What about outside the U.S.?"

His smile warmed. "Kelly, *sex* isn't illegal anywhere. It's only soliciting that's illegal."

He had that look. That bemused look she'd seen on the models going out for their first shoot. A few months or even weeks from now that innocence would be gone. Damn. The timing was perfect. The innocence was part of what made him so attractive.

Kelly swallowed hard. "So, ummm, if someone -- if I -- wanted to hire you, as my companion, how much would you charge me?"

That hint of color crept back into his skin. "This might not be the best place to have this conversation. Stay here a minute, would you please? I'll be right back, I promise."

Before she could argue, he was gone. Kelly started to feel a little nervous as Terry crossed the waiting area back to the ticket desk in a few strides of those long legs. He handed the woman something.

Had she done something illegal? Just by asking him? Could this be some sort of reverse sting operation? Entrapment. It had to be entrapment, if she'd done anything wrong.

Why was he smiling like that as he crossed back to her? She --

"The agent needs your boarding pass."

"My boarding pass?"

"I have enough frequent flyer miles to cover an upgrade. The agent said the seat next to mine is available." His face clouded over. "Unless -- sorry. That was presumptuous of me. I should have asked first. I --"

"No!" Kelly shoved her boarding pass into his hands. "I'd love to sit with you. Thank you."

The smile turned back on again, that wondrous little boy smile that made her feel almost guilty for what she had in mind.

He was gone again, then back with her ticket, upgraded to first class. Kelly stared at the paper in her hands, a little self-conscious now that she had time to talk and he couldn't talk about the one thing she wanted to talk about. She scrambled for a safe subject. "I guess you would rack up a lot of frequent flyer miles as a networking consultant. You must have traveled a great deal."

"Six months in Toronto last year. Was there twice -- six weeks in March and April, then four and a half months starting in August. Dallas in between. Seattle over the winter before. Usually come home on long weekends. The cat misses me."

Had she traveled with him? This woman who'd left him and emptied the bank account? Kelly didn't want to ruin the mood by asking. "You have a cat? Where did you find an apartment that would let you have a cat?"

"I have a house. Had a house. About an hour from here. New Jersey. On the coast."

"She got the house, too?"

"Not exactly. I had the house before Cleveland. But last month's mortgage payment bounced too, so I won't have it much longer."

"Cleveland? You mentioned Dallas and Toronto."

"The ex. Her name was Cleveland. Is Cleveland. She's not dead. Yet."

Kelly held up her hand like a traffic cop. "I don't want to know if you're planning to kill her. Don't tell me shit like that. I don't want to have to testify against you later."

He laughed again as he stood and reached for her chair, pulling it out for her as she scrambled hastily to her feet. Was it time already? What had he heard that she hadn't?

His hand on the small of her back steered her gently toward the ticket counter. "Kelly, I want you to know something."

"What?" She hoped her voice didn't sound as alarmed as she felt.

"Whatever else happens or doesn't happen between us, you've made me laugh. No one's done that in a long time. I just thought you ought to know. Means a lot to me. I was pretty sure if I told anyone what I was doing they'd laugh at me -- or worse. You've made me feel like a lot less of a fool."

Kelly stopped and turned to face him, tilting her head back a little to look up at those brilliant blue eyes. "Terry, I'm not laughing at you."

She felt his breath hitch in surprise as she slid her hands up onto his shoulders, but he didn't say anything. He didn't resist her when she pulled his head down either. His lips were soft, hot, and incredibly sexy. She took the bottom one in her teeth and nipped gently. "I'm not laughing at all."

His hands cupped her ass, pulling her tight enough that she could feel his erection where he pressed against her. Hot, like a branding iron leaving its mark on her. "*Ummm*," she murmured. "You feel delicious."

His eyes slid half closed, brilliant blue overshadowed by thick dark lashes that seemed too impossibly beautiful to belong to a man. His hands practically fisted into the wool of her skirt, as if he'd forgotten where they were or who was watching or anything but the feel of their bodies pressed together. Warmth spread through her like liquid fire. She would have stripped out of her jacket if her arms hadn't been occupied. He didn't kiss her. He devoured her, like he was trying to catch every last drop of ice cream before it melted.

She was melting. With every touch of those soft, warm lips, with every press of his body against hers, she was melting into a pool of molten lust. She would cease to exist if he quit touching her. Surely she would melt away into nothingness. She had to have him. Had to possess him. Here. Now.

"American Airlines Flight 44 to Paris Charles de Gaulle, first class passengers now boarding."

Well, maybe not *here* and now. They had a plane to catch and a long flight ahead of them. But she had his business card and his e-mail address. She could find him anywhere over the Internet.

11:30 PM, Tuesday, 7 February, 2006
American Airlines Flight 44

She'd flown before. Flown with Martha to visit their parents in Florida. Flown to San Francisco to hand carry contracts to Richard when he'd left his briefcase in the airport in Miami after one too many sex-on-the-beaches in the rooftop lounge.

That had been nothing like this. She'd never had the prospect of sitting so close beside a man who made her more aware of her body than she had been in ages. A man whose eyes smiled down at her as his hand curved around her hip, ushering her gently down the boarding ramp.

A man who'd just kissed her the way every woman deserved to be kissed at least once in her life. Damn, but he was a wonderful kisser. The small triangle of absorbent material in the crotch of her panties was already damp where it rubbed against her. She hadn't wanted a man this badly in a very long time. Maybe forever.

Why? Why had he affected her like this? Was it just those gorgeous blue eyes, such a surprising contrast to his dark good looks? Or was it the fact that she knew, for the right amount of money, he would do whatever she asked of him?

If he asked her, what would she do?

But that wasn't the line of work he was in, was it?

It was all too easy to picture him bound before her, naked and kneeling at her feet, all that power under her control.

Would he run if he knew what she was thinking?

Did she have the strength to control a man like

that? It wasn't physical strength that would count. It was the strength of her will, to make him believe he had no choice but to do her bidding.

What would make a man want to surrender that kind of control? What would make it worth his while to play her game?

The money?

Somehow she didn't think that alone would do it. There had to be more than that to it. Damn. There had to be schools. If you could rent a man for a week online, surely you could find a school to teach you how to become a good Domme.

In the meantime she'd settle for a good straight fuck. He didn't have to know how badly she wanted to see him bound and helpless before her. All he had to do was let her run her hands over that magnificent body.

What would he think when he saw what she was wearing underneath her dress? Would it turn him on? Or scare him so badly she'd never see him again?

"Watch your step." His hand slid a little farther down her back than it needed to as he paused to let her go first into the cabin. She bent to stow her carry-on bag under the seat and he pressed up against her, his hands on her waist, the thick bulge of his cock hot against her ass.

Could he feel the seams of her leather bustier through her conservatively styled business suit? Did he know her nipples were bare, with only the thin fabric between his hands and two tight little knots of need that awaited his touch?

Seven hours. Seven hours till they landed. Seven hours of having everything she wanted close enough to touch. She'd never make it. She would combust. She would --

"Hold this for me for a moment, would you please, darling?"

The flight attendant smiled as Terry pulled out two neatly folded and wrapped blankets. Oh, God. Blankets would only make things more difficult. Her hands could do whatever they wanted underneath those blankets. She licked her lips as he pushed the arm dividing their seats up out of the way.

Now the extra wide first class seats resembled a high-backed loveseat.

Great. So much for constraint. Kelly sat silently beside him, properly buckled in place, waiting as if her body were a time bomb set to go off. The flight attendants passed out drinks while they waited for takeoff. Maybe a glass of wine would help. She was ready to try anything.

Taxiing down the runway took forever. Takeoff was an eternity. Then the flight attendants passing out more drinks. Kelly downed another glass of wine, praying for the fatigue of the day to take over. If she could just fall asleep…

* * *

She was floating, nestled in a warm cocoon while the cold air nipped at her nose. Waking up enough to realize Terry had lifted her into his lap, she turned to snuggle closer against the warm skin beneath her head. Even in this state of half-sleep where reality and the dreaming met, she knew what she wanted. She unbuttoned his tailored silk shirt, pushing the fabric back, raking her fingers across wisps of short, curling hair.

There. That was what she wanted. She bent her head toward the treasure she'd found. Small, soft, hardening under her touch. His breathing stopped as she brushed her lips over his nipple. "*Ummm*."

She felt him groan into her hair. "I thought you were asleep."

"I was. I was dreaming about you."

"Must have been some dream."

Kelly searched her sleep-befuddled brain for an easy lie. "We were in bed together."

He laughed against her hair as she teased his nipple, his cock jutting hard against her hip. "I figured that part out. What else? Do you have a favorite dream? Tell me your fantasies."

Kelly swallowed hard. "I -- no."

He tilted her head back to kiss her, taking his time, raising her blood to the boiling point as he savored her like some expensive dessert. "I won't laugh at you, Kelly. Trust me. Tell me what you want."

No. He wouldn't laugh. He didn't know her. He was a stranger she'd never see again. If she told him her fantasies, he'd quote her a price, and they'd make all the appropriate arrangements. She could live out her fantasies.

For a price.

Why not? Men had been paying for their fantasies for thousands of years. Why shouldn't she? What made such things wrong, just because she was a woman?

Kelly took another deep breath. "It was a scene from an e-book I read -- *His Mistress* by Treva Harte. It's set during the Revolutionary War. I was a widow, and you were my bondsman. There was an old-fashioned four-poster bed. You were naked, and your wrists and ankles were tied to the bedposts."

She felt his cock jump hard against her. His voice came back thick and husky. "And where were you?"

She slipped her hand down between them, cupping his balls with greedy fingers. Unbuttoning the waistband of his slacks, she rested her fingertips on the zipper pull. "*Ummm*. On top of you. Making you beg."

He wasn't laughing. His cock was practically jumping out of his pants. "You're on top of me now. And I'm begging. Do anything you want with me. God knows I won't try to stop you. Fuck me, Kelly. Please. I feel like I'm eighteen again, alone with a girl in the backseat of my father's car for the first time. I want you. I've never wanted a woman more."

Did he know what it did to her to hear a man in an Armani suit say *fuck me*? Kelly licked her lips, her heart pounding. "Oh, God. Everything about you makes me want to fuck you. But I -- we -- we can't do this now, here, can we? We're in an airplane. People will see us. And we haven't even talked -- about -- about money."

He turned his head to bite down on her shoulder as she flicked her tongue over his nipple again. "You own me, remember? You don't have to pay me. Just fuck me, please. It's been so long… I didn't think I could feel like this again. I need you, Kelly."

The overhead lights were off, and the blankets sheltered them from passing flight attendants. First class was nearly empty. Almost everyone else here was asleep. If they were quiet…

Her fantasies were getting mixed up with her common sense. He was just playing the scenario she'd described. What would happen when he wanted her to pay him later? She didn't have a great deal of cash on her, and automatic teller machines were only good for a few hundred at best.

She could always write him a check.

Yeah. Right. He wouldn't even talk about money and he was going to accept her check. The hard realities of a financial transaction took some of the edge off of her desire. Maybe she'd pushed this just a little too far. She'd been so caught up in the novelty of the idea -- of actually being about to get exactly what she wanted from a man -- that she'd lost sight of reality.

"I want to touch you. Tell me I can touch you. Untie my hands."

Kelly turned enough in his arms to meet his gaze. "We're not in a four-poster bed, and as much as I'd like to be there with you, I don't own you and you're not tied up. I don't even know you. You don't know me. There are some things we have to talk about."

He sighed, straightening slightly in the angled seat. "I'm not going to be any good at this, am I?"

"What do you mean?"

"I can't even get a woman who's obviously attracted to me to have sex with me for free. How the hell can I expect anyone to pay me?"

Kelly punched him playfully on the shoulder. "Idiot. You've already got a paying client. That's what you're doing on this plane, remember?"

"Yeah. But she hasn't met me yet. Not in person. I'm not sure I can do this for money. I mean, it's just sex. I know that. But I always thought there was more to sex than just a quick lay in the back of the car, you know? I thought I ought to feel something for a woman."

Kelly chewed on her lip, trying to decide whether she was angry or not. "So you want to practice with me? To find out whether you'll be any good at this?"

"Yes. I mean no, not like that. I've tried to date since my divorce. I haven't met anyone I even wanted to go out with. When I saw you tonight, I felt something electric in the energy between us. I think you felt it, too. If I'd met you in a different time in my life, I'd know where you live, and what your favorite color is, why you're afraid of cats, and how many brothers and sisters you have. All I know about you right now is I'll always remember the way you feel in my arms, the smell of your hair, and that for some reason I can't understand you find me attractive. And I don't know why that scares you so badly."

"You scare me," Kelly whispered. "I can't play the game if I don't know what the rules are."

"There aren't any rules. Well, maybe a couple. No children. No animals. No blood. I practice safe sex and I expect you to do the same."

"All right. That's pretty straightforward."

"Is that what you want? Terms, like the contracts you write up?"

Was it? Was that all she needed to make her feel safe? "Maybe," she admitted. "I like things spelled out, so we both know what to expect. That way no one gets hurt. Nice and neat. No surprises."

He didn't turn cold and formal, the way men always had whenever she asked for any sort of definition to their relationship. Instead he nipped at her ear again, sending shivers down her neck. "My terms are pretty simple. Whatever you want, whenever you want, wherever you want. I make your fantasies come true. The agency sets the rates. One hundred Euros an hour, three hour minimum, a thousand a day, six thousand a week. A non-refundable deposit, made by electronic transfer, balance either billed to your credit card or payable in cash."

There was a hint of something in his voice that pulled at things other than her wallet. He was still an actor, playing a role. A year from now, maybe even a month from now, that insecurity would be gone.

"You did that very well," Kelly assured him with a kiss on the tip of his chin. "It wasn't so difficult, was it?"

He laughed, and his carefully crafted persona fell apart. "Yes. I can't believe I'm doing this. Or that anyone would actually hire me."

Desire shot through her like a white-hot pain. She'd be his first. No matter what happened later, she'd be his very first customer. Almost like seducing a virgin. "I'd like to hire you. You have any plans for that layover in Paris?"

* * *

She talked about tomorrow and Paris, but her breath still fluttered the hair on his chest, and her fingers slipped inside his pants, gently stroking his balls. He hadn't wanted a woman like this in a long time. He'd never realized what an incredible turn-on it would be to have a woman want him enough to pay for the privilege. She finally eased his zipper down, freeing his cock. Her fingers tightened around him as he circled her earlobe with the tip of his tongue.

His voice nearly broke. "Do any of your fantasies include joining the mile high club?"

She shuddered deliciously under his touch. "What's that?"

He'd managed to work his hand up under the silk lining of her skirt. To his surprise, the tops of her stockings attached to an old-fashioned garter belt. When he ran his hand up her thigh, there was nothing but a small, soft triangle of fabric between him and warm, wet woman. The fabric easily slid out of his way. She struggled to open herself to him within the confines of the seats as she purred under his touch. "People who have managed to have sex in an airplane at an altitude of over 5280 feet."

"Do you charge extra for that?"

Damn. What was it about her that made her want to define everything as if it were a business deal? Did it make her feel safe? Had someone hurt her? Or was she just looking for ways to avoid emotional entanglement?

Well, he had some experience in that department. He didn't need anything from her, after all. Nothing but sex and money. And the money was fast losing its importance. "This one's on the house," he whispered against her ear.

"Tell me how much you want me. Tell me you'll do whatever I tell you to."

That was easy. "You make me so hard just thinking about you. I'm going to die if I have to wait till tomorrow."

She rode the heel of his hand as he slipped his fingers inside her. "*Ummm*. I don't want to wait either. I want you now."

Knowing he could have what he wanted gave him the patience to move slowly. He ducked his head under the blanket to graze her breast with his teeth, then set about the slow process of unbuttoning her blouse one-handed. Damn. She was wearing a leather corset that ended just below her nipples.

"*Ummm.*"

That little growling noise she made was driving him wild. She could make it mean a dozen different things. His cock jerked hard against her hip.

Her hand was still busy, too, ignoring his cock in favor of a slower torture as she rolled his balls in her fingers like some Chinese exercise toy. "Kelly, do you have any idea what you're doing to me?"

She ran one sharp, pointed nail up the length of his cock. "What?"

"Witch."

Laughter flowed across his chest like a heat wave. "I like the way your skin feels under my hands. I like the way your body responds to me. I really like knowing you'll do whatever I want."

Control. That turned her on? Damn, he was slow. The bondage fantasy. Her concern over money. It wasn't about the money. It was about knowing he'd do exactly what she wanted. "I spent eight years in the Air Force. I know how to follow orders. Tell me what you want. Tell me what you like."

She raised her hips enough to help him slide the silk panties down her legs, where she kicked her feet free of her low-heeled black pumps. He watched her tuck the scrap of fabric into one shoe with her toes. Discreet and mostly out of sight. To anyone walking by, they'd look like -- they'd look like two lovers, making out under a blanket. He grinned at the thought. What was the worst that could happen? They couldn't exactly be asked to leave the plane.

"Tell me you didn't pack the condoms in your check-in luggage," she giggled.

"Back pocket. I was a Boy Scout. 'Always be prepared.' Scout motto."

He wriggled his ass away from the seat. Feeling her fingers exploring his pockets was a torture all of its own. She took her time, her hands gliding over his ass, eventually producing three small foil packets linked together and his package of breath-strips. He didn't even want to think about what she had in mind for the breath-strips.

"You look like a Boy Scout. Clean-cut, all American type." His cock felt like it would explode any moment as she rolled the condom down his length, taking longer than she needed to, enjoying the way he jumped under her touch, he was sure. "Tell me you'll do whatever I tell you to, Boy Scout."

"I'll do anything for you. Whatever you want." He itched to help her, to touch her, anywhere, but she hadn't told him he could. She turned to face him, tucking her knees on either side of his hips, stretching herself over his lap so that his cock danced between her thighs, just a hair's breadth from her clit. He slid down in the seat a little, making himself as accessible as he could.

Her hands covered his, guiding them across the length of the leather corset to her breasts. *Yes.* She felt hot and heavy in his hands, a gentle brush of his fingers over her nipples letting him know they were spearing straight out, hot and hungry for his touch. He rolled them between his fingers, then stretched them slightly, finding that making her squirm brought her closer against his aching cock. "I love the way your tits feel, all hard and hot for me. Let me fuck you."

"*Ummm.* I love it when you talk dirty to me, Boy Scout. I want you to be so hot for me you beg."

Her fingers tightened over his cock as he nipped at her collarbone. "I already am. Please, Kelly. I need to fuck you. *Now.*"

"Touch me."

He knew what she meant. He let his fingers make their way slowly down across her bunched-up skirt to that waiting triangle of soft, springy fur concealing the entrance to her pussy. She opened up to him with a soft moan. Her clit responded eagerly, already as distended and engorged as her nipples. His cock trembled against her as he slid his middle finger deep within her. "So wet. So hot. I love the way your pussy feels. So ready for me."

She clenched her thighs around him, making his

waiting cock shudder in response. If it was to be torture, two could play at this game. He finger fucked her as slowly as he could, sucking her breasts in the same rhythm.

She stifled her moan against his shoulder, her lips searching now for something to attack. Could you come from the feel of a woman's tongue outlining your nipple? He thrust his pelvis hard against her. "Can you feel how hard my cock is for you? Let me fuck you, please," he begged again, trying hard to keep his voice whisper-low.

"Not yet." He could tell the power was turning her on as much as the feel of his fingers buried with her. He changed his tactics, withdrawing, caressing her instead with the heel of his hand, slow strokes that made her buck as he moved over her clit. She curled, rocking toward his absent fingers, but he didn't slide them back in. He wouldn't. Not unless she ordered him to.

He heard a snap and wondered what she was doing. In a moment he knew. *Christ-almighty*. Her lips closed over his nipple, sucking hard, the freezing cold of a breath-strip sending a jolt of exquisite pain through his nipple. Despite his resolve, a moan slipped from his lips. He tried to twist away, but her teeth pinched sharply, warning him, reminding him. There was no doubt in his mind, she was in charge.

The muted tap of the flight attendant's heels against the carpet warned them she was on her way back. He pulled the blanket back up so that only the top of her head showed, trying to look as much like any other sleeping couple as he could manage, all the while shivering as the cold fire of her breath shot through his nipple straight to his aching balls.

2:30 AM, Wednesday, 8 February, 2006
American Airlines Flight 44

The flight attendant walked through the cabin, then turned on her heel, her gaze meeting Terry's as she headed back again. An amused smile pulled at the corners of her lips as she paused for a moment beside them. "I see you're still awake. Buzz me if you need anything."

"Thanks," he managed, his breath hitching as Kelly squeezed her thighs shut around him. She reached between them to stroke the length of his cock, her nails raking him through the thin latex of the condom.

"You're trying to kill me, aren't you?" he whispered against her ear as the flight attendant disappeared.

She made a circle of her fingers just below the head of his penis and drew her fingers slowly upward until he wanted to scream. "I want to feel your cock inside me. *Now.*"

He lifted her up, dropping her down over the burning length of his shaft. God, she was tight. Tight and wet and slick. Why he was here didn't matter. Nothing mattered but the feel of this woman around him. Good. So good. So...

"Don't move. Not yet."

By the time she was through with him there would be nothing left. "You're so hot. Your pussy's so tight around my cock. I love the way you feel around me. Like an inferno, and I'm engulfed in your flames." He took long, slow, deep breaths, trying to regain his equilibrium.

That might have worked better if the scent of her

hadn't overwhelmed his senses.

"*Ummm*. You feel good inside me," she whispered. She wriggled a little, experimentally.

"Too good," he groaned into her hair. "If you do that again, I'm going to come."

"I didn't give you permission to come yet, slave."

"Yes, Mistress." She sounded deadly serious. He didn't know what else to say. Was she teasing him? Or testing him? Trying to see if he knew the rules of her game? *Could* a man keep from coming just because permission hadn't been given? What would she do if he failed?

There were ways... devices. He'd seen them online. Leather strips called lassos. Cock rings. Cages. And... other things. He shuddered at the thought.

When he slid his hand back between them to brush through the springy mound of her pubic hair, she bit his arm, smothering a cry. Her pulse beat against the length of his cock, the pounding of her blood driving him wild.

Holding still wasn't helping. He rocked his hips experimentally, grinding their bodies together in a slow, tortuous dance. If he was going to suffer, so would she.

She tightened around him, trembling violently as he stroked her clit with his fingertip. Her hips curling, she rode his cock with small jerky movements that made him ache to thrust into her, hot and hard and heavy. But she was in control. Her hand moved over his now, dictating his rhythm as he worked her clit faster and faster.

Her nipples stabbed at his chest through the thin fabric of her dress. If only he'd taken the time to undress her properly, he'd be able to suck them, bite them, lick them the way he was aching to. But if he pushed her back far enough to play with her tits, it was going to be pretty obvious to anyone who walked by just what they were doing under that blanket.

Not that it wasn't now.

"Fuck me, baby," he whispered against her ear. "Ride me hard. Come for me. Please."

She bit her lip as she came, the contractions coming hard and fast, a vise closing around him. "Now!"

He didn't have to ask what she meant. He came so hard it was more pain than pleasure. She clenched again and again as he spurted into the condom, milking him until he thought he must be dry, then taking a little more.

"I can't wait to get you into a real bed," he teased as he nibbled on her shoulder.

"I have to meet a courier at the airport first thing in the morning. After that the day is all mine." She curled against him, laying her head on his chest as she ran her fingers over his nipple. "I can't wait to get you into real restraints."

She wanted to do more than just play at bondage? He should tell her he wasn't into that. This was all fun and games, but real men didn't submit. Men shouldn't want to submit.

So why did the images her words conjured up make his sated penis suddenly spring to attention again?

This was a job. Only a job. And he needed the money.

A lie he could live with…

10:00 AM, Wednesday, 8 February, 2006
Paris, France

Paris was everything she'd expected and more. Old and new blended, with no real restraint, amid a chaos of traffic noise and confusion that was as impossible to sort out as her feelings. Terry's hand rested in the small of her back, his light touch an anchor in the storm of emotions that threatened to send her flying loose on the winter wind.

Sex. This was all about sex. Nothing more. She'd met him less than twenty-four hours ago. So why was she feeling so possessive as they headed toward the hotel Lady Elizabeth had booked for him?

Kelly clutched her carry-on bag tightly against her side. He'd be her first. She'd been to a few clubs, watched the carefully choreographed scenes. Places like No Bounds and *The Fetish Club*. She loved the feel of leather against her skin, and she almost always wore one of her corsets under her business suits.

She'd read every erotic e-book she could get her hands on. She had her favorites loaded on her PDA -- Angela Knight, Ann Jacobs, Diane Whiteside, Treva Harte. She'd planned to read them over again on the plane.

Meeting Terry had changed her plans.

He seemed willing enough. For him, it was just a job. Still, despite the research, this would be her first time. She felt like a virgin. Would he know? Could he sense that despite her words, she'd only ever fantasized?

Control. It was all about control. Reading the sub, understanding what he wanted, needed, pushing his buttons, making him want to submit.

The light pressure of his fingers on her arm pulled her focus back to their immediate surroundings. Why were they stopping? The magnificent old building in front of them looked like a palace.

She swallowed hard. It wasn't a palace at all. It was the *Hôtel Amarante Elysées Star*. The place was awash in lights -- floodlights competed with the first sweep of dawn to make the huge old building look even more incredibly unreal.

The lump in her throat grew. She'd been right the first time. This place wasn't a hotel. It was a palace. She could never have afforded a hotel like this. But it wasn't *her* room, after all.

Lady Elizabeth could afford whatever she wanted.

Lady Elizabeth could afford Terry.

Well, she could afford today. Even if it was just sex.

"Kelly, I --"

She stopped his words with her fingertips. "We have today," she whispered. "Let's not waste it."

"Right." He scooped her up with the luggage, making her shriek with delight at his idiocy as he carried them all in the door, depositing the luggage in the arms of a bellhop who rushed to greet them.

Damn. Despite herself, she was impressed. She wasn't exactly a lightweight. Not anymore. Terry didn't look like a body-builder type. Well enough built, with muscles in all the right places, but damn. She hadn't expected him to be so strong. On the other hand, she'd yet to see him with his clothes off…

"*Ma femme reste avec moi.*" *I'll keep my wife*, Terry told the bellhop with a laugh. He set her on the counter next to the registrar. "*Nous sommes nouveaux mariés.*"

Just married? Kelly swallowed hard.

"We're here on our honeymoon."

It wasn't a scenario she'd have picked, but it would do. Terry's French wasn't perfect, but the desk clerk smiled and slid the room key to the bellhop.

Terry's fingers rested against the curve of her breast under her jacket, chafing her nipple with the edge of his thumbnail. Kelly smothered a moan as the hand under her ass moved just a little, positioning her so that the sharp jutting of his cock branded her hip.

She nearly gasped as the bellboy unlocked their door. She didn't have to ask whether the brocade drapes and sateen comforter and sheets were real. Again she thought of a palace.

Terry turned her in his arms to kiss her, sliding her slowly to her feet. God, she loved his cock. Hot and hard and ready for her use. And today she didn't have to share him with anyone. Today he was all hers.

The room was gorgeous -- and well equipped. She could think of more than one use for the bucket of iced champagne sitting on the nightstand next to the bed. Terry tipped the bellman and sent him away.

Alone. The moment of truth. Her heart pounded as if she'd run a marathon.

It wasn't an old-fashioned four-poster bed, but there were bedposts. They were shorter than the ones in the book, but they looked sturdy enough for her purposes. She slipped her hands inside his suit coat. His nipples pebbled beneath the shirt, hardening at her touch.

"If at any time you feel you are in any real physical or mental danger, you will use the safe-word *alert*. Do you understand?"

"Alert. I understand about safe-words."

Kelly pushed him away, falling into the character she'd practiced over and over again in her mind. She was Mercy, and he was James. Young, randy, irrepressible James, always sporting a hard on for his mistress. "I own you," she reminded him. "Until the term of your apprenticeship is over. Never forget that."

"Kelly, I'm not --"

"You will address me as Mistress. And you will not look directly at me. Such actions are arrogant. I will not have an arrogant bondsman."

"Yes, Mistress." He flushed a little as he dropped his gaze, whether from the reprimand, or from excitement, it was hard to tell. After all, this was her fantasy, not his. Wasn't it?

"Take off your clothes."

He drew in his breath. A little too sharply?

He started to toss the suit jacket over the back of a chair. She was no neat-freak, but she hated to see clothes strewn about. "In the closet!" she barked. "On hangers."

"Yes, Mistress. I'm sorry."

His back was to her now as he stripped. What a back it was. Long and lean and covered with muscles that were as well defined as any of the models she'd worked with. He followed her orders precisely, hanging up the jacket, then the shirt, then the pants. He carefully folded his socks as he pulled them off, laying them in his shoes in the bottom of the closet. Then there was nothing left but those silk boxers.

Slowly, deliberately, he dropped the shorts on the floor. His eyes came up, just a little, as he turned to face her, sparkling now as he tried to hide his smile.

He wanted her to punish him? Why? Just to see if she could -- or would?

His cock was standing straight up, so hard she could see the dark blue vein throbbing along its underside.

Her mind searched frantically for some way to carry out her threat. She didn't have a whip or even her flogger with her. Nothing but her one carry-on bag. A change of underwear, her personal toys, and two clean pair of --

"On your knees, slave."

Slowly, very slowly, still watching her from behind those thick, curling lashes, he dropped to his knees. She walked past him to the luggage piled on the chair near the door. Spilling her toys -- a pair of lifelike gel dildos, full sized and anal -- onto the thick comforter, she searched the bottom of the bag for the small mesh zipper pouch. She hadn't had room for much -- a hairbrush which she set out now on the nightstand, and a few things for emergencies. There they were. Two pair of sheer silk stockings. This wasn't quite the emergency she'd had in mind, but they'd do. And in the outside pocket, a pair of small jeweled hairclips. Perfect.

She circled him, the stockings in her hands. "What did I tell you to do with your clothes, slave?"

"Hang them up in the closet," he answered promptly.

"And where are your shorts now?"

"On the floor, Mistress."

"You *want* me to punish you."

"I have been disobedient, Mistress. I beg your forgiveness."

"You will have to earn my forgiveness." Before he had time to argue, she looped the stocking around his wrists, drawing them together tightly behind his back. Another sharp intake of breath. Still, he didn't try to fight.

Good.

"Don't try to fight me. Stockings aren't the best

restraints. They can be dangerous. They can pull too tight and cut you or even burn your skin. I want you to promise me you'll remember our safe-word."

Another deep breath. "I spent two years in the Gulf, Mistress. I don't frighten easily. I think I can handle anything you might do to me. But if things get out of hand, I'll *alert* you. You have my word."

Her low-heeled pumps made no sound in the thick pile carpet as she walked across the room to the bed, dropping her clothes on the chaise lounge. First her jacket. Then her skirt. Then her blouse. She let him get a good look at what was left -- the black leather corset with its row of shining brass eyelets laced tightly up the front.

Next time she flew she'd find one with nylon eyelets. Airport security'd been a real bitch. She'd set off their metal detectors. Not the kind of strip-search she'd had in mind while she was dressing. This was far more her flavor.

She left her black pumps, stockings and garters in place. His cock danced against his belly as she crossed to the bed. She knew how good he'd feel buried balls deep in her. She was getting wet just watching his reactions as he knelt there, waiting for her. She wanted to push him onto his back and ride him, long and hard.

But he needed to be punished. And leaving that cock alone was the best punishment she could think of. But that was also punishing her.

Hmmm. She shouldn't have to wait just because he'd disobeyed her.

Sitting on the edge of the bed, her legs spread wide, she found the vibrators she'd left on the bedcover. Terry made a sound like a whimper as she slipped the larger one between her wet folds, sliding it into her pussy. "This could have been you, slave."

"Forgive me, Mistress. I won't disobey you again."

She ignored him as she slid the large ribbed head in and out of her soaking pussy, turning the speed setting to fast. She almost forgot her audience as she fucked herself, riding the vibrator harder and harder.

"Let me help you, Mistress," he begged.

"I don't need," she gasped, "a disobedient slave." She didn't. She cried out as she came, her muscles clamping down hard on the now-hot plastic.

She left her legs spread wide as she sprawled backward on the bed. She was almost relaxed again by the time she felt his warm breath on her sated pussy. "Please, Mistress."

He didn't wait for her permission. Instead he bent his head, reawakening her desire to fever-pitch as he first kissed, then sucked, her clit, the tip of his tongue darting back and forth over the tiny head.

She screamed when he moved to thrust his tongue deep into her. Her heels came up to wrap over his shoulders, pulling him closer against her, close enough to tangle her hands in his hair. "Yes!"

His overnight growth of beard raked her skin, driving her wild with lust. Desperate for satisfaction, she ground her pussy against his face, riding his tongue. So close… shuddering, she broke, her pussy drenching them both in a hot glaze of release.

Before she could protest, cool air hit her overheated flesh. She wasn't sure how he did it, with his hands tied behind his back, but he made his way to his feet, standing at the foot of the bed, her legs still hooked over his shoulders, his cock hovering near her wet and wanting pussy.

That was as close as he got.

"Christ," he muttered. "Kelly, I'm naked."

"Of course you're naked." She propped herself up on her elbows, thoroughly annoyed. "Did I tell you to speak, slave?"

He lowered his eyes, falling back into character. "Forgive me, Mistress. I'm not wearing a condom."

Christ. She pulled her feet to the front of his shoulders and pushed, hard, sending him staggering back a few steps. How had things gotten so out of control so fast? *She* was supposed to be in charge. She wasn't in control of anything.

Kelly paced the room, picking up her clothes and folding them neatly into a pile. She had to restore her credibility as a Mistress, or the fantasy would never come close to being anything more than just sex. Great sex, but nothing like her dream.

She had to get back to the scene in the book. That was what she wanted, after all. James, tied down to the bed, completely under her control. The thought turned her on again instantly. This would be good. Better, even -- she could add her own kink.

Terry stood naked before her, eyes downcast, every hint of a smile gone now. She ran her nail up the underside of his cock again, along the dark blue vein, watching as small drops of pre-cum leaked from the tip to drip slowly over the ridge that formed its head. He leaned into her touch, his body trembling slightly, like a guitar string someone had just plucked.

Good.

Moving the heels of her hands on his shoulders, she shoved, sending him sprawling face-forward on the bed. "Don't move," she ordered.

His breath rasping in sharply, he strained at the bindings on his wrists. Grabbing her hairbrush from the nightstand, she slapped him hard on the ass with the broad, flat wooden back. "I said don't move."

"Ouch!" he yelped.

She smacked him again on the other side, brightening that cheek with a red blush as well. "What did I tell you about stockings?"

"Forgive me, Mistress." His body trembled as he lay there, but not a muscle twitched otherwise.

She let him wonder what she was doing as she collected her dildo, washing it with the body wash the hotel had so thoughtfully provided before she stowed it back in her suitcase. Digging in her bag again, she found a bottle of lotion, a small tube of lubricant, and the selection of condoms she'd packed for her toys. That would do nicely.

Looping a stocking over one of his ankles, she secured it to the bedpost. He didn't fight her. Not when she rubbed body lotion down the length of his back and over the cheeks of his lovely ass. Not when she slid her fingers under him, teasing his cock from behind.

He made a strangled, gurgling sound when she circled the small, tight opening of his anus, using the lube, spending extra time making him softer and slippery. His hips bucked off the bed when she pressed harder, but still he didn't fight her. Not even when she pressed her fingers in, probing gently for the hard bump of his prostate, though he groaned into the comforter.

Not until she withdrew her fingers, adding another measure of thick, greasy lube, and pressing the condom-sheathed anal vibrator's head against his tender ass did he fight her. He stiffened, bucking wildly, trying to twist himself over.

That was easy enough to deal with. Kneeling with her knees on the backs of his thighs, she pinned him down. "Relax," she ordered. "Take a deep breath, then breathe out slowly."

She felt as much as heard his whimper of protest, but he did as instructed. Pausing with the vibrator's head just inside his tight passage, she let him get used to the feel, then pushed again, waiting as the length of it slowly penetrated his ass.

* * *

He had to get loose. He couldn't, he wouldn't submit to her. Not this way. Not when it wasn't a game anymore.

Why? Why fight her? Wasn't this what he wanted?

Be a man. Real men don't --

What are you going to do, Terry? You don't want to fight her. Admit it. The only thing that really scares you is that you'll like what she's doing.

An excited shiver ran through his body as she spread lotion along his spine and over his ass cheeks. Christ, that felt good. He couldn't lie to himself. He was tired of being the responsible one. He *wanted* her in control.

His world narrowed down to a tiny focus. One woman who held his soul in her hands. No decisions to make. No one to be responsible for. Nothing to follow up on. Only her. All he had to do was obey her every command. So simple. So focused. Nothing else in his life had ever been this easy -- or this rewarding. Because when he got it right, when her hands were on him like this, when her body was touching him everywhere at once, her breasts dragging over his heated, oiled skin, the world outside ceased to exist.

Anything she wanted. He had no pride. No limits. His only purpose was to please her. *Anything. Anything, Mistress. Anything for you. Just touch me.*

Please.

Anything but *that.* What the hell was she doing playing with his asshole? No! Fuck! He wasn't gay, for Christ's sake. He'd never --

Her finger forced its way in, past his tight sphincter. Christ Almighty, that felt... Oh, God. What was she... his cock jumped as if she'd hit him with a cattle prod. What was she -- fuck that felt good. No wonder gay guys... No. He wasn't going to allow himself to enjoy this. He couldn't. But --

He whimpered when she withdrew her finger, missing that intimate, invasive touch as much as he had feared its violation. Why --

The tip of something cold and hard pushed against his anus, demanding entry. Her dildo? She wanted to use *that* on him? It was too big! It wouldn't fit!

Sure, gay guys managed cocks, even big cocks, somehow, but that thing...

He'd watched, fascinated despite himself, as she played with the ugly toy as if it, and not he, had been her personal sex slave. The thing was huge and knobby, with ridges and bumps, and squeezable balls molded to its base. She'd played with the balls as she rode it, thrust it into herself in rapid, jerky movements. He'd watched her come -- come for it, and not for him...

A lesson. He could be replaced. He *would* be replaced if he didn't obey.

Still, there were limits. He didn't want that big ugly thing in his virgin ass. It wouldn't *fit.* But she pushed relentlessly, and it did fit. It felt smaller, somehow, less painful than he'd expected, and smoother. That wasn't right. This wasn't supposed to be easy. He wasn't supposed to like this.

He whimpered again, responding already, despite himself, his cock so impossibly hard he knew he would come any moment, even without her touch.

It felt so good. But he wasn't allowed -- he couldn't -- this was wrong. Wrong.

"I want you to turn over, slowly. Don't try to fight me. I don't want you to get hurt. Do you understand me?"

He understood. *Everything you are, everything you have ever been, has just ceased to exist. You're mine, slave. Whatever you think, whatever you feel, whatever you want, it doesn't matter. I am all that matters.*

He had no will of his own. No choices.

All he could do was feel. And obey.

He turned slowly, making sure he didn't dislodge her carefully positioned toy. Not because he wanted the toy within him, stretching him, filling him, making him more aware of his body than he'd ever been. No. He didn't want that thing stuck in his ass, so tight and hard it made him wince with every play of his muscles. But the Mistress had put it there. He didn't need to think about why. He needed to obey.

She ran her hands over him again as she tied him in place. He didn't bother to check the tightness of the bonds this time. He wouldn't try to get away. What was there to go back to? A world with responsibilities, decisions, people who wanted, needed, demanded.

Here there was only one woman. One woman who commanded him with her every touch. Good. So good. The feel of her hands on his skin. The smell of her sex where she'd touched him. The feel of her cock within him. In his state of heightened sexual awareness, even the dip of the bed where she knelt to slide the condom over his throbbing dick made him harder.

Her toy started to shift in his ass, sliding out as his hips rose to thrust toward her touch, and he pushed down, ramming the dildo back in until he felt the flared base lodged flat against his ass. Good. That was what she wanted, after all. He was just the cock. She was the one doing the fucking.

Anything. Anything you want, Mistress.

She wanted to own him, body and soul.

She had what she wanted.

He dared to look up, his gaze hot with lust. "I'm yours, Mistress. I want you in control. I'll do anything you want. Whatever you allow me to do."

A slow smile spread over her lips. She slid her greased fingers beneath him. His hips jerked off the bed as the toy within him began to vibrate intensely.

He screamed. He knew he screamed, although the sound of his voice was muffled by the roar in his ears as he came like 4th of July fireworks. Not like this! He sobbed out his denial even as his balls pumped more and more cum into the condom. He wanted to be *in* her. He wanted to feel her tighten around him, knowing he'd made her come first. All that was gone now. Gone. Gone.

Then her hands were on him, stroking him through the impossibly long orgasm that shook him like a helpless child, caressing the length of his cock, massaging his aching balls.

Even when it was over, it wasn't over. That damn plastic cock still hummed within him. He pushed back against it, his body jerking from the pain that was pleasure as it pushed deep within him.

"I -- *can't* --" he sobbed. "Turn it off, please turn it off."

"You *can*." She slipped the condom off of him and walked away, leaving her toy buried within him, shattering his psyche with its low-pitched hum.

She returned what seemed like hours later with a damp, steaming washcloth, which she used to cleanse him thoroughly. Her hands on him, stroking. The vibrator in him, pulsing. Her body over him, tempting, as she bent forward to kiss him.

Yes. Yes! He sucked her lip between his teeth, nipping, demanding. She fought back with him in a parody of combat, sucking, pinching, twisting, biting. "Fuck me. Please. I beg you."

She moved her head, licking his nipples.

"Fuck! Jesus fucking Christ! What the fuck?"

Smiling, she licked him again around the small jeweled clip she'd clamped on his nipple. It hurt like a son-of-a-bitch. Denial rushed through him like the flow of blood to his cock. *No.* The sound came out like a moan…

He barely jumped when she clamped the other nipple. At least he hadn't embarrassed himself by arching toward her, the way his body wanted to. He saved that for her hands, as they unrolled another condom down the aching length of his dick.

Smiling, she reached for the wine bucket the hotel had thoughtfully provided for the newlyweds. Setting the champagne aside, she pulled two handfuls of crushed ice from the bucket.

No. Oh, no. Surely she wouldn't…

A ragged voice screamed as the sharp tang of the ice encased his nipples. Before he could recognize the voice as his own and regain some measure of self control, the ice moved, sliding its way down his chest along a path that led straight to his cock.

It was like watching a train wreck. He couldn't get away. There was nowhere to go. With his hands and feet lashed securely to the bedposts, there was nowhere to go except up. Right into the hands of waiting ice. And down again, hard, with her nearly forgotten dildo screwing his ass. And still the ice was there, cupping him, molding around him like an ice-bride's cunt, making him scream again with wanton disregard for what the occupants of the neighboring rooms might think.

Oh God. No more. Too much. Please, please stop. He couldn't take any more. "Please," he managed aloud, his voice sounding pitiful in his ears. She had to stop. She…

The room went dark as she rose up on her knees, dropping her hot cunt down over his frozen, pussy starved cock. The melting ice pooled around his balls, tiny spots of icy-hot pain dripping down and over him as her pussy consumed him.

Wet. So wet, so hot. Hot as a summer day in the desert. Oh God. Fuck me. Please. Fuck me. He wasn't sure whether he'd managed to say it out loud, so he tried again. "Please, Mistress. Fuck me."

She rode him hard and fast, her fingers stroking her clit as she rose up and down on his latex-wrapped cock. His hips jerked up off the bed, shoving hard into her, but when they did, her vibrator slid out of his ass. On the down stroke his body weight thrust it back in. *Too much. Too much!* He jerked hard against the restraints, desperate to get to her, desperate to hold, to touch, to possess, as he bucked helplessly back and forth.

But he couldn't. He couldn't do anything but thrust against her and then ram the other cock back again, fucking his ass and her cunt until he made a rhythm of it, a frenzied, out of control, demanding rhythm that had her gasping as she rode him, had her coming hard around him, screaming his name as the orgasm took her over the top.

She'd move away, now that she was done -- she'd leave him alone. No. He wasn't done. He had to come, damn it! Desperation drove him faster, faster, his cock thrusting at a frenzied pitch as she tightened around him again. He wanted -- he needed -- it was his turn!

He didn't matter. *She* wanted. *She* needed. Her hands stroked her own nipples, the ones he wanted so badly to touch, pulling and tweaking them until they shone like bright coral beacons. She rode him like a half-broke stallion, and it was her desire driving them on. He sobbed as he strove desperately to please her.

Reaching down, she yanked off the nipple clamps. "Now," she ordered. "Now!"

He screamed at the pain as the blood flooded back into his sensitive nipples, his cock erupting in tune to his scream. She came around him again, her contractions fisting him tighter than any hand job, her cunt engulfing him like a white-hot flame. He shot into her, hot and heavy, wave after wave of searing cum, the most intense pleasure/pain he'd ever known.

When the light crept back into his vision, she lay atop him, quiet at last, even the hum of the vibrator gone now. He had no awareness of her turning it off. He needed to hold her, to assure himself this was real, and not just some dream a lack of release had forced from his subconscious mind. As if she read his thoughts, she slipped the bonds from his wrists, allowing him the comfort of her touch, the reassurance of her feel as he held her against his trembling body.

She had broken him, turned his whole world upside down.

Nothing would ever be the same again.

The silence was devastating. She had to say

something.

He'd let her so far inside him. If she didn't...

"Thank you," she whispered against his cheek.

Thank you? She'd just given him the most-mind blowing, life-altering sex in the world and she said *Thank you*? Raising his head, he saw the tears glistening on her cheeks. He bent his neck to kiss her silken eyelids. "Thank you, Mistress."

"Terry, I -- I'm new at this. I've been to the clubs and the websites and I've read the books, but that's not the same. You're my first. You're so perfect. You'll always be very special to me. Leaving here this afternoon is going to rip my heart out. Tell me you'll e-mail me when we both get home. It might be a while before I can afford you, but I have to see you again."

She wanted to see him again. He hadn't done it wrong. The fears he'd been harboring leaked out in a choked sob against her skin. "Anytime, anywhere. You don't have to pay me, Mistress. I don't want your money. All I want is you. Once this assignment is over, once I get home, I won't work for the agency again. I don't want to take this assignment now. I don't want anyone but you to touch me."

Her hands were on him again, stroking him gently, holding him together as she eased the ache. "It's all right. I understand. I know you signed a contract. And you need some time. You're very vulnerable right now. We both are. You may not feel the same about me a week or a month from now. I won't pressure you. But I will leave you my e-mail address. I want to hear from you again. When you're ready."

"I'll always be ready for you." He nudged at her now, letting her feel the tip of his cock rubbing hard and needy against her pussy. "Did James and his

Mistress ever have sex any other way?"

"Yeah." She wound her leg around his hip, kissing her tears off of his cheek as her hands caressed his raw emotions. "They had sex just about any way you can think of. Maybe we could invent a few new ways."

"Yes, Mistress," he promised. "Anything." As long as he could hold her.

The tip of her tongue crept between her teeth as she eyed him. "You look like my cat when he's thinking about pouncing on a dust bunny. What are you thinking?"

"I'm trying to decide whether I have the energy to pounce on your nipples. You'd probably try to get away. I don't feel like fighting you at the moment."

"Pleasing you is all that matters to me." He shifted her in his arms until she curled close to his chest. "You don't have to tie me up to get what you want, Mistress."

"No?" She flicked her tongue over his nipple experimentally. His arms closed around her convulsively, crushing her head against his chest. "What if I do this?" Her fingers brushed down across his belly to capture his cock, playing over his length inquisitively as she covered him in another condom.

She leaned in closer, using his cock in her hand like a dildo to outline her clit, seemingly unaware she was driving him totally insane.

He captured her hands, rolling with her until he was below her, pulling his knees up so she could slide slowly down onto his waiting cock. She made no move to resist him. Instead she linked fingers with him, helping him position her perfectly. Her smile stretched across her face as she came down on him, burying his cock up to the balls in her steaming wet pussy.

She rode him hard and hot, the cowgirl riding the bucking Brahma, though no one blew the whistle at precisely eight seconds. She screamed out his name when she broke over him, her pussy clenching like a closing fist around his cock as she exploded. It was more than his slipping self-control could manage. He bucked hard against her, yanking her down to where he could feast on her breasts, pounding against her harder, harder, feeling her body respond to him again and again.

He broke like a summer thunderstorm expelling its first burst of pent-up energy, branding her, claiming her, trying to recover the pieces of himself he had lost.

He could not. He could not undo what had happened. He had given himself over to her, allowed her total control. And it had been good. Better than good.

It had been what he'd always wanted. What he'd secretly dreamed of. She'd captured his soul and held it in the palm of her hands.

But it was only for one day. After that she'd be gone, as if she'd never been part of his life.

If one day was all he had, it would have to be enough. If he wanted something more, that was the one power over him he would not give her. He would not let her know she owned his soul. Not now. Not yet. But he knew he would never surrender himself so completely to any other Mistress.

9:00 AM, Monday, 3 April, 2006
C.H.A.S.E. Headquarters, New York, NY

"Martha, coffee!"

Kelly wadded up a sheet of paper and threw it at her boss, hitting her target straight on. David held up his hands defensively, laughing too hard to make much headway on his stern-faced façade.

Jennifer shushed them as she reached for the phone. "You've reached The *C.H.A.S.E.* Organization. May I help you?" Her professional frown of disapproval brought them all back in line.

Still smiling, David made his way to the coffeepot, handing Kelly a cup as he parked his long, lean frame on the corner of her overburdened desk. He kept his voice low. "You know that's the first time you've smiled all day."

"Sorry. Guess I'm a little stressed."

"You wanna talk about him?"

Kelly drew back a little, almost startled, but then, this was David. She didn't have to wonder why Candy had dumped Brasden-Marten and everything it stood for to follow this man. "I'd ask how you know it's a man, but you always know."

"Kelly, when my fiancée tells me someone's 'frighteningly efficient' -- an exact quote, mind you -- I trust her judgment -- enough to hunt you down and hire you. A decision, I might add, that I've found quite advantageous. But when the Mistress of Efficiency has a week's backlog piling up on her desk and her nose buried in web pages, I figure there's something wrong. With most women, I'd assume that something to be some asshole who didn't know what a treasure he had in you. However, in the six weeks you've worked here,

I've never known you to go out on a single date. Beautiful women who don't date usually have a reason. Still points back to some asshole somewhere."

"David, I love you. Give up on Candy and marry me."

David shook his head. "I love you too, but you know you wouldn't put up with me for ten minutes. I've seen the way you look at my office. Besides, we both love Candy."

Kelly sighed again. "Yeah." A click of her mouse brought the web page back up. Terry's provocative smile stared at her, his naked chest begging for her touch as he posed for the camera, his shirt unbuttoned a few more buttons than was necessary, and his tie slung carelessly over his shoulder.

"Wow."

That was Jennifer, looking over her shoulder. "Yeah."

"Oh my God. He's an *escort*? Kelly, you know this man? You've been out with him? Is he as hot as he looks?"

"Even better."

"E-mail me that link!"

Kelly shook her head. "The link doesn't work anymore. This is from my Temporary Internet files. He's gone. The whole agency's gone. All I get now is the damn clock."

"Clock?"

"Windows wait screen, clocking, trying to find the site," Jennifer explained automatically. Sometimes David was hopelessly behind the times with computers. "So maybe they changed names. Sites like that change their names when things get too hot."

"I e-mailed him at the agency over a month ago. No response. Then I e-mailed the agency directly. Still no response. Now the website's down. I tried doing a search for him by name. He's a -- he *was* a computer network consultant. Private contractor. I thought I could find his company. Nothing."

David ran a hand through his hair, a deep frown settling across the bridge of his nose. "Would he have any reason to avoid you?"

"Do you mean am I a sex-crazed stalker? No. We parted on good terms, and I paid my bill. But he never cashed my check. At first I was hurt, then pissed. Now I'm worried."

"You might have a reason to be worried."

Kelly moved her hand away from the mouse without looking directly at David again. "That's why I showed you this picture. Something's wrong. I can feel it. Terry needed money. That's why he went to work for the agency. Even if he was pissed off at me, he would have cashed my check." She pressed her fingers against her eyes. "I might not be so worried if I hadn't come to work for you, but I've learned way too much here."

"What do you know about this man? Tell me every detail you can think of. Well, not everything. I don't want to know about the sex. Just the facts."

Just the facts. Kelly took a deep breath as she picked up the complaint form she'd already started on. "Terry Bradford. Thirty-four years old, six-foot-one, two-hundred pounds, dark brown hair, blue eyes. Oldest of four brothers. Did two four-year enlistments in the Air Force, then moved back to his home town. Ex made him promise not to re-up a third time. Her name is Cleveland. He owns a house on the New Jersey coast. Lives alone with his cat Squire, who's white with a black hat and black boots. Terry likes his coffee black and his steak medium-well."

"He has a cat?" Jennifer was the first to pounce. "People with cats don't disappear."

"No," David agreed. "Let's hope he's just avoiding you. How did you meet him? Through his website?"

"No. I told you about the courier assignments? I met him in the airport the first time out. He kept staring at me. Eventually I introduced myself. He bought me coffee and gave me his business card."

"Do you still have his business card?"

Kelly handed it over.

David studied the card. "Looks like this was done on a laser printer. High grade cotton paper, 110 lb bond, laid finish, watermarked. Expensive stock. Has to be special ordered most places."

Jennifer stared over David's shoulder at the card. "There's no address or phone number on the card. He didn't say where in New Jersey?"

"Just on the ocean front."

"He said it like that? The ocean front? Not the beach?"

"Ocean front. I pictured one of those places where the coast is rocky. Not a tourist area."

David nodded. "Did he drive to the airport?"

"I don't know. Wait. He must have. His car keys were in the screening basket at airport security."

Jennifer looked again at the picture on Kelly's screen. "He printed the cards himself. Probably a small town. Not the sort of thing he wanted to take to a local print shop. If he's the oldest, he wouldn't want his brothers to know he needed money badly enough to prostitute himself. Probably didn't tell them where he was going."

"But one of them is watching the cat," David agreed. "And by now the brothers are all just as worried as you are. Who would they call?"

"Cops," Kelly speculated. "Already checked missing persons. No reports that matched him. And I didn't just search under his name. I figured it wouldn't be that easy to get an international passport in an assumed name, but if Terry Bradford's his real name, why can't I find any reference to him or his business anywhere?"

"It's not that hard to get a fake passport. Dangerous if you get caught, though. Foreign police departments don't take kindly to that sort of thing. Hardly worth the risk. Did you actually see his passport?"

Kelly shook her head. "No. And I don't think I ever heard anyone call him by name."

Jennifer reappeared at their elbow with a road atlas in hand. "He flies out of JFK, so I'm betting he lives somewhere close to the New York line. If it's a private beach house where it's not too crowded, then he's somewhere between Union Beach and Highlands. Past that and it's too commercial. That's about a ten-mile stretch of coast, a lot of it pretty built up. I guess you could start by driving down the road reading mailboxes in the rural areas."

"I live in New York!" Kelly argued. "I don't own a car. I don't even have a driver's license. Never needed one."

"The phone would be more practical. Did you try information?"

"There are twenty-one Terry Bradfords in the state of New Jersey, if that's his real name. I started on the list two nights ago. So far mostly answering machines that didn't sound at all like his voice. A few really lewd offers I'd rather not repeat."

"Stationery stores," Jennifer suggested. "Call

office supply places. Tell them your friend showed you some paper he ordered and you want a ream. If it's pricey enough they'll want to make sure it's the right paper."

"*That* I can do."

* * *

Two hours later, Kelly had three possible leads in hand. The last one looked the most promising. "Hazlet, New Jersey, the guy at the office supply place says he knows exactly what paper I'm talking about. A Terry *Bradley* ordered that paper for his business cards more than once. Apparently he always makes his own. Laid finish, twenty-five percent cotton, watermarked. Twenty-eight dollars a ream -- a short ream at that. Only one hundred sheets."

"Come on. I'll drive," Jennifer volunteered.

* * *

It was a relatively simple matter to get the store manager to show her the sample of the paper he'd kept -- with a copy of Terry's receipt still stapled to it. Kelly did her best to memorize the address as she paid for her order, repeating the number over and over again in her head. "North Beach Drive, number seven-three-one-seven."

The sun was at the right angle to wash the place in a red-gold blaze. The weathered bricks took on an eerie glow, as if the house had caught fire. There was a car in the driveway. Somewhere near the back of the house a light flicked on.

Kelly felt her heart pounding insanely. All this time, and she'd been worried over nothing. Anger knotted her hands into fists. She was tempted to tell Jennifer to take her home, but she'd come too far for that. She marched up the steps, purpose giving her courage where anger failed.

The door opened before she could knock. Tall. Gorgeous. Shirt half-open and a beer in his hand. Looking so much like the picture on the website. "Oh, yeah," Jennifer whispered at her elbow.

"You're not Terry." Kelly stared at the man, stunned, her hand still poised to knock.

"No, I'm not. And you're not Cleveland." The man eyed her speculatively as he took another draught on his beer. "Dallas? Toronto?"

Kelly flushed slightly. "Paris."

"Paris? As in France?" He took a step closer, setting down the beer bottle. "What is this, an April Fool's joke? Terry's never been to Paris."

"Where did he tell you he was going when he left in January?"

"Toronto."

Kelly shook her head. "I met Terry in the airport on the way to France. We promised to e-mail once we both got back home. I didn't hear from him. Now his e-mails are bouncing. I got worried."

A huge white cat with a black hat and black boots shoved at the man-who-wasn't-Terry's legs, meowing loudly. "Squire!" Kelly cooed. "Come here, fat-cat."

"Do you have a name, little brother?" Jennifer managed to make her voice sound a hell of a lot sexier than it did when she was hollering the length of the office.

"Paul. Paul Bradley. Brother number four, and Feeder-of-Cats. And apparently the last to know anything."

"Jennifer." She held out her hand. Paul raised it to his lips in a familiar gesture that made Kelly feel a little queasy.

"Have you heard from Terry at all? Please tell me

I should be angry, not worried. Maybe he meets women all the time and promises to write and never gets around to it. Tell me Dallas and Toronto were here yesterday. I'd rather feel foolish than worried."

Paul led them into the house, Jennifer's hand still in his. "If you're worried enough to come looking for him after one flight to Paris, I ought to have heard of you. I'm betting I would have if he'd bothered to come home. As far as I know Terry hasn't dated since Cleveland. I was always teasing him -- said he had a girlfriend in every town, which was why he dated the town, not the girl. He never bothered to argue with me. Just gave me that big-brother look."

The cat jumped onto the counter as Paul opened a can of food. "Anyway, Terry was supposed to be gone two months this time. That means he should have been home over a week ago. He hasn't called. Hasn't e-mailed. Nothing. That's just not like Terry. He's the responsible, reliable older brother type. The one who always made us younger brothers look bad, you know?"

Kelly laughed at that, grabbing Squire back from the can opener. "I know exactly what you mean. I have an irritatingly perfect big sister. Adorable husband. Three kids. They all eat dinner at Mom's every Sunday."

Paul nodded. "That was Terry until Cleveland left. Now everything's upside down. There was a termination notice for the power bill hanging on the door last Monday. Bunch of overdraft notices from the bank in the mail. Certified letter from his mortgage company yesterday. Couple of nasty letters from the IRS. So I called Toronto. He wasn't at the hotel where he usually stays. The client he works for up there said he tried to hire Terry back again -- they're expanding --

but he hasn't gotten any response to his e-mail either. I'm getting a little freaked."

"I know about the IRS." Kelly hugged the cat tight against her chest where he squirmed, clearly more interested in the food than being held. "Cleveland emptied the checking account when she left. The IRS check bounced. That's why he took the assignment in Paris."

"Assignment? What assignment?"

Kelly chewed on her lip. "Terry found an ad on a website. A way he could make a lot of money fast."

Paul sat down hard on a barstool. "Damn. He hooked up with that escort service, didn't he? God damn it, it was just a joke! A stupid joke! We even clowned around about trying it out together. A great way to get some action. I wasn't serious. I never thought he'd actually try anything like that!" Paul pitched his empty beer bottle into the recycle bin forcefully enough to disturb the cat, who shrieked in protest at the noise. "Why the hell didn't he just tell me he needed money? I would have helped. My brothers would have helped."

"Oh, right." Jennifer snorted loudly. "That's what I'd do if I were in trouble. Call my baby sisters. Yeah."

Kelly laid a hand on Paul's shoulder. His eyes told her he was already afraid of what she was going to say. "Paul, Jennifer and I work for C.H.A.S.E -- *The Coalition for Humanitarian Aid for the Subjugated and Exploited*. We're working on a case that has me more than a little freaked. I think I know where Terry is, and I'm afraid he's in a lot of trouble."

Suspicion rode up the length of Paul's long, straight nose until it wrinkled his brows again. "I never heard of *C.H.A.S.E.* and I'm not in the habit of making charitable donations to anyone just because they know my brother's cat's name."

Kelly smiled despite herself. "You can check *C.H.A.S.E.* out at CHASE.org, but we don't want anything from you. Nothing you can give me, anyway. I wanted to find Terry and tell him what a jerk he is because he didn't keep in contact. But if you don't know where Terry is, I'm betting no one else does either. I think I better go find him."

9:00 AM, Tuesday, 4 April, 2006
C.H.A.S.E. Headquarters, New York, NY

"I need the organization's backing on this, David. I think Terry's being held against his will. If I'm wrong -- if he's not there, or if he *is* there and he wants to stay -- that's his choice. But if I'm right, we could bring down a well-established white slavery ring. I can't do it alone. I need your help."

"Kelly, you're not a field agent. Even if you were, you're too close to this case to be objective. The board would never agree to send you in."

"I have to do this, David. Who else have you got?"

"Almost anyone else would have more experience."

"Name one agent who has the experience to infiltrate a place like Lady Elizabeth's *l'Ecole de Dominatrix*. It'll take anyone else a month just to learn the lingo. I can do this. You know the board will agree if you give me your backing."

David's eyes turned hard. "I'll go in."

Kelly laughed at that. "You're gorgeous, David. But it's a Femme Domme school. I just can't picture you in a black leather corset and thigh-high stockings. If you're into that, I just don't want to know."

"I can go in as a sub."

"Are you ready to let any woman who wants touch you any *way* she wants? With her hand or a whip or a flogger? Are you ready to lick her feet if she tells you to? Are you ready to let her fuck you with a strapon? Because that's what we're talking about. Total domination. Some of these guys are so far under they don't want to think for themselves anymore."

David's face paled, but he squared his shoulders resolutely. "This is too dangerous. You don't have the training. You don't --"

"I know what I'm doing." Kelly took a deep breath before she played her final card, pulling the tie and letting her cream silk wrap dress puddle around her feet.

"Kelly!" Jennifer shrieked as she slammed the office door shut. "What the hell are you -- oh my God." She moved forward, almost hypnotized, to get a better look at the black leather corset Kelly wore beneath her dress. "That's real leather, isn't it? Not the cheap stuff you see in the costume catalogs. You never told me you were into that."

"Jennifer, you're a good friend, but domination isn't exactly a topic for everyday discussion over the lunch counter. I never really figured it was anyone's business. We bust up real slave rings, not arrangements between consenting adults. But if these complaints are real, Lady Elizabeth is offering more than just consensual sex. I suspect the escort service was in on this. They sent her the vulnerable ones -- men with no families who would miss them. Terry wouldn't have listed family. He didn't want anyone to know what he was doing. In some cases the men may not have even been kidnapped. A lot of subs would jump at a chance to serve in a place like Lady Elizabeth's."

She crossed the room to splay her hands on David's desk, her breasts close to tumbling out of the top of her corset. "It's not the real subs I'm worried about. The invitation I received says she has 'wild' ones. Lady Elizabeth has issued a challenge. The Domme who can tame one of her wild ones can purchase him and take him home. Twenty-five thousand, cash. That doesn't sound consensual to me."

David was still staring at her, his expression more worried than shocked. "How did you get an invitation to *l'Ecole de Dominatrix?*"

"I told you, I'm into this lifestyle. I'm no top Domme running my own stable, but I know enough. I'm just the kind of client Lady Elizabeth looks for. Or we'll make her think I am. I can do this. I can take her challenge and win. I'm going in. I've got to get Terry out. But I'm not sure I can do it alone. I'd really like some backup."

"Put your dress back on. If Candy sees you in that outfit she'll kill us both. Or worse yet, she'll want one of her own." David glanced down at the paperwork on his desk. "We've been trying to plant operatives in *l'Ecole de Dominatrix* for some time, but apparently it moves. The only way to locate the 'school' is with an invitation. You've taken care of that part. But I won't send you in alone. I want you to recommend two other agents to Lady Elizabeth. If we're going to do this, we'll do it right."

"I don't get to wear my little outfit to the board meeting this afternoon?" Kelly laughed as she slithered back into her dress.

"I don't think that will be necessary."

"I dare you," Jennifer challenged. Her voice dropped as she headed for the door. "I wonder if that would work on all the Bradley men…"

2:00 PM, Sunday, 23 April, 2006
Paris, France

"This way, please, *Maîtresse*."

Maîtresse. The smiling uniformed driver gave no other sign that he was anything but what he appeared to be. She could almost believe he was part of the vanilla world she was about to leave behind. Kelly inclined her head slightly, acknowledging his deference as he held the door for her.

Just a little farther. One ride in a limousine was all that separated her from the man she couldn't get out of her mind.

She would find him and win him and take him home with her.

Assuming he wanted to go home with her.

Assuming he wanted to leave.

Assuming he was there at all.

"May I serve you some refreshment, *Maîtresse*?"

"Water, please."

"*Bien sûr.*" An ice-cold bottle of Evian appeared in front of her, bestowed with a flourish. "Will there be anything else, *Maîtresse*?"

"Just get me there," she snapped.

"*Certainement.* As you wish, *Maîtresse*."

Her eyes wanted to fall shut, her brain wanted to shut down as well, but she needed to keep track of the route, needed to know that if all else failed, if she had to get herself out…

Who was she kidding? She'd never find her way through the French countryside alone. If her cover failed, she'd be at the mercy of the same people who had Terry.

If they had Terry.

Where was he now? Was he frightened? Resigned? Happy? For a natural sub, no other place could offer what Lady Elizabeth offered -- total immersion. There were men who wanted to know they had no way out. Men who wanted to feel compelled, trapped by their own desires. A man might find exactly what he wanted, what he needed, in a place like that.

Had Terry found what he wanted in their sex play? Or had it all been just an act? Had she introduced him to a way of life that would claim him? Or had he simply allowed her to play out her fantasies?

How far would a man like Terry go to maintain the image of himself he wanted his family to see?

Perhaps only in secret places like this could he actually allow himself to let go.

She prayed he was one of the wild ones, untamed, fighting his captors, waiting for the woman who could conquer him, claim him, make him her own.

She could be that woman. For him. If that was what he wanted. But if it was only a game he'd gotten caught up in, if he was simply an accidental victim, could she let him go?

Was she that strong?

What if he wasn't even there? What if the whole slavery ring was yet a deeper immersion into the lifestyle, and the men involved were there by choice?

No. This couldn't be a hoax. Once, perhaps. Someone might have found her name on a guest book somewhere and sent her a piece of spam e-mail. Once. Or even twice. But not three times in one month. Not three times with the same message. She'd held one piece of information back when she brought her arguments before the board. The e-mails had all been addressed directly to her, to her special e-mail address. She had to believe Terry was reaching out through Lady Elizabeth's clients to the only person who might understand where he was and what kind of trouble he was in.

If she was wrong, if this was all some conspiracy theory she'd made up to explain away the fact that he hadn't wanted to see her again, she wouldn't let it break her.

If she was wrong, she'd find a way to convince herself that some other man really could take his place. After all, it was just sex.

Right. She could walk away any time.

Which was why she'd followed him halfway around the world.

Again.

* * *

"We are arrived, *Maîtresse*."

Kelly woke up with a start. So much for memorizing the route. Where was she, anyway? The beautiful blue of the Mediterranean beckoned to her from a few feet in front of the car. A boat dock? They were at a marina?

"The *navette* she will be here *dans un moment* to carry you to the yacht, *Maîtresse*."

A shuttle? Lady Elizabeth's *l'Ecole de Dominatrix* was a yacht? The driver said this as if she was to know, to expect, such accommodations. Very well. She would not let him know he was wrong. If, as she'd expressed in her letter of inquiry, she'd been briefed by other members of the club, she *should* know what to expect.

Made sense, really. A yacht could remain in international waters, not subject to any governmental interference. Would make prosecuting a hell of a lot more work.

The shuttle was easy to spot. The driver carried her bags to the *Lady Elizabeth*. Kelly almost laughed. Lady Elizabeth wasn't a woman. It was a ship. Or maybe it was both…

The sight of the small crowd gathering on the shuttle didn't make her laugh, however. These women were serious. Even in their street clothes, they looked like what they were. Powerful women who never bothered to ask for anything.

They'd see through her in a minute. They'd know she was only a novice.

But she wasn't, really. Not anymore. All that had changed when she'd met Terry. She'd come into her own with him -- graduated from observer to participant. Whether his submission was real or just a part of his job, she'd owned him, at least for the moment. That had changed her. She'd never be an innocent again.

Neither would he.

Kelly straightened her shoulders and took her place among the elite. She was *la Maîtresse*, after all. It wasn't just a role she was playing. She was *the Mistress*.

2:00 PM, Sunday, 23 April, 2006
Lady Elizabeth's *l'Ecole de Dominatrix*

She's not coming, idiot. Not today. Not any day.

Only a fucking moron would pin all his hopes on a woman he'd met once in an airport. Even if one of the Mistresses he'd confided in had gotten Kelly an invitation to Lady Elizabeth's "School," how would she know it was from him? She couldn't possibly know what a mess he'd gotten himself into.

He wasn't her problem. She was just a client who'd paid him to do a job. She wasn't going to show up here like some avenging angel. Time to face reality -- learn to live with the hand he'd been dealt. He'd gotten himself into this. Should have known better. No woman was ever going to pay a man six thousand Euros for sex. If he was going to escape, he had to find a way to do it on his own.

There was something tempting about this place. Some strange allure that made him want to forget who he had been. If Kelly didn't want him, what reason did he have to escape? What did he have to go back to? He shouldn't fight. It would be so much easier to just give up.

Someone would feed the cat…

* * *

"On your feet, slave."

A heavy hand jerked his chain. How long had it been? He'd lost track. His latest Mistress had given up on him after the first day.

It must be time to let the new Mistresses get a look at the goods. *Here we go again.* His legs, stiff from the confinement of the hold, nearly refused to cooperate. It didn't matter. The hands on the chain forced him along. He could go willingly, or they would drag him. No sense in fighting the inevitable.

On deck, the slaves received the usual treatment. Cold seawater pumped over them in a hard spray from a fire hose while they tried to scrub away the filth from the hold. A brief pass through freshwater at the deck-side shower. Coarse toweling and a brief inspection before they donned the only clothing they were allotted -- leather collars and cuffs, and for some, like him, the hobbles.

He was one of the "wild ones." The troublemakers.

They were right not to trust him. At the sight of the sun, his determination returned. He wouldn't give in. Not this time. Not ever. He wouldn't give up. He'd lived through worse things than this in the Air Force. He knew how to withstand almost any kind of torture. He wouldn't give up hope... There was only one woman he would submit to. Ever. He refused to give up on her.

The slaves were herded up the stairs to line the walls of the salon, standing ready, heads bowed, eyes down, waiting, naked, on display like pieces of meat. After this, nothing would ever embarrass him again. Nothing as superficial as clothing.

This much he would cooperate with. This much. The new Mistresses were coming. *She* might be among them.

If one of the other Mistresses had understood what he wanted. If she'd received the invitation. If she'd been able to come up with that kind of money.

If, if, if.
Idiot. It's the hope that will kill you.

Eight new Mistresses strolled in to inspect the merchandise. As always, he was torn. To be picked meant freedom from the hell of isolation in the hold. Clean sheets. Fresh water. Decent food, too, if his mistress chose to allow him to eat.

To be picked meant punishment when he did not cooperate. Eventually, inevitably, punishment meant being returned to isolation.

"These are the wild ones. We keep them shackled for your protection. The blond here has the biggest cock. Show yourself off, big boy."

Beside him, he felt Denis stiffen in defiance.

The parade stopped as Lady Elizabeth moved to stand at his shoulder. A shiver of fear coursed through him as she laid her hand on his cock. So far she hadn't cared enough to put her full attention into breaking him. If Lady Elizabeth made him her personal pet project, things would get much, much worse.

"You'll notice our pretty dark-haired boy here comes with leg shackles as well as wrist-cuffs. He can be *very* dangerous." She made dangerous sound sexy. Shit. The woman should be a used car salesman.

Tick. Tick. Tick.

The women circled, their heels tapping the floor like the slow ticking of doom marching home. Legs moved in and out of his field of vision. Smooth, curvy, female legs. Legs in spike heels. Tanned legs in sandals. Darker legs in low-heeled black pumps.

Oh, God. His mistress had worn shoes like that.

The black pumps stopped, turned three-quarter profile to him. He felt a soft breath of air caress his skin as she moved. A single sharp red talon on a dark-skinned finger ran down his breastbone and continued on down, nearly slicing his flesh. His cock went hard, jumping to full attention beneath the woman's touch. His Mistress had done that. Just one nail, up the underside of his cock.

She'd smelled like that, too. Fresh, clean, soft -- like sex.

He was deluding himself. Seeing what he wanted to see.

Damn. Get a hold of yourself. He was starting to see her in every woman who came here. *Fool. It's the hope that'll kill you*, he reminded himself once again.

It didn't matter. If he was wrong, what was there to live for?

Dark waves of silken hair cascaded across his chest as she leaned forward to run the tip of her tongue over his nipple. He tried to jerk back, but she held him a moment too long with the suction of her lips. "*Ummm.* You taste good."

Fuck. Christ Almighty. Fuck. Oh, fuck. God, please let this be real. Only one woman made a sound like that, a sound that drove him insane with lust just hearing the hum of her voice. He wanted to sob with relief. He wanted --

"Look at me, slave." Sweet, soft, sexy steel in her voice.

He kept his eyes focused on her feet, afraid to look up.

The woman knotted her hand in his hair, jerking his head up. "Look at me!"

The jolt of recognition shot straight to his balls, even though he knew, he knew, he knew…

"I'm your last hope, slave."

"Yes, Mistress." His voice sounded dry, hoarse… powerless.

"You have a choice. One choice. You will obey me in all things. Anything, everything, when I want it, because I want it. Or you can go back to that hole they brought you out of." She jerked on his hair again, forcing his head to her level, assaulting him with her lips, her tongue, her scent, her taste. "I'm offering you your freedom, slave. Freedom to be who you were meant to be. My slave. I don't think you're going to get a better offer."

Freedom. She was speaking in some kind of code.

She wanted him to know she'd come for him.

But he didn't want freedom. He wanted her. He wanted everything she offered.

Terry did the only thing he could think to do. He dropped slowly to his knees and kissed her black pumps.

A whisper of surprised disbelief raced through the room. *No. Not that one. He wouldn't submit. Why? Why now? Who is she?*

"This one is mine. Remove his shackles."

"Mistress --"

"Now!"

"But --"

The sharp crack of a leather popper landing its blow across unprotected skin. Trembling fingers fumbling with the straps around his ankles. More fingers fumbling with the straps on his wrists. "Remove the collar, as well. I have my own."

A murmur of disapproval. A sharp hiss threatening those who did not obey. Hands on his throat, fingertips brushing, palms caressing, soft, silk lined leather brushing against him. Fingers under his chin, raising his head until their gazes locked. "This collar identifies you as mine. You will not remove it. Do you understand me?"

Identifies... A tracking device? How -- it didn't matter. It was her collar. Nothing else mattered. He bent his head to formally kiss the collar before she buckled it in place. "Yes, Mistress."

"Pick up my bags and show me to my

stateroom."

He scrambled shakily to his feet, trying his best to remember the things he'd been taught. Always on her right. One pace behind. Quiet. Always quiet. Eyes on her at all times, reading her body, anticipating her desires.

Please, God. If there is a God. Don't let this be just for a week. Don't let me be reading her wrong. She can't be here by chance.

Suitcase on the stand. Turn down the bed. Everything on hangers, in drawers, secured, neatly put away.

"Terry."

Draw water for Mistress's bath.

Hands on his skin, touching his shoulders. "Terry."

Hot, but not too hot.

"Terry, look at me."

Please, God. I know it's been a long time. How did you pray to a God you no longer quite believed in? *I know I haven't talked to you much, probably since I was around twelve…*

"Terry, stop. Look at me." The firm tone of command in her voice would not be ignored.

He shut off the water, slowly, slowly turning to face her.

Fingers in his hair, tilting his face, warm lips against his, soft lips, kissing his eyelids. The tears came now, when they were alone.

No. A man doesn't cry…

"You haven't done anything wrong, Terry. Everything's OK now. I'm going to take you home."

"Mistress -- others -- have touched me."

Arms around him, holding, comforting. "You weren't wearing my collar then. No one will touch you now but me."

He whimpered in shame. "You shouldn't touch me, Mistress. I'm not clean."

"Help me undress. We'll bathe together."

Yes. He could do that. He could hold himself together long enough to take care of her. She was his Mistress.

Silk. He loved the feel of silk against her skin. "You should always wear silk. It's soft, like you, and strong, like you."

"Get in the tub with me, Terry."

How long had it been... The hot water stung the welts on his back, but he didn't care. He slid his head beneath the water, reluctant to surface again. Only her hands on him reminded him to come up for air. Her lips brushed his. Sweet, sweet lips. His arms tightened around her, pulling her close, letting her feel his desire, a raw wound that bled for her. "Please..." Tears streamed down his face. He didn't care. Not anymore. "I need you, Mistress. I need you."

"Who am I?"

"You are my Mistress."

"Say my name."

He hesitated, afraid to break the spell.

"Say my name."

"Wonderdomme69@aol.com."

She sucked in her breath. "I knew somehow you'd convinced those other Mistresses to get me an invitation." She buried her face against his chest, her tears mixing with the hot water, hot and hotter. "I'm sorry. I'm sorry I didn't come sooner. I could have spared you so much pain."

"No, Mistress. I had no right... It was only one night."

Her fingertips healed wherever they touched. "It was a lifetime..."

He couldn't meet her eyes. "I was afraid it was just sex."

She plucked a condom wrapped in bright red and shaped to look like a rosebud from its stem in the vase next to the tub. He trembled as she unrolled the protective barrier down the length of his burning cock. "It was never just sex. It's not *just* sex now. But I want to feel you inside me. I need to know you're mine."

He lifted her, her legs wrapping around his waist as he settled within her, two lost souls coming together in the tumult of the ocean. "I am yours, Mistress. Yours alone. No one else can ever touch me the way you do. You own my soul."

"I've been waiting for you to say that all my life." She kissed him again, not just his lips but his cheeks and his nose and his eyelids, easing away the pain with every swipe of her lips. "I love you, Terry *Bradley*. And I love your crazy cat and your house and your family."

She knew his name. She knew... Horror crept back in. "My brothers? My parents? They know?"

"They know you took an assignment in a dangerous place and you've been kidnapped. They're pretty worried. They're more than a little mad at you, too, for not coming to them for help."

"I couldn't ask for help. I didn't want them to know what a failure I was. I'm the *responsible* one. I'm the oldest. I'm supposed to set an example."

She nipped at his ear, a hint of reprimand in her tone. "And they're your family. It's OK to need help sometimes. That's what families are for."

"Do they know I'm going to prison?"

"Do you think I'd let anyone take you away from me again?"

He didn't care about the reproof in her tone. A surge of hope shot through him, so strong that he felt his cock tremble within her. "I don't want to know how. Not now. God, I need you."

Her arms tightened around him, her fingers combing through his hair, drifting down over his back, reading the marks there like Braille. She clenched hard around his cock, pulling him even deeper within her. He groaned into her hair, afraid to move, afraid to start what would only eventually lead to an end. "I don't want it to be over."

"Trust me. It'll never be over. I'll always want you as much as I do tonight."

"Then fuck me," he whispered against her neck. "I need you, Mistress. My Mistress. Kelly."

"*Ummm.* I love it when you talk dirty to me, Boy Scout."

Below the surface of the water, they rocked together, small movements at first, then harder, lust, fear, worry, doubt combining until the water washed everything away, and there was nothing left but the hunger. She screamed out his name as the water slopped over the sides of the tub. He held on as long as he could, his body shaking with the effort, as she tightened around him again and again. Then there was nothing left, no more control, and he shot into her like fireworks on the 4th of July.

She collapsed against him, small and soft and vulnerable now. She was almost asleep in his arms when he carried her back to the large four-poster bed. Tomorrow there would be time for other things. Tonight he held her in his arms while he fell asleep at her side, a prayer of thanks on his lips.

9:00 AM, Monday, 24 April, 2006
Lady Elizabeth's l'Ecole de Dominatrix

The first thing she noticed when she woke up was the meat hook hanging from the ceiling. Funny. She hadn't seen it last night. But then she hadn't been looking up. She'd been concentrating on Terry. Broken, wounded Terry.

Terry who refused to look her in the eyes.

The space beside her was empty now. Had she heard the door click? Was that what had awakened her? Kelly sat up in the bed, taking stock of the room. Her clothes were all put away. She could tell because her empty suitcase stood next to the armoire, and her comb and brush sat on the dresser.

She'd slept for almost ten hours. In the early morning light the room looked barren without him. Where was he? Had he slept at all? Why had he left her? Had he gotten bored and restless, watching her sleep, with nothing left to do?

The latch clicked again. She saw his backside first, long and darkly tanned from the sun, absolutely naked except for her collar. Her fingers itched to trace the curves of his ass. Her mouth watered at the thought of the taste of his skin. Her whole body hungered for him.

He stood straighter this morning, his shoulders back, his head raised a degree or two. He turned, a smile lighting his face as he realized she was awake. He'd brought her coffee. A steaming mug of cappuccino. She didn't have to ask to know he'd ordered two extra shots of espresso.

His cock, which seemed to exist in a perpetual state of arousal, bounced against his belly when she smiled up at him. So easy to please him. Just a smile or a look.

As he turned to place the mug into the hollowed space on the nightstand, details began to fill in the holes from the missing weeks. Darker spots beneath the lovely brown of his tan. Fading welts across his ass. A bruise over his hipbone.

Mistress -- others -- have touched me... You shouldn't touch me, Mistress. I'm not clean.

What was he trying to tell her? Damn. She'd heard, but she hadn't been listening. Hadn't thought past the awful hollow, lonely place he filled within her.

Had he been raped?

She'd had to supply a current physical, including blood work, to get in here, but that didn't mean everyone was perfectly safe, or emotionally healthy. She needed to get him out of here, get him home, have him talk to a counselor. It wasn't fair to take advantage of him now.

But that was what she wanted to do. She wanted to hold him and fuck him until nothing else mattered.

No. He was more than just a sex toy.

He was *her* sex toy. And she was his Mistress. There were other ways to work through the hurt that had been done to him.

Kelly turned back the covers and crooked her finger. Terry slid in beside her, his arms already around her, his head curled against her chest. He practically purred as she feathered her fingers through his dark curls. She slid a finger under his chin. "Look at me. We need to talk."

"Yes, Mistress." She might as well have struck him. He sat back, looking down at her, his eyes half-veiled by those thick, curling lashes. All the light and happiness drained from him.

"You understand how important it is to me that you trust me."

"Yes, Mistress."

"Then why do you look as if I'm punishing you when I ask you to talk to me?"

His eyes darted away, then back again, conflicting emotions showing in his body language.

"When I ask you a question, you will answer me."

"Yes, Mistress." Still, he hesitated. "I do trust you, Mistress. I do not trust *me*. I'm not a very good slave. I'm disobedient and willful and I don't have the proper attitude for a slave."

"Did the ones who beat you tell you that?"

He flinched, as if she'd struck him herself. "Yes, Mistress."

"Did you like what they did to you?"

"Mistress?"

She traced a finger over the welts on his ass. "You've been to school here, Terry. What have you learned about yourself? Do you enjoy pain? If I whipped you would you get hard for me, just thinking about the next stroke of my flogger? Or would you be frightened and angry? What do you like? What turns you on?"

His eyes slid closed. "You turn me on, Mistress. Everything about you turns me on."

"You didn't answer my question." She pinched him, hard.

"Ouch!" Those beautiful blue eyes flew open, radiating baffled resentment.

"How did that feel?"

"That hurt!"

"What does that tell you?"

"How have I disobeyed you, Mistress?"

Kelly ran her fingers along the underside of his jaw. "You haven't. You haven't done anything wrong. Nothing. Do you understand me?"

A puzzled frown settled between his eyes. "You said that last night."

"But you still don't believe me, do you? Yet you're angry because I hurt you for no reason. The people on this ship had no reason to hurt you either, and no right. You didn't ask for their pain. When I became your Mistress, you had a choice. What we did was consensual. What happened to you here was not consensual. You fought back. That does not make you a willful and disobedient slave. That makes you my hero."

He just stared at her. "I fought, but I lost."

"Then why were you beaten?"

"I... I wouldn't -- I couldn't -- do what they wanted."

"What did they want you to do?"

"Submit."

"If you had done that, you wouldn't have been wearing ankle cuffs when I got here. So who won?"

A slow smile spread across his face. "You did, Mistress."

She laughed as she ruffled his hair, pulling gently, coaxing him back to her side. "Who won, Terry?" She ran her hand over the curve of his hip, letting her fingers rest there, close enough to feel the heat of his cock dancing inches from her fingers.

He laid his head against her chest again. "It's easy to submit to you, Kelly. I'd do anything to please you. If -- if I hadn't met you first... You gave me the strength to hold on. I couldn't let anyone else -- I couldn't submit to anyone else. I'm yours."

"That works both ways. I'm yours, too. I was

scared coming here. I was afraid you wouldn't be here, that I'd just invented some conspiracy theory to explain why you never got in touch with me. I wanted you to be here, waiting for me. I don't want any other sub. I want *you*." She felt his cock surge against her and smiled.

"Kelly, if we -- *when* we get out of here, I want to -- there's a contract a slave signs for his Mistress. I'd like to do that for you."

"I'd like that." She kissed the tip of his nose. "I'd like something more, too. I think we should share more than a contract. I won't share you with anyone ever again. I want you to live with me."

"Think what you're saying. I'm broke. Worse than broke. I'm wiped out. Even if you could somehow make the IRS go away, they're only the first in line after me. I don't have a career anymore. I --"

"Shhh." She placed a finger over his mouth. "You've got to learn to trust me."

"I do trust you, but you --"

"I know about the IRS. Do you think I don't know about the rest?"

He shuddered as she ran her nails down his skin. "I trust you, Mistress."

"Completely?"

"Completely, Mistress."

"You unpacked my suitcases. You know I brought other toys with me."

A delicious shiver ran across the surface of his skin, his cock surging against her again. "Yes, Mistress."

"Which of my toys frightens you the most, slave?"

"The blindfold, Mistress." No hesitation there.

"Hmm. Curious. My other toys don't frighten

you?"

"All of them frighten me, Mistress. But the blindfold is the worst."

"Fetch it for me. And the other toys, too."

He whimpered. "All of them, Mistress?"

"All of them. We're going to have a lesson in trust."

* * *

Trust me.

Trust. He *did* trust her. Hadn't he proven that? He'd let her do things to him no one else ever had. Wasn't that enough? Why did she need to blindfold him? He fought the blindfold resentfully, trying not to panic as she tightened the chain that held him suspended from the three foot spreader bar separating his cuffed wrists.

That she hadn't had packed in her carry-on luggage, though God knows there'd been plenty of other toys in there. *l'Ecole* provided the bigger items. Restraints. Tie downs and spreaders. Swings and harnesses. All meant to work with the remote control hook anchored to the central beam in the ceiling.

The damn thing would hold his weight, and more. He'd seen its uses demonstrated. Knew without a doubt there was no damn way he was getting loose. Blindfolded, helpless, his weight supported more by his grip on the bar than by his toes where they brushed the floor, he stood, waiting. He felt more than heard her circling, her feet nearly soundless in the thick pile carpet.

Take it off! Take off the blindfold!

"You can fight if you want. It doesn't matter."

He took a deep breath, trying to quiet the pounding of his heart, letting the sound of her voice soothe him. He swallowed his fear. He'd submit to anything for her. He could handle the blindfold. He could handle pain. He could handle whatever she wanted -- because she wanted it. Because he had to. Because if he didn't she'd know he had lied.

There was nothing in her collection of toys that frightened him the way the thought of her leaving him did. She was still here. That was all that really mattered. If he fought her, she might lose interest in him as the others had. He couldn't take that chance.

"Who's in control?"

She needed to ask? He was suspended from a hook in the ceiling, bound and helpless. Worse yet, she'd made him bring her the wrist and ankle cuffs, presenting them ceremonially, then slide the cock harness on himself, pulling the soft silicone cock ring down, hard against the base of his dick. He'd helped her adjust the bar that separated his ankles, making sure he'd be ready and open for her, no matter what she wanted.

And he knew what she wanted. The last thing he'd seen was a vision burned into his brain -- he'd watched as she slid her new double-ended dildo deep into her pussy, then fasted its harness so the end meant for him jutted proudly from her cunt, ready and waiting.

Then she'd tied the silk blindfold over his eyes.

Where was she? Had she changed her mind? Decided to ignore him while she satisfied herself with that long, thickly knobbed cock?

He hated this -- not knowing when she would move or where she would come from. He turned, as far as he could without falling, twisting at the waist, trying to get any clue as to her position.

"Who's in control?"

She was behind and to his left. Nowhere near the

bed. His body trembled violently. He was also hard enough to come the moment she touched him.

Please. Take the blindfold off. Let me see what you're doing. "You are, my Mistress. You are in control."

"You want me to control you, don't you? You need me."

Did he have to say it?

She was close now. He could smell her. Where was she?

He nearly jumped away when she sucked hard at his nipple, her only point of contact. He pushed himself at her, needing her touch, nearly screaming when she shoved him away. "Say it!"

He'd say anything if she'd touch him. "I want you in control, Mistress!"

"You like the blindfold, don't you? Now you're not responsible for anything. You can't fight me."

Her cock scraped along his inner thigh, making him jump again, his own cock quivering violently, cum leaking out, dripping to run down over his balls. "Yes!"

"Answer me properly, slave."

"Yes, Mistress. Thank you for blindfolding me."

She chuckled softly. "Tell me what you want next. Tell me what you need."

"Anything," he begged. "Anything, Mistress. Just touch me."

The hard crack of the popper bit against the backs of his knees. He cried out in pain as he lost his balance, dangling helplessly from his wrists.

And his cock jumped as if he'd been hit with a cattle prod.

"That was a touch. Did you like that?"

"No!" he insisted.

Another crack, hard across his ass. "Don't lie to

me. I don't like it when you lie to me."

"No," he moaned. He *couldn't* like that. He *wouldn't*. His cock stabbed at the air helplessly.

"Then I'll stop."

"No!" he screamed. "Mistress Kelly, please. Fuck me. Please. I need you."

She ran her hands over his chest, up and down his arms, stroking, calming, reminding him that there were other ways she could please him.

Terry took a deep breath, pulling himself back together. "I'm sorry I lied to you, Mistress."

"What happens to slaves who lie?"

"I must be punished, Mistress." He whimpered in anticipation, knowing that whatever punishment she chose, it would only make his cock swell harder.

One crack of the flogger over his ass. Swallowing all that was left of his pride, he replied as he'd been trained. "Thank you, Mistress. Please whip me again."

The flogger came down harder this time, its lashes warming his ass to a dull glow. Then again, and again. "Thank you. Please whip me harder."

Exquisite pain shot straight to his balls, dragging a long, low moan from his throat. *Oh God. Oh God. Oh God. Please stop. Please don't stop…*

No. No! He cried out, trembling with need, as the room went silent again. Where was she? Where had she gone? "Please, Mistress…"

He shuddered with fear and delight as warm, moist heat wrapped over his nipple. She kissed, then sucked, running the tip of her tongue around the hard ridges and the tiny dent in the middle. He tried to twist away, knowing what was coming, but it was no use. His traitorous nipples stabbed out for her. He screamed as she pulled away and the nipple clamps -- real ones this time -- bit into his tender flesh.

The urge to climax surged in his balls, but he couldn't. Her ring trapped him there, while the blood pounded in his cock like a tidal wave about to break. Could he just keep getting harder? Was there no limit to the punishment -- and stimulation -- his body could sustain?

He heard the low mechanical whir of the ceiling hook's motor as she lowered him back toward the floor. His legs didn't want to support his weight. "On your knees!" she ordered.

Oh, God. He wasn't ready. He couldn't take that, not now, not --

Her thigh between his legs forced his knees even further apart, one hard shove knocking him off balance. He had to catch himself, support himself with his shackled hands or be knocked face down in the carpet.

The jerk of his chest muscles as he sprawled there trying to catch his balance sent the nipple clamps digging in all over again. He bit his lip to keep from screaming. Again. "Thank you, Mistress."

The lube warmed in her palms, like a balm to his bruised ass. He shook with desire as she rimmed the edge of his asshole with her greased finger, around and around, but not in. She didn't have to tell him to beg this time. He knew her too well. Knew what she wanted to hear. "Please fuck me, Mistress," he pleaded.

"Fuck you how?"

"Please fuck me with your big, hard dick, Mistress."

"No."

He felt more than heard her move.

"Suck my cock, slave."

Oh, God, no! But it was useless to object. Worse

than useless. She'd leave him, find another slave who was more obedient, who was worthy of her. "Yes, Mistress. Anything, I --" The long, stiff jelly shaft slid into his open mouth.

He'd never sucked cock, never had any desire to, but he'd seen it done, had his own sucked. Running his tongue around the base of the thick, flared head, he hummed, letting his tongue transmit the sound waves down its length. Taking the cock deep in his throat, he nuzzled her clit with his upper lip. He wanted to suck her, lick her, taste her deep inside, but he couldn't. Not with her cock in his throat. Up and down, in and out, he sucked, doing his best to give her what she wanted.

He could smell her sex, dripping wet for him. "Let me fuck you, Mistress," he begged as he stopped at the cock's head for air.

Her cock pulled away from his mouth, leaving him cold and desolate. But only for a moment. The flogger flashed over his ass and thighs again. At last she stopped that as well, resting the tip of her strap-on against his anus. He could feel it vibrating within her. "Straighten your knees," she commanded. "Lift your ass for me."

She was going to make him do it himself? Push that thing into his ass with legs that refused to even support him? He wouldn't. He *couldn't*.

He had to. She was waiting for him.

Slowly, an inch at a time, he forced his hips up and toward her, pushing the well lubricated dildo deep inside him until it filled him, pressing in all the way to the balls. "Thank you, Mistress," he managed as he stood, hands still flat on the carpet, folded neatly in half before her.

"This is what you wanted all along. Admit it."
"Yes, Mistress. I want you to fuck me."

"Why?"

Why? His mind was reeling, his body was screaming, and she wanted to know why? "Because..."

"Say it, Terry."

"Because I trust you. Because I need you to be in control. I know you'll make me like what you're doing."

Her fingers hovered at the tip of his dick, just brushing where he quivered against her. She bent, and he felt her warmth, her full breasts press against him -- right before she bit his ass, hard, making him jerk forward, finding himself impaled in a waiting condom as he pulled away from their joining. Her hands closed around him as he thrust back against her, and then she was in total control, setting the rhythm, her hips driving him forward, her hands pulling him back, her teeth and her lips inflicting devastating damage as he screamed out her name.

He felt her coming, thrusting harder and harder against him now, her breathing fast and ragged as she gasped for breath. He could feel his balls drawing up tight in his scrotum, her hands milking him, pumping him, demanding he come for her.

But he couldn't. Not with her ring holding him. No matter how desperately he needed to come, the ring would not allow his release.

He felt a sharp sting as she tore the ring loose. In one swift move she yanked the nipple clips off, the pain so intense he screamed as the blood flowed back into his nipples in hot waves.

The pain was like nothing he'd ever felt, dark and addictive, so far beyond pain that he reached for it, trying to hold it inside him, but her hands on his cock, fisting him again and again, brought him back, pushing him over the edge. They climaxed together, a cacophony of screaming, beautiful music, both of them sobbing at the intensity of their release.

Then her hands were on him, her fingers fumbling as she unfastened the restraints, slipping the blindfold off. Picking up her limp body, he cradled his precious cargo against his chest, carrying her to the deep softness of the bed. She trembled in his arms, still sobbing, as he kissed her, worshipping her with his hands and his mouth.

When their breathing grew quiet, he spoke in a whisper, his lips next to her ear. "Do you trust *me*, Mistress?"

She curled more tightly against him. "I -- of course."

"Tell me why you need to be in control."

Her breath hissed into her lungs. "I don't *have* to be in control."

"You *need* the control as much as I need you. Talk to me. Who hurt you, Kelly?"

"I -- no one. No one hurt me."

He waited, his silence speaking louder than any words could have.

"Men just don't stay in my life."

"Then they're fools."

"I -- I'm the kind of woman men want to have sex with. Not the kind they want to marry. But that's not such a bad thing. I like sex. I love sex. Sometimes women prefer uncomplicated relationships, too. I don't -- I've never needed a man in my life before. Not permanently. I didn't mind them leaving as much as how they left. Sneaking off in the middle of the night. Or me suddenly finding out they had a wife. Now I set the rules. I say who comes and who leaves. And when."

"I don't have a wife. Not anymore. And I won't

sneak off in the middle of the night. I won't leave you. You're all I've ever wanted. I need you, Kelly."

"I need you, too. This time I want more than just a night, or a week, or a year. I want you. I want… I want to keep you."

"Yes," he promised.

"Yes?"

"Your place. My house. It doesn't matter. I don't want to let you go. Wherever you are, that's where I want to be."

"Is it always going to take this much work to get you to agree with me?"

"Probably. I've been told I'm stubborn."

Kelly sighed. "I'm going to have to start working out again. Build up my stamina."

"You need a good massage, to relax your overworked muscles." He didn't wait for an answer. He let his hands skim over her shoulders, then down her arms, laying her out straight and even on the bed. He chose a blue condom this time from the arrangement beside the bed, taking his time, soothing her muscles with long, easy strokes before he slipped into her, resting easily inside her. There was no need to rush now. She was his. She owned him, body and soul. But he owned more of her heart than he'd ever hoped for. "I love you, Kelly," he whispered as he kneaded her shoulders.

She tightened around him, her body responding to the words as much as his touch. He would learn more, in time, about her past. For now, this was enough. "I love you, Mistress."

Her smile was worth everything that had brought them to this point. "I love you, Terry."

Lady Elizabeth tapped on her wine goblet with the edge of her olive fork. A clear chime rang through the length of the salon. Nine slaves moved forward in unison to fill their Mistresses' goblets. "Ladies, as we share our last meal together, on behalf of myself and the entire staff of *l'Ecole de Dominatrix*, I'd like to thank you for joining us. A toast to another successful mating of minds aboard the *Lady Elizabeth*."

The Mistresses clinked their glasses.

"Several of you chose from among our more challenging candidates. Congratulations to Mistress Diane, Mistress Stephanie, and Mistress Pearl for your fine work in breaking the untamable ones. You will all, of course, have the opportunity to purchase your slave, as we advertise in our brochures. But first we'd all like to hear from you as to how you tamed these wildlings."

"Mistress Stephanie?"

The tall, willowy black woman held out one elegant finger, dangling a leash attached to a short leather strap holding five metal rings that made even Kelly feel squeamish. "Five Gates of Hell. Ball spreader. Works every time."

A roar of unladylike laughter rumbled down the table.

"Mistress Diane?"

Diane grinned mischievously, the slight tilt of her head shifting her short cap of red-blonde hair away from her eyes. "Whips. Silk. And knives. I have quite a collection."

Sharp hisses of indrawn breath followed by

murmurs of approval.

"Last we come to Mistress Pearl." Lady Elizabeth swirled her wine delicately in her glass. "But that isn't your real name, is it, darling?"

Panic alarms went off. *Run. Flee. Escape.*

Right. They were on a yacht in the middle of the Mediterranean.

Lady Elizabeth nodded her head and her personal slave aimed a remote control at a curtain drawn across the far wall. The curtain whisked away, revealing a large screen projection TV. As the power flickered on, Terry appeared, blindfolded, hanging by his wrists from the spreader bar, while Kelly applied her flogger to his fine, firm ass. Her strap-on teased his anus as she bent in to rub against him.

Another crack, hard across his ass.

"Don't lie to me. I don't like it when you lie to me."

"No," he insisted.

"Then I'll stop."

"No!" he screamed. *"Kelly, please. Fuck me. Please. I need you."*

The slave hit rewind, and the scene played out again. *"Kelly, please. Fuck me. Kelly, please. Fuck me."*

Lady Elizabeth ran a sharpened nail down her personal slave's hip, carelessly stroking his balls as he turned to press against her fingers. "Fuck me, Kelly," she mocked, her voice a whining imitation of Terry's. Everyone jumped when she slammed her hand against the table. "Speak, slave! Who the hell is this woman and why do you call her Kelly?"

"I --"

"Speak, or your life will be forfeit!"

Kelly held up her hand, managing an impassive air. "He calls me Kelly because I commanded it to be so. What other reason is there?"

"You are a spy," Lady Elizabeth accused.

"I am exactly who I represented myself as," Kelly maintained. "My full name is Pearl K. Monroe. For the last fifteen years I have worked for Brasden-Marten, a legal firm representing actors and artists in entertainment law. I developed an interest in bondage after I worked with the models in a client's bondage and fetish wear catalogue. I've studied in New York and Paris, and now I have come here, at great personal expense, just so you can accuse *me* of being a spy? Is this the way you treat *les clients*? You *spy* on us, with hidden cameras in our *private* staterooms? Your establishment came highly recommended by several of your former clients. Perhaps I should question their motivations."

"You no longer work for Brasden-Marten," Lady Elizabeth pointed out.

"I didn't say I did," Kelly responded, managing to keep her voice calm. "I took an early retirement. I made a good income while I was at Brasden-Martin, and I invested well. I've made a nice portfolio for myself."

"Perhaps I have been hasty," Lady Elizabeth offered, though her eyes brooked no apology. Kelly wondered if she even consciously noted that her fingers still stroked her handsome young slave's balls, or that he was close to collapsing against her.

Lady Elizabeth snapped her fingers and the slave regained his composure, scrolling the curtain down to hide the projection monitor. Kelly watched in fascination as glistening drops of cum leaked from the tip of his cock. Lady Elizabeth handed him an elegant linen table napkin and shooed him away with a flick of her fingers. He retreated to the corner, moaning softly as he stroked himself to completion. Lady Elizabeth frowned, and he swallowed the cry that had broken from his lips. Immediately another handsome man, this one dark and possibly Greek, came to stand at her elbow.

"Explain to us, then, Mistress Pearl, why a slave who managed to endure and even defy eight of the most skilled Mistresses in the world should drop at your feet like an obedient puppy." Her slave bent to whisper in her ear, shooting a menacing glance at Terry. "Or why since you've been on board this same slave has assumed the demeanor of a well trained domestic of many years in service."

Terry cleared his throat softly. "Mistress? May I answer?"

Kelly looked him over carefully, knowing him well enough by now to see the tenseness hiding just beneath the surface.

Strong, hard, dangerous. That was what had attracted her to him in the first place. She'd seen him stripped, naked to the core, broken and sobbing at her feet, but he'd never once reached for their lifeline.

Do you trust me, Mistress?

Did she? If he said the wrong thing… "You may speak."

He knelt beside her, his beautiful golden brown skin a dark contrast to her formal white gown. "Forgive me, Mistress. I have lied to you."

A sharp hiss silenced the room. Kelly didn't look up.

"The invitation to Lady Elizabeth's did not find you accidentally. I was too much of a coward to admit that I was wrong. I asked other Dommes to let you know of this place. I thought without me you might be on the alert for a new slave."

That was a damn complicated way of working

alert into a sentence. Kelly quit focusing on his words and started watching his hands. His fingers were spread oddly across his knee, as if he were signaling to her. Three. If he was pointing, he meant Lady Elizabeth and the two entrances to the room at her back.

"I was at a crossroads, not knowing which way to turn. I decided to take middle ground, hoping you would find me, rather than me returning to you. It was a coward's way out. Forgive me."

Kelly gave him her best reproving frown, nodding her head just slightly.

He rose to face the patroness. "I ask your forgiveness as well, Lady Elizabeth. My deception was unintended. I could not submit to your Dommes. I already have a Mistress. If she'll have me back."

Lady Elizabeth pursed her lips angrily. "You ran away from your Mistress only to arrange for her to come here and buy you back from me?"

"Yes, Patroness."

"I would not have allowed you back into my service."

"Fortunately my Mistress knows my weakness and is kind and forgiving."

Lady Elizabeth shrugged, turning her attention to Kelly. "A convincing argument for branding. Unfortunately, I don't believe either of you. You're both spies. Seize them."

Kelly spun with a whirling kick as she leaped to her feet, the precious white gown splitting neatly down the side seam as the younger of Lady Elizabeth's personal slaves launched himself at her. With her peripheral vision she caught a glimpse of sweet, submissive Terry pinning Lady Elizabeth to the ground as she scratched and kicked and gouged with all the finesse of a street fighter. Two of the other slaves, Diane's newly tamed Shawn and Stephanie's Denis, had already taken out the subs who moved in on Terry's right from the doorways. Diane and Stephanie were covering the doorways now, small caliber handguns appearing from hidden recesses within their skimpy formal gowns.

"*Lady* Elizabeth, you are under arrest for trafficking in persons for profit," Diane announced. She snapped her fingers and Shawn came instantly to heel.

"Mistress!" a terrified voice screamed. "There are men on the docks, with guns..."

The pilot, the only clothed male Kelly had ever seen on board the ship, threw up his hands when he saw the muzzles of the two pistols pointed at his chest.

"By all means, go ahead and dock," Lady Elizabeth replied calmly from under Terry's knee. "The sooner this case is turned over to the authorities, the sooner I will be exonerated."

"Good," Stephanie offered with a smile. "Then we can talk about your financial ties with the I.R.A. -- I believe Scotland Yard wants you next."

7:00 PM, Tuesday, 4 July, 2006
New York, NY

They looked like the perfect couple. He walked at her side, his hand resting easily on the small of her back. He wore his Armani suit once again. His eyes met hers when she spoke. He laughed. He talked. He joked. He chose the restaurant and the wine. To the casual passerby, they appeared so… vanilla. A handsome man and his exotically beautiful woman celebrating Independence Day at a classy New York restaurant, enjoying the hours before the fireworks began.

Under the table, his foot slipped out of its shoe to trace its way up her leg. At the top of her thigh he found the edge of her stocking, held in place by an old-fashioned garter belt. The lace of her corset tickled his toe. His smile deepened. Laughter glittered in his eyes that had nothing to do with whatever comment she had just made.

His throat was dry. He sipped the wine, too excited to do more than pick at his food. The food must have been good. Everyone complimented the chef here.

"I have a present for you," he blurted, no longer able to contain himself.

"What? And you made me wait all evening? Give it here!"

He laughed as he withdrew the foil wrapped box from his coat pocket. "The evening has just begun. Perhaps you shouldn't open it here."

"You want me to open it now, I can tell. I know you too well. Will the *maître 'd* be scandalized?"

"Would I do that to you?"

"You certainly would." She ripped the foil paper

off anyway, as excited as another woman might have been had she been expecting a diamond tennis bracelet. She snapped the jewelry box open, withdrawing a small leather leash, and leaned across the table to place an extravagant kiss on his mouth.

Under the table her toes crept up his thigh to brush at his crotch. "I want to try it out tonight. After the fireworks."

He wanted to tell her they could make their own fireworks. But instead he smiled, saying the words he knew made her hotter than his gift ever could. "Yes, Mistress."

As they left, the waiter came to pick up his tip. Noticing the jeweler's box amid the littering left on the table, he thought to flag them down, then stopped to take a quick peek.

The box was empty except for a receipt.

His face blanched as he read the name of the store, then blanched again as he read the name of the item purchased. Under his formal black pants and vest and his starched white shirttails his cock twitched violently against its constraints.

Oh yes, he'd heard of *The Five Gates of Hell*.

He watched the perfect couple walk away, fear and longing in his heart. Somewhere… somewhere, there was a woman waiting for him, his leash in her hands.

Would she sit at his table and smile up at him? Or would she meet him in a coffee shop after work on a long winter night?

Would she walk up and say, "Pardon me, but do you like to be disciplined?"

Yes. Oh, yes, Mistress. I'm yours.

Welcome to the Fetish Club (*C.H.A.S.E.* 3)
Deep Cover - in a Human Trafficking Ring
Shelby Morgen

"I'm not sure this is such a good idea."

"Trust me, this'll be a blast."

"Last time you said that I ended up with worm guts between my teeth."

Ani's stressed. She really needs to forget her asshole boss, Richard (Richard Marten, owner of Brasden-Marten). She also needs to get laid. (The two dilemmas are *soooo* not related.)

Crystal's got a membership at *The Fetish Club*. Two girlfriends. One bottle of tequila. And a charity auction... How bad can it get?

Crystal wants Ani. Ani wants revenge. Richard -- you remember Richard? -- Richard has... the Victoria's Secret underwear?

Dedication

For Crystal, Ani, and all the members of the League who listened to me bemoan the trials and tribulations of coaxing this plot out on stage. Like Ricky, it was shy...

Thanks for holding my hand!

"Come on, ladies, don't quit now. Just look at this beauty. Nine hundred dollars, what a steal. Nine hundred, I've got nine hundred. Do I hear one thousand?"

My oh my. Crystal's mouth watered just watching the sub strut down the runway and back. Tall, trim, elegant, bold, and yet charmingly shy, the stunning brunette -- Ricky, according to the program -- pirouetted gracefully, no easy task on three-inch spiked heels -- the ankle length red satin dress parting to reveal a flash of long, lean, perfectly waxed leg. Cool, slippery fabric over warm, silky skin. And beneath that skin, all the tone and muscle of a man's strength, submitting to her will. The contrast -- satin on steel -- a woman's looks, a man's strength -- always made her hot.

Crystal raised her placard and nodded her chin.

"One thousand. Do I hear --"

"Ten-fifty!"

"Eleven hundred."

"Eleven hundred, I need twelve, twelve hundred for this gorgeous sub here, who'll give me twelve? Come on, ladies, it's for a good cause!"

Marteeka turned away, feigning disinterest. Crystal knew better. She'd never seen this sub before. No one had. Which was exactly what was driving the price up. The sub had "fresh meat" written all over him. Breaking this one in would be a Domme's wet dream... tearing him down, finding out what made him tick, building him back up again... Marteeka wanted him all right, but this prime piece of beef was out of her price range.

Ani, on the other hand...

"Looks like it's down to you and me. Unless you want to bow out now."

Crystal shook her head. "Not this time, Ani. He's mine."

Ani smiled and raised her fingers. "Eleven-fifty!"

"Eleven-fifty, eleven-fifty, give me twelve hundred."

"You know you can't outbid me."

"Wanna bet?"

Crystal twitched her head a fraction of an inch.

"Twelve, I have twelve, give me thirteen. Thirteen hundred dollars, ladies! How bad do you want this pretty little sub?"

Little? Crystal almost laughed. Red satin gown and heels aside, the "little" sub might well be gorgeous, but he was close to six feet tall. And it was beginning to look like Ani wanted him *very* badly. Time to up the ante. "Fourteen hundred."

"Fifteen!"

"Seventeen-fifty."

"Bitch."

Crystal loved being right. Now to make her friend admit the truth. "Do you *want* him, or do you just want to win?"

"You said I was ready." Ani waved her placard at the auctioneer. "Eighteen-fifty!"

"For a sub of your own, yes. But not to break in fresh meat."

"I want *this* sub."

"I *can* outbid you. You know that."

"But *will* you? How bad do *you* want him?"

"Eighteen-fifty going once…"

Crystal shrugged. "I like to win." She raised one finger. "Two thousand dollars."

"We could share." Ani sounded almost desperate.

"We could." Crystal eyed her speculatively. "Why do you want him so badly? There are plenty of subs to choose from tonight. No reason to risk so much."

Ani tapped her placard against her palm, chewing her lip, as if trying to decide how much to reveal. Always a telling sign.

"Two thousand going once…"

"I know him," Ani admitted at last, desperation showing in the set of her shoulders.

"Twice…"

Interesting. "My place?"

"Deal."

"Sold!" The gavel banged on the wooden podium, echoing through the room like a gunshot. "To bidder #43. Remember, ladies and gentlemen, it's for a good cause. All proceeds go directly to the Foundation for Aids Research."

Crystal let her gaze travel across the room to where the gorgeous brunette in a long red satin fuck-me dress was being led from the stage. "So, who is he?"

"My *boss*. Richard-the-Asshole."

Richard slouched lower in his chair, staring down the hall. What the hell? There she was again, his secretary -- Ani, this one's name was -- dressed in a stylishly cut man's suit. She looked damned hot in it, too. Talk about double standards. Just let him walk in to work in a designer dress, and there'd be hell to pay. He shifted uneasily in his chair again, adjusting the satin panties so they didn't ride over the burn on his tender skin.

To add insult to injury, that witch -- the one who'd dumped the pot of coffee all over his freshly waxed skin -- had not only burnt the insides of his thighs, she'd also ruined a brand new pair of Victoria's Secret satin panties. There was no way he'd ever get the stains out of them. Not once they'd set. He couldn't exactly run to the ladies room and wash them out while the stain was still fresh, either.

The men's room would have been worse. Oh, yeah. He could see it now. Stripping down to his poor scalded skin in front of the prying eyes of a dozen male models. Not a straight one in the bunch.

Not that it mattered. They were models. Clients. They could do and say -- and wear -- whatever they wanted. Not him. He was the president of the firm. There were proprieties to be observed. Clients to impress. Rules.

Always, always, there were rules. The rules started from the time he learned to walk. *Act like a gentleman, Richard. Say thank you, Richard. Excuse yourself, Richard. A gentleman doesn't do that, Richard.*

You can't wear that, Richard. What would people think? Oh, no, you can't date her, Richard. She's not one of us. Of course you're going to law school, Richard. Your father's alma mater. It's all been arranged. You can't do that, Richard. We must keep up appearances.

Why? Fuck them. Fuck them all. Them and anyone else who expected him to do the *right* thing. He'd tried to play by their rules, and what had it gotten him? Forty-five years old, divorced, and miserable. True, the firm was doing well, but not by his parents' standards. What's more, they expected him to remarry -- an *appropriate* woman, from their social circles, this time -- give up this foolish idea of running a modeling agency, join the family firm, and produce the prerequisite heirs to the family fortune.

Maybe tomorrow he'd ditch the Armani suit and come in wearing three-inch spiked heels and a raw silk dress split clear up to his perfectly waxed thigh. That ought to send a few whispers of shock rippling through Mother's social circles.

He'd be the only one in the office wearing a dress, too. And he'd like to see any of the women around here try wearing spiked heels. He was tired of hiding, damn it. He wanted more. So much more than forbidden underthings hidden beneath his perfectly tailored Armani suit.

Richard opened his desk drawer and pulled out the invitation once more.

You Are Cordially Invited To Attend The 19th Annual
Fetish Club New Year's Eve Bash
The Gala Event Of The Season
Please RSVP To Reserve Your Table Today

The Fetish Club. Totally inappropriate. He couldn't be seen in a place like that. Why hadn't he thrown the invitation away? The party'd been nearly two weeks ago. He didn't have any idea why he'd gotten the invitation in the first place. Or why he'd kept it. He started to shut the drawer.

Hell. What did it matter who sent it, or why? He knew why he'd kept it. If he was ever going to find someone who'd accept him for what he was, it was time to make a move. Maybe *The Fetish Club* was the place to start.

7:00 PM, Saturday, 10 February 2007
The Fetish Club

Loud, strident, angry. The music penetrated every orifice, whether you wanted it to or not, like an uncaring lover. The place was packed, the dance floor writhing with near naked bodies, clad only in bits and pieces of black leather.

Fetish Club indeed. This was definitely not her kind of kink. These people were over the top. Too noisy. Too out of control. Too… too *young*.

"Please, Mistress, let me suck your toes."

Crystal grimaced in distaste. "Go away." She didn't need to watch some handsome young stud wearing nothing more than a black leather G-string and a studded black collar get down on his hands and knees and crawl to the bar to fetch a drink for his Mistress. She'd always preferred a less ostentatious lifestyle. She liked structure. Order.

"I'm not sure this is such a good idea," Ani mumbled for the twentieth time.

"You can do this, Ani. Trust me. You're ready."

"Last time you said 'trust me' I woke up with worm guts between my teeth the next morning."

"I also warned you to stay away from the tequila," Crystal reminded her. "You've got to learn to do things in moderation." It wasn't advice she took herself, of course. She'd never done things halfway. Which was exactly why she'd ended up here. With Ani. Waiting for the 5th annual Valentine's Charity Sub Auction to begin.

Because Ani wanted to be here. And, well, because Crystal just couldn't risk letting Ani attend alone. God knew what she'd bring home.

It had started out innocently enough. An invitation to the famed Fetish Club for their 20th Annual New Year's Eve party. The invitation said she could bring a guest, and naturally, the first person she'd thought of was Ani, the Domme she'd been mentoring for the last year and a half.

Then, while they were sipping drinks and watching subs perform anatomically amazing feats, Ani had spotted a flyer on the events board. "Hey! They're having an auction!"

"Whatever thought just popped into your head, Ani, douse it. Remember last time, the male dancers at the strip club, the tequila?"

"It's a charity sub auction to raise money for AIDS research. For Valentine's Week. 24/7 Power Exchange." Ani brought a copy of the flyer back to their table. "I want one of these. I'm going."

Crystal could have pointed out that the same subs could be had by simply joining the club and letting it be known she was in the market. She didn't. She could see too many possibilities in this. Because while Ani was indeed going to make a fine Domme, Crystal knew Ani better than Ani knew herself. And in her heart, Ani would always be a sub. Crystal's sub.

Maybe it was time she reminded Ani of just how well they worked together. She hid her grin in a melodramatic sigh. "I'm going to regret letting you talk me into this, aren't I?"

"Hey, don't blame me. I'm not talking you into anything. All I said was that I'm going to go buy me a toy-boy."

"Well, then, someone has to keep you out of trouble."

Ani raised one delicately sculptured eyebrow. "Right..."

9:00 PM, Saturday, 10 February 2007
The Fetish Club

"I can't go through with this."

"Ricky? Baby? What's wrong?"

Half a dozen long-legged, broad-shouldered gurls swarmed around Ricky, their faces frowning in concern.

"I can't go out there. I can't."

Chandra put an arm around his shoulders. "Everybody gets stage fright the first time, Ricky, baby. You're going to be nervous, gurl. That's all right. You'll do just fine."

"About as fine as three-day-old leftovers." Richard fisted his hands in the satin, fighting the urge to rip off the stupid dress and go hide in his office in the politically correct Armani suit he wore like armor to protect himself from ever having to face a day like this.

He smoothed the red satin down carefully, making sure his fists hadn't left marks in the fabric. He'd spent a small fortune on it, just for tonight. *Not the dress's fault.* These were his friends, the "gurls" he'd rehearsed with for months, and they cared about him. Or leastwise they cared about Ricky. He'd found a home here. Family. More of a family than he'd ever known. And this was what they did. This annual fundraiser was about so much more than raising money for AIDS. It was about holding on to the dream that somewhere, somehow, there was a partner who was meant to find them. Meant to love them, just as they were.

He had to do this. *Ricky* had to do this, for all of them. He took a deep breath and did his best to pull himself back together. "What if someone I know's out there?"

"That could happen, baby, but you got to remember, any Domme who sees you here tonight, well, she's got to be a member, too. And there's a lot kinkier stuff goes on at this club than anything we do. You're going to raise a lot of money tonight, and it's for a good cause. Now you go enjoy yourself for a week and don't you worry about a thing."

"Entry number nineteen, Ricky Valley!"

"Go on, gurl! You can do this!"

Richard couldn't. He knew he couldn't. But Ricky could. Ricky gave a final tug to the deep red satin dress and twitched her hips, clicking her three-inch stiletto heels together once. "Wish me luck!"

"Break a leg, baby, break a leg."

"Ladies and gentlemen, a big round of applause for Ricky Valley!"

The crowd whistled and cheered. Ricky held her head up and shook her mane of carefully arranged curls back over one shoulder, cocking one hip as she turned to head down the runway. Yeah. Oh yeah. Ricky could do this.

"We'll start the bidding at five hundred dollars. Five hundred. Five hundred. Give me five hundred for this gorgeous sub..."

The voice faded into the background as the stage lights warmed her skin to a feverish glow. Ricky had been born to do this. No matter what happened, even if no one offered a bid, she'd had this night, this chance to be Ricky. Whatever the cost, it was worth it. Richard might hide in the shadows beneath that perfectly tailored Armani suit, but Ricky would never have to wonder what it would be like to fly free. Never again.

9:25 PM, Saturday, 10 February 2007
The Fetish Club

"I'm not going anywhere with *her.*"

Crystal held up a hand to stem Ani's angry retort, wishing for the thirtieth time in ten minutes she'd asked *why* Ani was bidding so insistently on this particular sub. She called on every bit of presence she'd learned from eight years as an MP and another half dozen as a Mistress to pull the situation under control. "Quiet. Both of you."

God, blessed, silence. Ricky crossed his arms over his chest, green eyes shooting daggers at Ani, while she scowled back at him, but they both held their tongues.

For the moment.

Calm. Crystal needed to project an aura of calm power and control. "Ricky, you entered this agreement of your own free will, and you agreed to the contract terms."

"I did *not* agree to --"

"Silence! There are only two words I want to hear from you, and you will say them, now."

Ricky snapped his mouth shut, though his frown couldn't have dropped any deeper. Finally, his jaw muscles straining with the effort, his lips moved.

"Try that again. I didn't hear you."

"Yes, Mistress."

"Thank you." Crystal turned her traffic cop hand toward Ani. "Ani, you agreed to the same contract terms when you signed up for this event. I brought you here. I sponsored you. You will act like the Domme I trained you to be, or Ricky and I will go home alone."

Ani closed her eyes and took a long, deep breath.

She straightened, rolled her shoulders once, and managed to recapture most of her poise. "You're right, as always, Mistress Crystal. I apologize."

Crystal nodded, then turned her attention back to Ricky. "Assume the position, slave." For a moment she thought he'd refuse. Slowly, still glaring, he pulled up the gown's skirt far enough to allow him to kneel. Even more slowly he folded his hands behind his back and lowered his forehead to the floor. "Good. Now make your vow."

One second. Two. "Thank you for accepting me as your slave, Mistress. I acknowledge that as long as I am in your service I have no rights other than those you choose to give me. I promise to obey you without question. My only purpose is to please you, Mistress."

Crystal smiled, her tension easing just a little. "Nicely said, slave. When you address me you will always refer to me as Mistress. You will treat me with respect at all times, and you will never again raise your voice to me. Do you understand my rules?"

"Yes, Mistress."

"You may sit up." She buckled her collar around his neck, carefully lifting the sweep of long, dark curls out of the way. Gorgeous hair. It wasn't a wig, either. "This is my collar, not yours. It is a symbol of my ownership. You wear it with my permission, and you will wear it at all times, as long as you are in my service. This is my leash. I will give it to whomever I wish, whenever I wish, and you will obey whoever I give it to as if their orders were my orders."

"Yes, Mistress."

"There are two kinds of pain. Erotic pain and punishment. You will do everything in your power to keep me from having to punish you. Punishment is not for your sexual enjoyment, and I assure you, you will not find my punishment enjoyable. Do you understand me?"

He shivered slightly, though she suspected it was not from cold.

"Pardon me? I don't believe I heard you."

"Yes, Mistress. I apologize. You will not have to ask me to speak up again, Mistress."

"Good." She handed Ricky's leash to Ani. "Would you please help Ricky get her bags? I'll call for my car and meet the two of you out front in three minutes."

Ricky looked alarmed -- and not about the hand holding his leash this time. "Mistress, I'll need a few minutes to change back to my street clothes."

Crystal let her gaze come to rest on Ricky's deep red-bronze lips. The most important part of being a Mistress was reading the sub, knowing what they wanted before they knew themselves. What would make a man like Richard Marten, a well-known contract attorney and head of a prestigious talent agency, put himself out on display as one of the "gurls" at a place like *The Fetish Club*? That was taking quite a risk…

Risk. That was the key to unwrapping Ricky. "Did I ask you to change clothes?"

"No, Mistress."

"Why would I want you to change? I just paid a good deal of money for you, slave, just as you are. I want exactly what I paid for. You look gorgeous. As a matter of fact, the three of us look far too good to go straight home. I think we deserve a night on the town. I'm thinking *La Escuelita*."

"*La Escuelita*? I've never been there." Ricky looked both excited and terrified, but he didn't say he didn't want to go. "Thank you, Mistress," he added as an afterthought. Good. He was learning.

Ani just looked surprised. Which was fine. If they were going to enjoy this week together -- and Crystal certainly planned on enjoying herself -- she'd have to help Ani forget Richard-the-Asshole and focus on Ricky, the sub.

What happened when the week was over and they went back to the real world was up to them, but this week was hers. Lots of hot, sweaty dancing, followed by lots of hot, equally sweaty sex -- one way or another she'd keep them both too exhausted to find time to fight.

2:00 AM, Sunday, 11 February 2007
Charter Limo, Midtown Manhattan

Ricky flopped onto the limo's soft leather seat. Laughing, Crystal dropped next to him, spilling comfortably against his shoulder, while Ani started to slip into the seat on the far side. Instead Crystal pulled her down onto their laps, where Ani sprawled bonelessly.

They were all more than a little tipsy. Ani turned her head enough to realize where she'd landed. Had he not been carefully tucked and taped, her mouth would have been very close to his cock. She giggled, but she didn't reposition herself.

Had anyone dared to ask Richard before today what color his secretary's eyes were, he'd have been clueless. Now he knew they were a vivid, shimmering blue. And her hair was a bright strawberry blonde, all the way to the roots, a fiery contrast to Crystal's golden brown. Both of them were incredibly hot -- and even hotter together. He hadn't quite figured out the dynamics between the two, but he was sure of one thing. He'd never had a better time in his life. True, *La Escuelita* was a gay club, but it was also home to just about anything goes. Especially on Friday nights. He didn't know if he'd have the nerve to go there alone, as Richard or as Ricky, but with Crystal and Ani… the night couldn't have been more perfect.

Except that now they were headed home. To Crystal's home. And he had a contract to fulfill. He was still, as they said, fresh meat. He'd never done anything outside *The Fetish Club*, where everything was carefully scripted and the atmosphere was carefully controlled. Things were… different. Outside. He knew the contract he'd signed specified that the auction was for the purposes of Bondage and Discipline only, no sexual intent either suggested or implied, but as a lawyer he also knew the language had been carefully worded to avoid potential charges of soliciting. As far as he knew, no one on either side of the stage had any expectations of celibacy.

The way Ani and Crystal had been touching each other -- and him -- while they danced certainly didn't lead him to believe they expected their relationship to be celibate. Hell, he couldn't ever remember being so incredibly aware of his body. He might be dressed like a woman -- and that itself was an incredible turn-on -- but beneath the shimmering red satin and the push-up cincher that netted him his B-cup tits beat the heart of a man who desperately wanted to have sex with these two beautiful women.

"Just look where you landed," Crystal teased Ani. "You expect me to believe that was an accident?"

Ani turned her head again and nipped at Ricky's crotch. "Wasn't. But Ricky did too good a job. Can't find anything to play with."

"You want to play, do you?"

Ricky stifled a groan as Crystal bent down to kiss Ani's scarlet lips. His cock, already more than a little aroused, struggled to break free from his careful taping job. He wanted desperately to touch, to join in the sensual play. Throwing caution to the wind, he slid his hand down Crystal's arm, over her shoulder, and down to her lovely ass.

Crystal sat up abruptly. "What do you think you're doing, slave?"

"I -- I -- nothing, Mistress. Forgive me."

"If you weren't doing anything, what is there to forgive? I think we just added lying to your list of transgressions."

Oh, shit. "Forgive me, Mistress. I was -- I was…"

"The term you're looking for is copping a feel."

"Yes, Mistress."

"Did you ask my permission?"

"No, Mistress."

Crystal looked at Ani. "I think the slave needs to be punished."

Ani smiled wickedly. "I agree, Mistress Crystal."

Before he could voice an objection -- or even decide if he wanted to -- Crystal's hand was on his forgotten leash, yanking his head down to her lap. "On your knees, slave."

He was too off balance to even consider objecting, though slithering out from under Ani wasn't exactly easy. Or graceful. What if someone saw him like this? The windows were heavily tinted, but still… Gathering the red silk up around his knees, he knelt on the floor of the limo, hands clasped behind his back, head bowed submissively, body trembling slightly, both from fear and desire.

As if he'd been nothing more than in the way, Crystal went back to kissing Ani, one hand in her hair, the other pushing her sequined gown to expose a pair of gorgeous legs and thighs. Crystal's hand blocked his view as her fingers slipped inside Ani's tiny thong, setting his poor trapped cock on fire. "You're wet," Crystal teased. "I think your pussy needs attention."

"I think you're right." Ani scrunched the skirt up further and worked the thong down those beautifully curving legs. No wonder she'd hidden that body in a man-cut suit.

"Umm. Gorgeous pussy, don't you agree, Ricky?"

He was allowed to look? Ricky swallowed hard

as Ani spread her legs wide, revealing a nest of strawberry blond curls just slightly darker than the hair on her head. He swallowed again, trying to find his voice. "Yes, Mistress."

"Ani's pussy needs to be serviced. If you do a very good job, I may forgive your transgression."

Serviced? There was no way he could un-tape his cock without getting undressed, first. Surely she knew -- *ohhh*. Understanding hit. His cock didn't have any part in Crystal's command. Now might not be the best time to admit he'd never preformed oral sex. Richard might have objected that such acts weren't proper. Ricky didn't give a damn. Couldn't see beyond the red gold curls Ani spread open with delicate fingers to reveal the swollen lips of her sex. Ricky positioned himself between Ani's knees, spreading his legs as wide as he dared, both for stability and to ease his aching cock.

"Keep your hands behind your back."

Ricky shivered, wondering what would happen if he disobeyed that command. Carefully shaking his hair back over his shoulders, he leaned in, inhaling the fresh, salty sweet smell of Ani's musk. What would a woman like? What would she want? Would her clit be as sensitive to his tongue as his cock was to a woman's touch?

Experimentally, he traced the opening to her slit, bottom to top, tasting the heady tang of her juices as he made his way to her clit. It was full and engorged, the little head jumping to meet his tongue. He circled it with the tip of his tongue, then sucked it into his mouth. It quivered and pulsed, dancing between his lips as he swirled his tongue around and around.

"Sweet Jesus!" Ani exclaimed.

Ricky wanted to laugh in pleasant surprise.

Apparently he was doing this right! He'd always been careful during sex, afraid to lose control. What would it be like to make Ani lose control? He let go of her clit and licked her slit again, then the lips of her labia, nipping gently there where apparently she wasn't quite so sensitive. She jumped, but didn't pull away, only slid down in the seat a little more, spreading herself open even wider. He took that as an invitation, then thought better of it. "Mistress, please. May I fuck you with my tongue?"

"Oh, God, yes!" Ani exclaimed, forgetting the proprieties of their relationship.

Ricky put his hands on her knees, spreading them wider, and licked the length of her slit once more before slowly slipping his tongue into her hot, wet pussy.

Before he could register a protest, Crystal was off her seat, her knee in the small of his back, forcing him hard against Ani's pussy as she yanked his right arm back behind him the way he'd seen cops do in TV shows. He heard the sound of Velcro ripping apart. Ani pushed her cunt toward him, moaning in evident pleasure, as Crystal fastened a soft velvet cuff around his wrist. "What did I tell you about your hands, slave?"

He tried to apologize, but it was difficult to speak with his tongue buried in a thrusting cunt. Crystal yanked his other wrist back to strap it to the first, pushing him even deeper into Ani's pussy.

Crystal's hand fisted in his hair, yanking his head back. "Answer me."

His cock swelled impossibly harder. "I'm sorry, Mistress."

"What are you apologizing for?"

"I apologize for disobeying you and moving my

hands, Mistress." Though if he'd known she had wrist cuffs about, he might have done it sooner. This was a lot more comfortable than trying to hold his hands behind his back. Now that she'd stopped torturing his shoulder, anyway.

"I don't think you're sorry at all."

OK. He'd give her that one. "I like the cuffs, Mistress. But I didn't mean to disobey you. I got caught up in the moment. For that I apologize."

With his head bent back, he could just see Ani, left to her own devices, rubbing her fingers over her clit. "Give him back," she moaned.

"Ask me nicely."

Ani's fingers stilled and her gaze focused over his shoulder on Crystal. "I thought we were sharing him."

"We never got around to the specific terms of that agreement."

"What do you want?"

He felt Crystal's hand on his arm tighten slightly. "Everything."

Ani's lips slowly spread into a smile. "I thought you'd never ask. Mistress."

Crystal let go of his hair and pushed him gently forward toward Ani's waiting pussy. As he thrust his tongue deep into her he caught a glimpse of fingers descending to work her swollen clit. Ani's fingers, Crystal's fingers, he couldn't be sure. Crystal's body pressed against the back of his head as she leaned forward. It didn't take much imagination to picture them kissing above him. Or perhaps their mouths aimed lower... and if those were Crystal's fingers, where were Ani's?

Fighting for breath in the suddenly crowded space, tongue fucking Ani as hard and fast as he could, hearing the women's moans above him, he wondered absently if it was possible for his cock to get any harder. One thing was certain. This was about as far from his orderly, perfectly boring life as he was ever going to get. Even if he never got to fuck either of them -- even if all they really wanted was to fuck one another -- he never wanted to go back. And he'd surely never look at his secretary in quite the same way.

With a moan and a cry, Ani came, hot juices washing over his face. Ricky smiled. His perfect makeup was definitely a thing of the past, but perfect just didn't seem all that important any more.

Someone's hand slipped down over his ass, stroking gently as he made a last few swipes over Ani's pussy with his tongue. "My turn," Crystal announced.

Ricky wasn't sure who was trading places with whom, but one thing he was sure of. His cock would never be the same again.

2:30 AM, Sunday, 11 February 2007
Charter Limo, Midtown Manhattan

Shifting his weight carefully, Ricky inched his way between Crystal's knees. Ani now had Crystal's gown shoved out of the way and the side opening zipper peeled down enough to give her access to Crystal's breast. Moaning in pleasure, Crystal pushed her breast against Ani's lips. At the same time she spread her lower lips open for Ricky's tongue, fingering her clit with hard, rapid swipes.

A small purple stud pierced the hood of her clit, bobbing in rapid time to the sweep of her fingers.

Fuck. At this rate she was going to come without him. Ricky dove in hard, licking and sucking the lips of her cunt before he speared his tongue deep inside her. Once, twice, three times he licked the walls of her pussy, but he wanted more. Bumping her fingers out of the way, he sucked her clit into his mouth, toying with the small metal barbell's studded ends, flicking them back and forth with the tip of his tongue.

Her hands fisted in his hair, pushing him against her wet pussy. He rubbed his chin against her slit, wishing he had his hands free to thrust his fingers deep inside her. Leaving her clit for a moment, he tongue-fucked her pussy long and deep again.

Ani moved from Crystal's side to slip to the floor next to him. He thought for a moment she was going to release his hands, but instead she straddled his legs to slide her arms around his shoulders. Her hands found his nipples where they strained against the fabric, kneading the already hard points through the thin satin.

He cried out, his voice vibrating over Crystal's

hot, wet pussy, his tongue thrusting harder, faster, in time to Ani's pumping fingers. His cock bounced and jerked against the confining, restraining tape, straining hard to free itself from its prison. He could feel his hips thrusting mindlessly in rhythm to his tongue, but it was no use. His cock was taped too securely to escape.

Ani rose up on her knees, shifting so that her left hand crossed over his chest to his right nipple, both supporting him and holding him firmly in place as her right hand slid down his ass. He raised up as much as he could, praying she was reaching for his tortured cock. Instead she circled his virgin anus with the tip of one questing finger.

Her hands withdrew, leaving him alone and off balance, falling face forward into Crystal's waiting pussy. Then Ani was back, her arm around his chest again. Oh, God. Oh fuck. She pulled his skirt up and cold lube hit his asshole. "Let me in. Let me fuck you," Ani whispered against his ear. "You know you want me."

No. He wanted his cock buried deep in her pussy. He wanted… it didn't matter. He was bound and helpless and completely unable to stop her as her lubricated finger teased him with long, slow circles.

Beneath his thrusting tongue Crystal raised her hips, thrusting back at him with growing momentum. Wanton cries ripped through the night. Despite the privacy screen, the limo driver had to hear them. He'd gotten a brief glimpse of the driver as he opened the car door for them. A huge Viking of a man, radiating raw power and strength. His predator roots were poorly disguised by the immaculate driver's uniform. The thought of this stranger listening to them getting off made Ricky even harder.

Ani's finger pushed past his sphincter and into

his channel in one slow thrust. He screamed, though the sound had nowhere to go, clenching tightly against the unwanted invasion. Never before had Richard made noise during sex. It simply wasn't proper. Waves of fear mixed with desire washed over him. He squirmed, whether to get away or to urge her on, he wasn't sure.

Then her finger found the hard bump of his prostate, sending long, searing waves of agonizing pleasure straight to his bound cock. Ani pinched his nipple, and he twisted, forgetting Crystal's pussy for the moment as the agonizing need to come shot through him. "Fuck me! Please, fuck me!" he begged. "Please, Mistress!"

Instead Crystal yanked him back to her pussy. "We're almost home," she promised. "And I'm almost there. Make me come!"

Come? He'd make her come, all right. He'd make her pay for the pain she caused him. He tugged on the stud piercing her clit, worrying it with his teeth and his tongue before he sucked her clit back into his mouth once more. Pain, pleasure, the lines blurred until he could no longer tell the difference.

He could feel Ani humping her fist as she ground her thumb into his ass now, sending painful spikes of pleasure rippling through him. Beneath him Crystal writhed and moaned, shuddering on the brink of release. The limo pulled to a halt just as the women came together, their cries shattering him as they collapsed in a pile.

Moments later the car door swung open. Apparently unfazed, the driver offered Mistress Ani his hand.

Something near panic hit Ricky. His dress was scrunched up around his knees, his makeup had to be a disaster by now, his hair was a wreck, and he was in handcuffs. Well, wrist restraints. Something. And he was supposed to walk across the sidewalk and through the lobby of her condo, past the doorman and residents and people on the street looking like he'd just had his face buried in pussy?

"Ricky."

He snapped his head around toward the voice. Mistress Crystal. A firm hand gripped his chin, and a wet wipe descended on his face. "There. That's better." From nowhere she produced a compact and dabbed the sponge briefly over his nose and chin. "Charlie, could you help Ricky out, please?"

The amazing Charlie set him on his feet next to the limo in one smooth, swift move. Ani reached down to twitch the wrinkles from their gowns and scoop up his leash. Charlie set his shoes on the sidewalk and steadied him as he slid his feet back into them.

Well. That was a bit better.

And then Crystal appeared, looking perfect, not a hair out of place, her tiny bag tucked neatly under her arm. The thing had to have magical properties, he thought rather abstractly. Wrist restraints, wet wipes, and a compact? In a bag that size?

Charlie reappeared with Ricky's suitcases, escorting them not only to the door, but all the way to the elevator. He waited while Mistress Crystal pulled her elevator key from her amazing purse. Key. Only the penthouse would require an elevator key. Ricky nearly giggled.

"Come on. Share."

He blinked like a deranged owl. "I apologize, Mistress. I'm not sure what you mean."

"Something struck you as funny. Share the thought."

Ricky allowed himself a smile. "My mother. She's always complained that I don't date women from the proper social circles. I was thinking she'd approve of your address."

Crystal and Ani both laughed. "She doesn't like the women you date?"

"I don't date. But no, she hated my first wife. Candy's a brilliant attorney, mind you, but she had to earn her degree. Remarkable ACTs, perfect 4.0 transcripts, scholarship, student loans, that sort of thing. But her parents are of the wrong social class, and she graduated from the wrong college."

"We should invite her over," Crystal laughed.

"My ex-wife?"

"Your mother. That would be so much fun! Send Charlie to fetch her, arrange a very proper tea, give her a tour of the condo -- all except the dungeon of course. And she'd never know what you had on under your respectable Armani suit. It is an Armani, isn't it?"

"Usually, yes, Mistress. But I didn't pack a suit this trip."

"Another time, then. But it would be fun."

Another time. Did that mean there would be other times? Was this more than just the week he'd signed his common sense away for? And what was that about a dungeon? She had a dungeon -- in a penthouse condo?

He waited in the middle of the living room, not sure which way to turn, as Crystal handed Charlie an obscenely large pile of cash. "Thank you, Mistress Crystal."

It struck Ricky as odd that Charlie called Mistress Crystal "Mistress." Did he…

"You're very welcome, Charlie. Care to stay and play with us?"

Charlie looked Ricky over, smiling. "Thank you for the invitation, Mistress, but I can't tonight. Got to go to church with Molly in the morning. But when I'm down on my knees in a few hours there's one thing I'm gonna be prayin' for, and that's a sweet ass like that all my own."

Oh Lord. It was *his* ass Charlie was admiring!

"Mistress…" Ricky flushed with embarrassment. "Yes?"

"I think I should tell you -- that is -- I'm straight."

Crystal glanced at the elevator doors. "Does that frighten you? The idea of Charlie's cock in your ass?"

Fuck. He'd known he ought to keep his mouth shut.

This was, in a sense, a contract negotiation. What he did for a living. He could do this. Give and take. All he had to give was the truth -- maybe more of it than he'd intended. "The idea of anything in my ass frightens me, Mistress. But Ani's touch also turned me on. The thought of Charlie admiring my ass doesn't excite me at all. I don't find him attractive."

"Ani's touch turns you on? What about me?"

"Everything about you excites me, Mistress."

"And if I gave you a choice -- my cock or Charlie's dick in your ass -- which would you choose?"

Her… Oh. A strap-on. As contract negotiations went, he was pretty sure he'd been outclassed. "If you were to offer me such a choice, I'd much rather you touch me, in any way you please, Mistress."

Crystal's smile turned feral. "But it doesn't matter, does it, slave. I'm not likely to offer you such a choice. And the thought of watching Charlie slide that big, thick dick of his into your ass turns *me* on. It's a shame he didn't have time to stay and play." She handed his leash to Ani. "It's late and we all need some sleep. Show the slave to the blue room, please."

"Yes, Mistress."

Ricky tried not to let his disappointment show. He'd assumed, after the limo, that they'd all be sleeping together. He wasn't sure he wanted to be alone with Ani, either. But before he could muster the nerve to voice an objection, Ani stepped behind him to rip off his wrist restraints. The Velcro made a harsh tear in the quiet of the entryway. He scooped up his bags and followed Ani down the hall.

And into a sea of blue. The room was opulent, luxurious, and very feminine. From the blue satin comforter on the four poster bed to the shimmering blue satin drapes and swags, all the fabrics in the room were shades of blue, no two the same. Even the carpet was a deep royal blue. He stopped just inside the doorway, feeling slightly lost.

"Unpack. I want to see what you've got in there. You may use the closet, and the highboy." Ani's voice sounded amused, but no longer malicious.

With the efficiency born of many years on the road, Ricky quickly emptied his suitcases, shaking out wrinkles as he deposited his wardrobe onto hangers and into drawers.

"Leave that one out." *That one* being a white satin fly-away baby-doll set. "Strip for me."

Strip? Not just undress. He'd never done anything that blatantly sexy for a woman in his life. His cock, which had finally calmed down, immediately jumped back to life. Turning to face her, he tilted his head down and glanced at Ani from under his lashes, just to be sure she meant what he thought she did.

She looked flushed, excited, almost hungry. His pulse raced as he reached behind him to unzip the red silk gown. Was she cherishing the thought of torturing him? Or was she really that excited about seeing his naked body? That would be a first.

How the hell did women get out of these things on their own, anyway?

"Turn around. I'll get the zipper." Her hands lingered in his hair for a moment longer than necessary, then scooped it over his shoulder. She took her time drawing the zipper open, slowly allowing the dress to fall open. "I love silk. So smooth and sexy. Never knew it would be such a turn-on on a man."

Ricky let the gown fall to the floor, then bent slowly to pick it up, still not quite ready to turn around again.

"Strip for me." Her voice was softer this time, huskier.

Still bent, he stepped carefully to either side of the puddled fabric, letting the gown trail over his inner thighs as he straightened. Turning to face her, he slid a finger along the edge of each of the cincher's removable cups, slowly peeling the Velcro apart. The Victoria's Secret thong came next, its silken triangle damp with the pre-cum that had managed to leak from his tortured cock. He shimmied it down his legs and let it fall to the floor beside the cincher's cups.

Strip. One would suppose that meant down to the skin, but...

"Leave the cincher on. I want to play with your tits."

"Yes, Mistress. Whatever Mistress wants."

"What do *you* want, Ricky?"

"Whatever Mistress wishes."

She ran one red taloned fingernail across his lips, over his chin, and down his sternum. "What do you want, Ricky? Say it."

"I want you to touch me, Mistress."

She made a quick slash with her fingernail. "That's a touch. Is that what you want?"

White-hot pain laced his vision. "Yes, Mistress," he moaned.

"Interesting." One sharp nail flicked his nipple. "What else do you want?"

Every sense of self-preservation he had left warned him not to tell her, but she was a Mistress. His Mistress. Even if it was just for this week. "Anything that pleases Mistress pleases me."

She pinched his nipple, twisting it sharply, and his hips bucked toward her so hard he nearly lost his balance.

To hell with self-preservation. "Please, Mistress. Suck my nipples. Lick them. Bite them. Anything." *Just touch me.* But he didn't say that out loud. Not yet.

She smiled, and he got a flash of small, perfect white teeth before she attacked. He tried to prepare himself for pain, but instead she undid him with a gentle kiss and a lick. The real pain came when the hand he hadn't seen coming reached between his legs and ripped loose the strip of medical tape.

Freed, his cock sprang to full attention, and only the fact that the blood flow had been restricted kept him from coming instantly as the pain washed over him. "Fuck!" he screeched. "You could give a guy a little warning."

"Like Band-Aids. Fast is better." She stroked his cock, as if in apology. "Besides. You like pain."

He wanted to argue with her. Real men didn't enjoy pain -- it simply wasn't proper. But the way his cock was behaving she'd never believe him, so he kept his mouth shut.

She rewarded his silence with a quick nip to his nipple.

His cock thumped against his belly, pre-cum leaking down its tip. It was all he could do to suppress the moan of pleasure that bubbled up into his throat.

"So careful. So controlled. I want you out of control, slave. I will break you. You will scream. You will moan. You will beg me to fuck you."

"Yes, Mistress," he agreed. What was the point in arguing? She knew his secret now. It was simply a matter of time. And pain.

3:15 AM, Sunday, 11 February 2007
Crystal's Penthouse

"I want to see you in the baby-doll set."

"Whatever pleases you, Mistress Ani." He pulled on the slinky white satin, relishing the tease of the fabric over his rigid nipples. Tying the ribbon bow that held the baby-doll closed, he accidentally brushed the tight little spikes with his thumbs, sending electric shock waves through his gut. "I'll need a moment to tape up."

"Don't bother. I assume Mistress will have her own restraints in mind."

His cock jumped again at the thought. He pulled the G-string on, though it tented out awkwardly over his flushed, swollen cock head. He could feel his balls drawing up. One more of those and he was going to come, hard and fast. He tied the string over his hip, trying hard to think about budgets and billing and anything but his raging erection.

"Turn around."

He spun obediently, giving Ani a good look at the shimmering satin fly-away.

"Face the wall."

Before he could turn fully she'd captured his wrist and wrenched it up behind his back. The tearing sound of Velcro hit his ears moments before the restraints fastened around his wrists again.

Ani's hand trailed down the line of his G-string. "You have a great ass. Armani should be held liable for the way your suits fit. Talk about distracting."

Ricky blinked in confusion. "I didn't know you paid any attention to my ass."

"We always watch your ass."

"We? I thought you all hated me."

"Eight women. Forty-five gorgeous and totally unavailable gay guys, one straight man, and he treats women like shit. Of course we hate you. That doesn't mean we don't admire your ass."

His former excitement melted. He swallowed hard, hiding his disappointment. Really. What had he expected? Ani wasn't going to lie to him and tell him his staff loved him. He wouldn't have believed her anyway. "I guess I should be flattered."

"You aren't, are you?"

That was Crystal's voice. *Mistress* Crystal. The one woman he really didn't want to think badly of him. Still, he couldn't lie to her. "No, Mistress."

"You'd like them to like you."

He shook his head, afraid to speak. His voice was going to crack, and that was so undignified. Though why he should worry about his dignity standing in his Victoria's Secret baby-doll set and a cincher that granted him a decent B-cup bust line, with his cock showing clearly behind the skimpy triangle of satin that covered his genitals, he didn't know. But no matter what his wardrobe, he was still a man, and men didn't cry. Especially not over something as inconsequential as office dynamics.

"Ricky?"

He took a deep breath, trying to calm his nerves. He was just tired. It had been a long, long day.

"Richard."

"Yes, Mistress."

"Tell me about Brasden-Marten."

Brasden-Marten? Why would she... It didn't matter why. Wasn't his place to ask. He blanked his mind and drifted to auto-pilot. "Brasden-Marten is an International Intellectual Property Rights law firm.

Contract negotiations. We represent male models to the advertising market worldwide. Very lucrative."

"And your staff?"

"One office manager, four junior attorneys, four legal aides, and my administrative assistant."

"All female?"

Why did Crystal want to know that? "Eight women. Two men."

"Why do you think they hate you?"

"I *know* they hate me. They call me Richard-The-Asshole." He shrugged, trying hard to keep the bitterness out of his voice. "We represent some of the most glamorous male models in the world to a clientele made up of some of the richest businessmen in the world. I have one simple rule. No screwing the clients. You'd think I asked these guys to cut off their balls. Any time we send a model out on an assignment that turns out to be a cover for a sexual liaison we all run the risk of being brought up on charges of soliciting clients for prostitution. And true or not, that would be the end of Brasden-Marten."

"So that makes it OK to be a dick to your office staff?" Ani made no attempt to keep the emotion out of her voice.

So much for leaving the workplace out of this week. "It's not easy to maintain a professional environment, but I try. If that makes me a dick, so be it."

"No, Richard. Asking your administrative assistant to fetch your coffee, never bothering to speak to anyone unless it's to issue an order, *that* makes you a dick. Half the time you don't even remember my name."

"I *know* your name."

"What?"

"I know your name, Ani. I know everyone's names. I know your date of birth, your home address... I know you take your coffee black, one sugar. And if I was nice to you every woman -- scratch that, the gay guys are worse gossips than the women -- everyone in the office would assume I was hitting on you. I do my best to keep a professional distance."

"You're saying it's all an *act*?"

"I didn't say that. I just don't get close to my staff. It's not professional."

"Then why are you unhappy?"

That was Crystal. Somehow he thought she might understand. "It's not enough anymore. I want..."

"Turn around." When he did, she picked his chin up and forced him to meet her gaze. "Why are you unhappy, Ricky?"

"No one gives a rat's ass about the company. I'm tired. I could close the doors tomorrow and no one would care about anything but their missed paychecks."

"I'd care." Ani's voice softened. "I'd miss watching your gorgeous ass as you storm down the hallway looking like sin waiting to happen."

"We can work on Richard's interpersonal skills later." Crystal handed his leash to Ani, changing moods so fast she made him dizzy. "Take the slave to the dungeon and prepare him. I'll join you shortly."

Ani tilted her head down slightly, her only sign of subservience. "Yes, Mistress."

A few minutes ago he'd have been excited, but the grim reminder of the workplace he had to return to had definitely kicked him out of the mood.

Ani led him down the hall to a locked door. She had to stretch to reach the top of the doorframe, where the key was kept. She wasn't precisely small, though she was trim, almost thin. It was more that the bulky Victorian style doors had thick headers. She unlocked the door to reveal a scene out of medieval legends. Three of the walls were painted to look like stone block. Heavy velvet drapes covered a booth in one corner and most of the fourth wall. Mysterious pieces of exercise equipment -- or torture devices -- or perhaps they were both -- filled every nook. The sight of a rack full of whips, floggers, and assorted leather gear was almost enough to make him hard again.

Almost.

Ani turned a crank on the wall and a heavy steel bar lowered from the ceiling. She unhooked one end and stepped behind him. Before he could register a complaint -- or even decide if he wanted too -- she slid the bar under his elbows. With the far end hooked back to the chain, she slowly ratcheted it back up.

The bar slid high under his arms, forcing his shoulders back and his chest out until his nipples stood out in sharp relief against the straining satin. He knew better than to argue. Not with Ani. This was personal. If she thought it was uncomfortable she'd just raise it higher. But if she didn't quit soon it was really going to hurt.

"Spread your legs."

He spread them as wide as he could, but apparently that wasn't wide enough. The toe of her short spiked heel nudged his feet out farther. When he was standing just the way she wanted him, she cuffed a spreader bar between his ankles.

Oh, shit. He wasn't sure exactly what that was for, but he was pretty sure he wasn't going to like it. He stretched to his toes, trying to take the strain off his arms.

"Very nice."

Crystal's voice. From behind him. He was helpless to turn and face her. He heard a small click and the heavy velvet drapes began to open. They had to be on a remote. Neither of the women were anywhere near them.

Oh, God. The entire wall was one huge glass window. Anyone with a view of this side of the building could see in. Could see him hanging here, helpless, dressed in nothing but a scrap or two of white satin.

And then his awareness of a possible audience faded as he caught Crystal's reflection in the glass. Honey brown hair tumbled down to meet the tightly laced black leather corset. But that wasn't what caught his attention. It was the large black dick she'd sprouted that had his gaze riveted on her pussy as she approached him from behind. So riveted, in fact, that he barely noticed the chains dangling from her fingers.

Until she stepped in front of him.

"I brought you presents."

Ricky raised his focus enough to stare at the ring Mistress Crystal held in the flat of her palm. It looked like a coiled serpent.

The other hand reached down to stroke over the small satin triangle covering his cock. She pulled the small bow loose and the G-string fluttered to the floor. Office politics fled his brain, along with every other coherent thought. He looked down to watch Crystal slip the ring around his penis, just below the head. His cock sprang to full attention. The bronze ring didn't hurt, but its weight commanded his attention, a continuing presence he couldn't forget.

Crystal slipped a leather lasso around the base of his cock, drawing it so tight he'd never be able to come unless she released it. Next she loosened the tie on the baby-doll. He screamed in exquisite pain when the nipple clamp bit into his tender flesh.

"Do you want me to stop?"

The voice seemed to come from far away. He tried to block out the noise like rushing water that filled his ears. He needed to focus.

"Ricky. Do you want me to stop?"

Stop? Hell no. He wanted... "Please, Mistress."

"Please what?"

"Please, may I have the other clamp, Mistress?"

Behind him he felt cold lube hit his ass. Ani -- it had to be Ani, right? Ani's finger rimmed his rigid hole, slowly pushing past his tight sphincter. He moaned helplessly as she violated his anus, pushing her finger in until she found the bump of his prostate. Crystal chose that moment to add the second nipple clamp.

"He's ready for you, Mistress."

The two women swapped places. Crystal's hands stroked over the smooth satin, rubbing the fabric against his skin. "I love the feel of satin. Almost as much as I love the feel of your skin. Smooth, soft fabric over hard male muscle."

"Touch me. Anywhere. Everywhere."

"Was that an order?"

"Yes!" Oh, shit. "No, Mistress. A plea. Please, Mistress. Touch me."

"I think it was an order. I think you need to be punished for such insolence."

She smacked his ass with the flat of her hand. Lovely, excruciating pain shot through him. "Thank you, Mistress! May I have another? Please."

Crystal's hand came down hard on his ass, again and again. His cock jutted straight up, so hard he thought he might come at each blow. But of course the lasso wouldn't allow that. Meanwhile Ani had become fascinated with his nipple clamps, and decided to lick her way around them in ever shrinking circles. "Please, Mistress, may I fuck the slave?" she whimpered.

His cock fully approved of that plan.

"Not yet. There's something missing."

What could possibly... "Yes, Mistress." Ani turned away, only to return with a condom. Placing it in her mouth, she knelt in front of him, unrolling it over his cock with her tongue and teeth.

Crystal's crack on his ass shoved his cock deep in Ani's throat. Moaning helplessly, he thrust into her mouth. "Please, Mistress. Fuck me. Let me fuck Ani. Please."

"I thought you'd never ask."

Ani pulled away, leaving his cock alone and bereft, but only for the time it took her to regain her feet. Despite their height disparity -- Ani had to be at least five inches shorter than he was -- the spreader bar had lowered him to the perfect height. With one swift move she impaled herself on his throbbing cock.

Crystal moved much more slowly than Ani had, carefully pushing past his reluctant sphincter with her thick jellied strap-on, sliding gently into his tight channel. "Fuck!" he moaned. "Oh, fuck that feels good." He didn't know whether he meant his cock in Ani's hot, pulsing cunt or Crystal's dick buried deep in his ass. He shuddered, moaning again as the women began to move.

Ani thrummed the clamp on his left nipple with her tongue, sending jolts of pleasure/pain tearing through his shattered nerves. He screamed mindlessly, thrusting his nipple and his cock into her as hard as he could. Behind him Crystal pulled back, nearly pulling the heavily lubed dong from his ass. Looking down he could see Crystal's hands on Ani's hips, while Ani clutched his.

They set up a rhythm, forward and back, Ani riding down hard on his cock while Crystal withdrew, Crystal thrusting in deep while Ani rode almost to the tip of his cock before she plunged back, as if they were fucking each other through him.

His knees would have buckled without the bar to support him. "Fuck me!" he screamed, near delirious with the pleasure and pain. "Please, Mistresses, fuck me!"

As if they'd only been teasing him before, they slammed down harder, pounding him back and forth between them till he thought his shoulders would pull out of their sockets before they allowed him to come.

Ani shrieked as she came around him, writhing convulsively over his flaming cock. He felt Crystal's punishing rhythm break as she shuddered against him, could almost feel her orgasm rip through from the other end of the dildo. He needed desperately to come, but he couldn't stop. Ani broke over him again as he thrust mindlessly into her, pushing himself back on the length of Crystal's strap-on with each stroke. Faster. Harder. He had to come. Had to…

He screamed out his orgasm as Crystal's hand flashed between the press of their bodies to release the lasso, shooting wave after wave of release into the condom. When he thought he was nearly spent, Ani pulled the clips from his nipples, sending waves of agony through him as the blood flowed back, another wave of cum pulsing through the ring that restricted his cock head.

Ani fisted her hand in his hair, yanking his head down for a kiss that shattered him. Exhausted, boneless, powerless to hold himself upright, he collapsed into her, tears streaming down his face as she claimed him with her lips.

Crystal released some hidden catch on the bar and the three of them tumbled to the thick padded carpet. Tomorrow. Tomorrow he'd try to sort out all the mixed emotions tumbling wildly through him. Tomorrow. Hell. It was tomorrow. Had been for hours.

Later then. For now, there were two sets of arms holding him, two sets of hands stroking him, two sets of lips kissing him -- and each other. Someone released his wrist and ankle restraints, pushing the metal bars off to the side, out of the way. Someone else pulled him closer, his face pillowed against soft breasts as together they tumbled into the sweet abyss of sleep.

* * *

Some time in the night -- minutes? hours? later -- he awoke with enough presence of mind to scout out the bathroom and then locate the master bedroom. One after the other he scooped up the two women and carried them back to Crystal's king-sized bed, carefully divesting them of their outfits. He knew from experience none of their clothes were the sort one should fall asleep in. When he'd have gone back to his room, Crystal opened her eyes enough to smile up at him. Sliding over, she patted the empty space beside her. That was one decision he didn't have to think twice about.

Crystal stretched languidly, savoring the feel of over-used muscles and the lingering scent of sex. Each hand brushed a warm body. Hmmm. That was interesting. Who…

The auction at *The Fetish Club* slowly came back. Then *La Escuelita*. Then the champagne. My, oh my. Champagne had been the perfect choice. Enough to loosen her two darlings up. And the action in the limo… priceless.

Ani lay next to her, curled into the hollow of her side. She looked so adorable in her sleep. Soft and vulnerable. Crystal smiled. Ani'd hate getting caught with that look on her face. On her right Richard lay facing away from her, his naked back one long, delicious sheet of muscle. Damn. The man put an awful lot of effort into maintaining that body, she could tell. He could be one of his own models. The three of them made quite a picture. The auction would prove to be a great investment.

She crawled over Ani and made her way to the bathroom. Brushing her teeth, she grimaced into the mirror. OK. Maybe she wasn't so photogenic at the moment. A quick shower and some coffee would help. And maybe a Tylenol or two. She wasn't getting any younger. One of these days she was going to have to give some thought to the future.

Eventually the week would end, and her toys would leave her. They'd all go back to their vanilla lives. Or find another Mistress. For some reason that made her sad.

Dominance was a voyage of discovery. Ani she knew well. While Ani could play the Domme, she liked things to go smoothly. When she gave orders she didn't want them questioned. She'd been more than willing to let Crystal be the one in control this time. Crystal suspected she'd had her fill of responsibility. What she really wanted was for someone to take care of her for a change.

As for Richard, he'd yet to really argue with a single command she'd given him. Oh, he'd made a few feeble protests, but mostly for show. He'd loved everything they'd done to him. All that physical strength -- all that lean, hard muscle -- and he hadn't even tried to fight her when she'd cuffed him. In the vanilla world, he'd never dream of doing anything that wasn't proper. But when she took responsibility, he was more than happy to follow her orders.

How far would he go to follow her orders? He had to have limits. Every sub had limits. She had five days to find them, and push him just a little bit farther.

Somehow she didn't think it would take her that long.

* * *

Richard came awake with a start, a sound like a gunshot echoing in his head. The body next to him -- a smaller, female body -- jumped as well. Instinctively he grabbed the woman and pulled her close, shielding her with his arms.

In the moment it took him to orient himself he realized his bed partner had to be Ani, because Crystal was standing at the foot of the bed, dressed once again in her black leather corset, holding a wicked looking crop in her hand. Its pop had brought him awake.

"Do you have any idea what time it is?"

"No, Mistress. I apologize for sleeping so late."

"Not nearly late enough," Ani grumbled.

"Silence! You have twenty minutes to get breakfast together and served."

"You know I don't cook!" Ani squealed.

"Then you better pray your partner can, or your ass is in big trouble."

Richard said a silent prayer of thanks for the Internet and two years of single, divorced male status. "What would Mistress like for breakfast?"

Crystal looked over her shoulder as she headed for the door. "Surprise me. But it better include coffee, and fast."

"Man, is she in a foul mood or what?" Ani groused as Crystal disappeared.

"I don't really want to find out how bad, or why." Richard glanced at the clock. Damn. He never slept this late. It was ten after ten. "You can have this bathroom. I'll take the one in my room."

Ani blinked at him, looking surprised. "Thanks."

Four minutes later she stuck her head in his room, holding a red silk bustier around her middle, its ties flapping in her wake. "Can you lace me into this? I can do it but it'll take way too long."

"Sure." Richard smiled. He'd loved helping the other "gurls" with their wardrobes at *The Fetish Club*. It took him mere seconds to flash the laces through their grommets.

"Tighter."

Surprised, he pulled the laces tighter, then tighter again, hoping Ani didn't pass out from lack of breath.

"Oh yeah." Ani pirouetted so he could see the finished product. His hands would span her waist. "Does this look OK?"

Her nipples were doing their best to shove their rigid points through the lace bustier. She was barely dressed and already his cock was painfully hard. "You look good enough to eat," he assured her. "We should serve you for breakfast. Maybe with a little whipped cream and a cherry."

Ani giggled as she belted a matching thigh length red silk kimono over the bustier. "Maybe for dessert. I sure hope you're better in the kitchen than I am or our asses are fried."

"I can manage. Can you give me a hand with this?" He held up his cincher and a sweet little maid's costume he'd picked up just for fun.

"Yummy!" She laced him in tighter than he usually did, giving his tits a shadow of cleavage, then helped him pin his hair up in a fast French twist and attach the silly little cap. "Make sure you bend over a few times. Shame to waste that neckline."

"I wish I had time to do my makeup."

Ani laughed. "You think women have time for full makeup every day? Powder base, lipstick, and a dust of blush takes thirty seconds." She ran her fingertips over his cheek. "You shaved already?"

"Waxed. I'll be good for another two weeks."

"Ouch!"

"Worth it not to have stubble under my makeup." A quick dive into his makeup case netted her arsenal. It was fast and light -- little more than a dusting of color -- but she was right. He felt immensely better for the effort. "We're out of time. Show me the kitchen."

And what a kitchen it was. Double wide industrial size stainless steel fridge, gourmand stainless cook stove with a built in grill, and granite countertops everywhere. Coffee was the first priority. Ani knew where the filters and beans were hidden, and she started the coffeemaker while he pulled out bacon and started it frying on the grill. Fortunately the freezer held readymade delicacies he was well familiar with. "Drop four of those waffles in the toaster would you please? And make sure it's set to light pastry."

"OK. I can do that. Anything else?"

"Top a handful of strawberries and cut them in half." He demonstrated by topping one with the point of a paring knife so when it was sliced it looked like a little heart. By that time the bacon was ready to flip and the toaster had popped out the waffles. He found a water glass and showed Ani how to use it to cut small round waffles out of the larger squares while he buttered the grill and fried up six perfect over light eggs, then decorated the plates with waffle rounds topped with whipped cream hearts with strawberry centers.

By the time he'd added the bacon Ani had the coffee poured and had located a serving tray and silverware. At exactly ten-thirty they arranged breakfast on the formal dining room table. Richard caught Crystal's quizzical smile for a brief flash before she wiped the look from her face.

Remembering Ani's advice, he bent forward a little farther than necessary as he served Mistress her breakfast. Ani set the table, adding delicate three-tined forks laid out on artfully folded linen napkins and orange juice served in frosted glasses. When he turned to place the empty tray on the sidebar, Crystal caught him by surprise with a swift pinch. "Ani's right. You have a great ass."

That surprised him more than the pinch had. "Thank you, Mistress."

"I'm guessing you cooked this. Nice job."

"We both did." He caught Ani's look of surprise and flashed her a quick smile.

Crystal was silent for a few minutes, munching happily. "After breakfast we're going to play a game."

"What game?" they both asked.

Crystal grinned, as if pleased with herself. Somehow he found that a bit unsettling. "Come to the dungeon as soon as the kitchen's presentable again and you'll find out."

"Yes, Mistress."

Whatever she was up to, there wasn't a damn thing he could do about it. The notion made him shiver with anticipation. "Do you think we should change outfits?"

"We better not take the time. She said as soon as we were done, not after we dressed."

"Might be worth it." He looked down at the once pristine maid's costume with regret. "I've got spots."

"It's just water. It'll dry. Trust me. We don't want to be late."

"Right," he agreed. "You'll have to tell me about that some time."

Ani shook her head. "Let's just say it's a lesson that doesn't need to be repeated."

11:15 AM, Sunday, 11 February 2007
Crystal's Dungeon

The heavy drapes were closed, now, blocking out the New York skyline and casting the room into shadows. The only light came from dozens of electric wall sconces bathing the room in artificial candlelight. He didn't remember seeing them before. The curtains in the corner were open, revealing a computer console and a camera.

Fear laced through him at the sight of the camera. If she had a live Internet feed…

A leather-covered bench built a bit like a gymnast's "horse" stood a few feet away from the camera. To the right of it sat a small table with an assortment of restraints, straps, whips, paddles, and chains. In her right hand Mistress Crystal held the riding crop with the leather popper she'd woken them up with, and in her left, a remote. "There you are, my pretties. Are you ready to play my game?"

"Yes, Mistress," Ani answered.

He knew what she was thinking. This camera was here, out in the open. Now. Had it been running last night? Where else were there cameras mounted? "I -- I…" He stuttered in his effort to reply, staring at the camera.

He'd wanted this, and there wasn't much he wouldn't do for his Mistress. But privacy was supposed to be part of the bargain. The camera wasn't. The Internet could be bad. Very, very bad.

"What's the matter, Ricky? Worried about your reputation?"

"Yes, Mistress."

Mistress came closer, her body between him and

the camera, trailing the end of the popper over the low V neck of the maid's costume. "It isn't proper, is it, Ricky. You don't want to be seen dressed like this in public. And make no mistake, my dungeon may be limited access, but it's viewed by thousands of people."

Fear coursed through him, warring with excitement. Limited access. Pay-per-view. So that's how she afforded a penthouse and a private chauffeur. If he really was a chauffeur… "Mistress, I can't." His protest sounded feeble even to him. Damn it, it was exciting as hell, but it could ruin his career. And his reputation.

"Did I ask your permission?"

What would she do if he argued? "No, Mistress. I apologize."

"You have one choice. You may wear either a hood or a mask to protect your privacy if you choose."

He let out his breath in a sigh of relief. "The mask, please, Mistress." A hood might cover more of his features, but it would be hot, and it would make his hair look like hell.

Mistress Crystal nodded to Ani. "Do you wish to wear a mask as well, slave?"

He looked up for a fleeting second, surprised. He hadn't really thought of Ani as another sub. Though, in retrospect, Crystal had treated her more like a sub than another Domme. If so, she was obviously the Alpha sub. Ani's gaze darted to the camera. "Yes, please, Mistress."

"Get them."

"Yes, Mistress." Ani extracted a pair of smooth black leather face masks from the rack along the wall, along with several straps and cuffs. She moved to stand behind him, slipping the mask over his face and lacing it snugly in place, then handing hers to him. He laced it tightly, so it wouldn't accidentally shift during the scene to come. For he was sure it would be a full-fledged scene, designed for the camera. His cock was on high alert.

"Assume the position," Crystal ordered.

He dropped to his knees, folding his hands behind his back, forehead as close to the floor as he could bend. Beside him Ani did the same. A ping sounded, and Mistress Crystal turned toward the camera, hitting a button on the remote. The red light on the camera blinked, then turned green.

He watched out of the corner of his eye as Crystal cracked the crop against her thigh, the noise echoing in the large cavern of a room. "Welcome to Mistress Crystal's Dungeon. I do hope you're not late. I expect all my slaves to be prompt."

With a smile that was far from comforting, Crystal turned her lovely backside to the camera and strolled the few steps it took to reach his side before turning three-quarter profile. "We're going to play my favorite game today. I call this game 'The Inquisition'."

Another pop of the whip. He flinched, almost expecting it to connect with his skin. That it didn't was of little comfort. Never had he felt so exposed. So vulnerable.

"One slave will be the prisoner. The other will play the part of the torturer." She trailed the lash of her whip over his exposed ass. "Do you wish to be prisoner or punisher, slave?"

Despite himself, he shifted slightly, almost making the mistake of raising his head. He was to be given a choice? What fool would willingly choose to be beaten? And yet… to lay a whip into Ani's soft, tender flesh? He swallowed hard. "I would be the prisoner, if it pleases you, Mistress."

She smiled, as if she'd known all along that would be his choice. "Let the games begin."

"Have you got some sort of martyr complex?" Ani hissed. She looked positively wicked in her shimmering red kimono and the black leather mask. "Don't think for one minute I'm going to be easy on you."

He did his best to hide his smile, sure now that he'd made the right choice. "Thank you, Mistress."

Smothering a laugh, Ani pulled his hands behind his back and cuffed them firmly into wide, padded leather restraints, connected so that his hands had to lie side by side. His shoulders pulled back sharply, making his tits strain against the thin fabric of his black satin uniform.

"The prisoner will be masked during the interrogation, to protect his identity, should he decide to cooperate," Crystal announced. "We will call this little sissy gurl Scott."

Ani flinched, then, smiling, cracked her whip for the camera.

Was the camera real? Or part of the game?

Crystal had donned a black barrister's robe, which swung open as she moved to reveal an overly large black dick, complete with dangling balls, protruding from her strap-on harness. Dear God that thing was fat. Surely she didn't think that would fit in his ass.

"I am the Grand Inquisitor, Bishop Stuart. My implement of punishment today will be Mistress Ani. I know from your letters how much you enjoy her work. Mistress Ani will now chain the prisoner to the interrogation bench."

Letters? He shuddered to think what sort of letter she might receive from the sick bastards who'd watch this on the Internet. Ani led him to the "horse" and kicked the point of her high-heeled shoe between his feet, nudging his thighs apart with her knee. Obediently he spread his legs wide, knowing what was coming. She secured each ankle to the horse's legs with more wide leather cuffs. His weight rode firmly on the balls of his feet, pinching his toes in the points of the slinky heels he'd chosen this morning. Had he known they were going to play a game like this... hell. He couldn't lie to himself. He'd still have worn them. They made his legs look damn good.

Next Ani added cuffs to his arms, just below the elbows. These she belted together, pulling his forearms as close to one another as possible without dislocating his shoulders. The last leather strap hooked to the horse on one side and across his back, toppling him onto his stomach over the hard leather bench. Ani swept his hair out of his face, grabbing a handful to lift his head so that he could meet Crystal's gaze.

Could she tell how excited he was? His cock was already leaking drops of pre-cum against the soft satin G-string. His nipples stood out so stiffly they had to show even through the frilly lace that adorned his bodice.

"Where were you last night, prisoner?" Crystal demanded.

Last night? Was this a trick question? "I enjoyed an evening out on the town, Bishop Stuart."

"Doing what, Mr. Scott?"

He felt himself flush, remembering. "Dancing, Bishop Stuart."

"That isn't all you were doing, was it?"

"No, Mis -- Bishop Stuart."

"You consumed large amounts of spirits."

"I did. I confess, Bishop Stuart."

"So you admit your debauchery?"

Wasn't he supposed to? "Yes, Bishop."

"Dancing and alcohol are a sign of the devil. Is the devil in you, prisoner?"

He was dressed in a French Maid's costume, spread eagle and cuffed over a horse, his cock swollen and stiff between his legs, like a cherry ripe for the picking. Too late to argue now. "Yes, Bishop. I have consorted with the devil. I have practiced deviant sexual behavior. I deserve to be punished."

Mistress Crystal moved close enough to run her hand over his ass and give his aching cock a squeeze. "Oh, look. The gurly girl has a dick. Before we begin the punishment we shall have to restrain your randy cock, prisoner."

Restrain? He swallowed hard as she plucked what he now recognized as a black rubber Gates of Hell set off the table. This was going to be good. So very, very good.

His cock securely fastened into the Gates of Hell, Ricky hung face down over the horse, his long black hair obscuring his vision. He might as well have been wearing a blindfold as a mask.

The click of her heels told him Mistress Crystal had moved to his side. "Tell me who led you into this wicked behavior, deviant. Who corrupted your innocence and led you to do the devil's work?"

Ahh. So that was the way it worked. Well, truthfully, he probably shouldn't have confessed so easily. She needed a reason to interrogate him, after all. "No one, Bishop. I swear it on my honor. I was alone in my wickedness."

"Oh your honor, peasant? You have no honor. Twenty lashes."

"Gladly, Bishop." He heard Ani pick up one of the whips from the table. What had she grabbed? He couldn't see, damn it!

"Are you ready, Mister Scott?"

"No, Mistress Ani. Please be gentle." Like he thought there was any chance of that. From the tone of her voice when she'd called him Scott --

Crack!

Heated ribbons of pain sliced through him. Not hard enough or sharp enough to slice the skin, but exquisitely hot, like an electrical charge running straight to his balls. Oh fuck. Yeah. Scott was not someone she was fond of.

"You will count the lashes, Mr. Scott."

Ritual counting, at that, he supposed. "One,

Mistress. Thank you, Mistress. May I please have another?"

Crack!

What the hell had she grabbed? No way he would make it to ten, let alone twenty. "Two, Mistress. Thank you, Mistress. May I please have another?"

Crack!

But he did. She changed sides at five, and again at ten, though his backside already burned with the heat of the stinging lash. Mistress Ani was a true artist with the whip, laying each stripe onto his exposed bottom right next to the last, like a painter laying out a field of grass. She changed cheeks again at fifteen… "Twenty, Mistress. Thank you, Mistress."

A hand fisted in his hair, wrenching his head up sharply so he could meet the gaze of an irate Bishop. "Who consorted with you, prisoner? Who else was privy to this debauchery?"

"No one, Bishop. I was alone in my wickedness."

"Confess, and I may yet be convinced to spare you further punishment."

Confess? He'd already pled guilty.

"Tell me their names, prisoner. Tell me their names."

Names? The pleasure/pain had taken him too high to think up even a remotely good lie. Besides. He deserved to be punished. He was the deviant, the sexual misfit, the man in a dress… the…

"Ten cracks with the paddle."

Dear God. He'd seen that. It was a long, narrow leather paddle with a snapper at the end. He'd be sleeping on his stomach for the rest of the week. "No, Bishop. Please." He did his best to sound cowed, though his cock had never been so hard.

"You will count the strokes."

Pop!

"One, Mistress. Thank you, Mistress. May I please have another…" The pain laced with pleasure that was sharper than anything he'd ever known. *May I please have another, Mistress. Make it stop. Don't stop. May I have another. Please, Mistress. I've been a bad boy. I've worn women's clothing. I've had deviant thoughts as long as I can remember. I want to touch you. Be you. Fuck you. Two, Mistress. Thank you, Mistress. May I please have another. Harder, Mistress. More. Please. More. Never stop. More…*

"Who was party to your wickedness, prisoner?"

"None, Mistress. There was only me."

Hands cupped his breasts, whose hands he didn't know or care, tweaking and pinching his distended nipples. He moaned even as his cock jerked against its restraint.

"Names, prisoner."

"I don't know, Mistress. Bishop."

"You lie, prisoner. Do you know what the punishment is for lying to me?"

He wasn't sure he could take another twenty lashes. "No, Bishop."

"Torture. Days of slow, methodical torture."

Days? He was to spend his week in this room, exploring various pieces of equipment, until finally, at long last, his cock fell off from being so hard for so long? Some rational part of his brain reminded him that it was just a scene, that scenes didn't last forever, but then cold lube hit his ass, stinging his sensitized skin, and he forgot everything but the feel of Mistress's fingers circling his anus, parting him, stretching him, pushing in hard, harder… and then Ani stood before him, her hand pulling his head by the hair, guiding his mouth to her waiting pussy.

The taste of her was as exquisite as the pain that wracked him when Mistress pressed her dong into his ass, pain that no lube could have prepared him for. His stinging flesh ground against her thighs. His neck arched and his back arched and his cock wanted nothing more than to explode, shooting cum all over them both, while he sucked and they fucked and he lay chained between them, helpless to do more than ride the wave and pray they wouldn't move away.

Mistress's fingers reached beneath him, unsnapping the loop around the base of his cock, pumping him slowly up and down in time to her thrusts into his straining ass. Almost instantly he felt the burn of cum pushing, straining, as the climax rolled through him, slowly, so slowly, the rings of the Gates of Hell still stretched around the length of his straining dick, constraining him. Pain shot through him at every thrust of Mistress's cock. Need filled him as he licked and sucked Mistress's cunt. Pleasure forced its way toward release in slow, excruciating waves.

"Please, Mistress," he managed as Ani fell back on her knees, gasping, too spent to stand any longer. "Please, Mistress, may I have another."

Mistress jerked and shuddered against him, her rhythm broken, the cadence of the march no more. She cried out in climax, her plastic dong slipping from his ass. Ani crawled over to unbuckle the straps that held him, sliding a condom over his straining cock as he tumbled to the floor. He cried out, too, as she rolled him to his ass, the pain rocketing through him from his blistered backside. Still he had the presence of mind to grasp her hips, pulling her cunt down hard onto his aching cunt. Cock. Whatever.

His hips hit the floor under her weight and he rocketed up, desperate to relieve the pain in his beaten ass, plunging into her hard and deep. He came down hard again, deliberately, riding the pain, transcending, glorying in the feel of the waves of agony rippling through his every nerve. Ani's climax came so hard the waves washed over him, her hot juices dripping down to sear his wounded flesh. He jerked into her helplessly, his cum bursting through the restraining Gates of Hell in slow, agonizing crests.

Ani's hot, dripping cunt milked him dry. Finally she folded over his belly, her head on his chest. He couldn't summon so much as a groan of protest as her weight forced his hips onto the rough carpet.

"Assume the position."

Slowly Ani crawled from his body, reaching back to tug at his hand, forcing him to focus his muddled brain on the sound of Mistress's voice.

"Assume the position, prisoner."

He crawled to her feet and slowly, slowly bent himself to her will. Beside him Ani's body trembled visibly, the red kimono shivering as if there were a stiff breeze in the room.

"I want a name, slave. Who was with you?"

"I was alone, Bishop."

"We will continue this interrogation tomorrow."

Crystal turned away, the remote once again in her hand, slowly stalking the camera. "Who among you is worthy? Who would be my next slave? Which of you pathetic worms has the balls to approach me? Are you willing to pay the ultimate price? Are you able to withstand the ultimate pain? Send your whining, sniveling excuse for petition to Mistress Crystal. I might let you kiss my foot, if you're a very, very good boy or gurl."

Mistress clicked the remote, and the green light went red again, then faded away.

Or maybe the whole room was fading away.

"Crystal?" he heard Ani's voice as if from a great distance. "… sub-drop…"

Sub-drop. That was bad, wasn't it. Who…

"Grab the blankets."

A long, rippling chill stole over his skin. Then there were blankets and hands and bodies pressed close. Apparently *who* was him. And then the room went black.

2:00 PM, Sunday, 11 February, 2007
Crystal's Dungeon

There might, possibly, have been a better way to wake up than sandwiched between soft, warm bodies, cocooned in plush blankets, the smell of sex thick in the air, but Richard couldn't think of any alternatives at the moment. "Mmmm," he purred sleepily, snuggling closer to the body in front of him.

The head tucked under his chin curled against him, warm lips pressing against his chest. "Welcome back."

"Was I out long?"

"Long enough." Ani's voice, behind him. She kissed his shoulder blade, the tenderness of her touch almost frightening. "You gave us quite a scare."

Naked truth hung in the air. Her lips against his skin told him as much as her words did. She cared. They cared. About *him*. Not just the sub Ricky, not just the part he played. Something in him wanted to bolt for the door, run, to where he didn't know, but somewhere, anywhere, safe.

No. It was just a game. That's all it was. "I apologize, Mistress."

"Ricky, look at me."

That was Mistress Crystal. And he couldn't. She could punish him if she felt the need. It didn't matter. He couldn't let her see the tears in his eyes.

"Ricky."

Long, sharp nails raked slowly over his scalp, sending shivers of pleasure running through him. Soft lips kissed his eyelids, wicking away the trace of dampness they found there, tearing a sob from his throat.

"Richard."

"I apologize, Mistress. I ruined your scene. Please forgive me."

"Richard. *Look. At. Me.*"

And he did, because she demanded it of him, blinking rapidly to push back tears no man was allowed to shed. It was hard trying *not* to look directly at her, anyway. Her face was only inches from his.

"You didn't ruin anything, Richard. The scene went perfectly. But now the camera's turned off. What we've been doing's been pretty intense. Now it's time for some fun." She leaned in, closer still, and she kissed him. Not Mistress. Just Crystal. The woman. He froze for a moment, too stunned to respond. Then his mind shut down, and his body took over. He kissed her the way he'd wanted too, from the first moment he'd seen her looking at him, smiling, but not laughing at the picture he made, just smiling. And looking hotter than any woman had a right to.

Combing his fingers through her hair, he cupped her head and plundered her mouth with his tongue. She tasted like cool sweet tea on a hot summer's day, so good, so right, he couldn't get enough. He could wake up next to her every day for the rest of his life and he knew it would never be enough.

But then there was Ani, behind him, beautiful, tempting Ani, kissing his shoulder, his neck, her hands stroking, sweeping over and around him till she found his cock. Her touch made him so hard he wondered if he could come just from the feel of skin on skin. How could he ever see her as his secretary, knowing the mysteries that her man-cut suit disguised?

How could he give either of them up?

"You're thinking again, Ricky. You shouldn't do that."

"Mmmm," Crystal agreed, pulling away from his kiss. "You think entirely too much." She pushed him to his back, which should have rolled him on top of Ani, but somehow didn't. Probably because Ani was now kneeling beside them, slipping a condom down over his cock.

Some dim analytical part of his brain wondered why his ass wasn't on fire, scorched like the nine hells as it was, instead of merely burning with a dull ache, but whatever the thought had been escaped him as Crystal straddled his hips and lowered her tight, wet pussy onto his cock. "Oh, fuck," was the most coherent thing he could utter.

Smiling, Crystal held out her hand, guiding Ani to straddle his chest. Crystal wrapped her arms around Ani, hugging her, while they kissed for a moment over Ani's shoulder. Then Crystal's clever fingers found Ani's nipples.

Dear God. He'd never seen anything so blatantly erotic. Ricky lifted Ani, urging her to sit up higher over him, where he could tease her clit with the tip of his tongue. She obliged, falling forward over him doggy style while Crystal's fingers worked her nipples. Pulling Ani down, Ricky licked her slowly from the bottom of her labia to the tip of her clit. He flicked his tongue over her clit, teasing, then pulled her down hard, thrusting his tongue as deep into her hot, wet cunt as he could reach.

Moaning with need, Crystal slid up the length of his shaft and came back down hard, taking him balls deep as she ground against his pelvis. He slid a hand between Ani's ass and Crystal's thigh, working Crystal's clit as she rode him harder. Her tight, wet cunt gripped him hard, milking him as she came. Ani screamed as she bounced harder on his tongue, her hips driving wildly against him. He licked and sucked, meeting her thrust for erratic thrust as she came over his mouth.

The weight of the two of them slammed into him, scraping his burning ass into the carpet over and over again. Had he really thought the damaged skin didn't hurt? He was so wrong, on so many levels. He wanted to scream as the icy-hot erotic burn seeped through him, searing his raw nerves with exquisite pain.

Just when he thought he couldn't hold out any longer, Crystal rolled to the floor, her fist closing over his cock to strip off the condom she'd coated with her juices. Ani slid on a new one before she moved to kneel on all fours over Crystal's weeping pussy. Ani swept her hair back out of the way, giving him an unobstructed view as she sucked Crystal's clit between her lips.

That left him naked and alone, and hard as Crystal's plastic dong, with Ani's ass in the perfect position. Surely they hadn't meant for him to waste this condom. He knelt behind Ani, his poor abused buns finally free of the stinging carpet, reaching beneath Ani to guide his cock into her waiting pussy.

"Fuck, yes!" Ani screamed.

Crystal moaned, her nails biting deep into his hips. She pulled him down hard, as if his cock were thrusting through Ani right into her waiting cunt.

His balls pulled up, slapping against Ani in time to her thrusts into Crystal's waiting pussy with her tongue. His hands found Crystal's tits and milked them in rhythm to his thrusts. He should have come by now, had never lasted this long, but then he hadn't come so many times in so few hours since he'd been a teenager watching forbidden porn flicks in time to his own clumsy hand jobs.

Ani broke around him again, screaming in release as she came. He could feel her muscles working as she turned fingers and tongue to her best use against Crystal's exposed flesh. He wanted nothing more than to come, collapsing over the two sated women in blissful agony, before they had no further need of him and tossed him aside, but the harder he worked the farther away his own release seemed.

And then the women shifted again, this time with Ani on the bottom, sixty-nine to Crystal's pussy. That left Crystal's ass facing him. Ani handed him yet another condom, and the ever-present tube of lube.

Dear God in heaven. His balls felt like they might explode at the mere thought of his dick in Crystal's tight ass. He worked her carefully with his fingers and the lube, knowing better than to thrust in before she was ready. She opened to him willingly, her tight sphincter relaxing at his touch, moaning in pleasure at something, his fingers, Ani's tongue, what he couldn't be sure.

This weekend had been littered with firsts, and this was no exception. Never before had he felt the tight fist of a woman's anus sheathing his cock. "Oh, fuck, that's good," he moaned as he slowly slid in.

Below him Ani's lips captured his balls, sucking them one after the other into the warm cavern of her mouth. He jerked hard, burying himself to the hilt with one final push. Then Ani's hands were on his hips, urging him in and out in rapid jerks that matched her own undulating hips.

Crystal screamed -- he hoped it was from pleasure -- and he could feel the strength of her orgasm milking his cock in strong, insistent pulls. "Now!" Crystal ordered.

Whether she meant him or Ani didn't matter. His body reacted as if given the permission he'd needed. Long, hot gushes of cum pounded unrestricted from the base of his balls through the length of his cock. He roared out his release, thrusting wildly into Crystal's tight channel. Ani's nails dug into his tender ass and he screamed, shooting spurt after spurt into the condom.

Ani's hips bucked hard off the floor and Crystal came with her, holding her tightly as she lapped at her pussy. Ricky could smell the hot juices that spilled from both women. Slipping from her ass as he finally went soft, he pushed Crystal aside to lick Ani clean. Crystal pulled the condom off and ran a soft cloth over him, then pulled him back down between them. "Feeling better?" she laughed, pushing the hair back from his face.

"Yeah," he agreed.

"Definitely," Ani answered as well.

"Good." Crystal yawned and stretched. "Let's go get some lunch."

6:00 PM, Sunday, 11 February 2007
Charter Limo

"Park in the garage, Charlie."

In the garage? Not at the front door? Why?

"Yes, Mistress."

Was there a note of anticipation in the big chauffeur's voice? Ricky shuddered, remembering the way Charlie had eyed his backside. He hadn't given a lot of thought as to why Crystal had called for the limo at the time. Not when it meant full dress just to go riding through Central Park in search of a Coney Island Dog vender who hadn't already closed up shop for the day. They'd all been having too much fun.

Now, though, the thrill of being out in public faded. Crystal's plastic dong up his ass was one thing. She was the Mistress. Sharing him with Ani had its benefits, too. But Charlie…

Did he dare protest? All Mistress had done was ask Charlie -- tell Charlie -- to park in the garage. Perhaps there was nothing to worry about.

Before he could decide, Charlie pulled the limo into an extra large space that might very well have been lined off just for it. The big man held the door for them, then escorted them to the rear entrance and through the lobby. The doorman gave the women a too-friendly smile, then looked at Ricky a little more closely. "Evening, ladies," he offered politely.

"Evening, Gregory," the ladies responded. Ricky merely waved. He was too nervous to be sure his voice wouldn't crack like a twelve-year-old's.

"I was disappointed that you couldn't join us this morning, Charlie."

Charlie squirmed uncomfortably. "I go to church

with Molly every Sunday morning, Mistress."

Crystal studied the Viking, her slow perusal far from flattering. "I don't think you went to church this morning, Charlie. I think you watched fuck flicks till four AM and slept in till I called for you."

"No, Mistress."

"Molly answered the phone when I called earlier. You were still asleep. You lied to me, Charlie. That's a transgression that must be punished."

There are two kinds of pain. Erotic pain and punishment. You will do everything in your power to keep me from having to punish you. Punishment is not for your sexual enjoyment, and I assure you, you will not find my punishment enjoyable. Do you understand me?

Ricky could see he wasn't the only one who remembered that warning. Charlie dropped his gaze to the carpet. A fine bead of sweat stood out on the big man's forehead. "I apologize, Mistress. I overslept."

"What was the last instruction I gave you, Charlie?"

Charlie bit his bottom lip, as if to still its trembling. "Not to touch myself, Mistress."

Oh, good God. He'd been under an order prohibiting masturbation while he was driving the limo home last night? Amazing his dick hadn't fallen off.

"I tried, Mistress," Charlie whimpered. "Honest, I tried."

"We both know why Mistress Molly sent you to me, Charlie."

"Yes, Mistress."

"I'd hate to have to report to her that you failed. I'd feel like I failed, Charlie. And I don't like to fail."

"It is an honor and a privilege to serve you, Mistress Crystal, and I regret that I have disobeyed you. It will not happen again."

Who the hell was Mistress Molly and why had she sent this man to Crystal? Did Dommes regularly farm out their undisciplined subs? What sort of punishment would a Mistress like Crystal bestow on a man who'd both broken his vow against masturbation and then lied to her? One thing was for certain. Ricky was damn glad he wasn't the one who'd made such a blunder.

"Are you still wearing your cage?"

"Yes, Mistress. Mistress Molly will not allow me to take it off."

Oh God. She'd put a chastity cage on him? And then that ride with them in the limo last night? Somehow Ricky wasn't nearly as worried about Charlie and the direction of his gaze any more. Seemed like he was a whole lot better off than Charlie.

The elevator opened with its characteristic whoosh and Crystal waved her hand. "Wait for us in the dungeon, Charlie."

"Yes, Mistress." He sounded worried. Well, he had damn good reason to be worried…

"Ricky."

His attention snapped to Crystal. "Yes, Mistress!" Charlie be damned. He'd best look after his own hide.

"I want you to go to the leather room with Ani and change into something special for tonight."

Something special? Ricky blinked in surprise, but he knew better than to argue. "Yes, Mistress," he croaked out.

"Come to the dungeon as soon as you're dressed." With that she disappeared.

Did she mean for him to play the Inquisitor? Could he do that? Could he take a lash to Ani's tender backside?

Funny. Had anyone asked him a month ago what the worst outcome he could think of for this week was, he'd have said having someone he knew showing up at the auction. But then, he hadn't really known Ani a week ago.

He had to run to catch up with Ani as she hurried down the hall. "Ani, wait!" he called, keeping his voice pitched low so it wouldn't carry.

She looked over her shoulder, one eyebrow slightly raised.

"I don't think I can do this. I don't want to hurt you."

Ani laughed. "Not me. Charlie."

"Charlie?" he squeaked.

"Charlie is in really deep shit. Mistress Molly sent him to Crystal because she caught him cheating on her with his clients. Rather than making him give up the business -- I take it the limo service pays very well -- Molly loaned Charlie out to Crystal. Now he's broken the rules. Again."

"Oh, shit. Dumb bastard. What the fuck was he thinking?"

Ani laughed again. "Thinking is not one of the things Charlie is best at."

No shit. "Ani?"

She glanced back again.

"Who's Scott?"

"My bastard ex-husband. He ran off with a bubble-headed bimbo with big tits."

"Idiot," Ricky snorted. "Give me a smart woman any day over one with big tits. Your tits are perfect."

Ani stopped in her tracks, wrapped her arms around him and kissed him full on the mouth. She tasted like ketchup and mustard and possibilities. He closed his eyes for a moment and dared to hope.

"You're one special man, Richard. When I saw you up on that stage, all I could think about was making you miserable. Now all I can think about is making you mine."

He opened his eyes and gently nipped her lower lip. "When this week's over it's going to kill me to go home."

Ani bit him back. Harder. "Somehow I don't think either of us will be leaving at the end of the week. But that's for Crystal to say." She swatted his ass. "Stop distracting me. We have a man to flog."

It was not, Ricky decided, a good day to be Charlie.

6:30 PM, Sunday, 11 February 2007
The Grande Inquisition
Bishop Stuart's Dungeon

A sharp crack rent the still of the dungeon. Charlie, who knelt naked at Crystal's feet, jumped as if she'd struck him. But then, from that position, he hadn't seen the whip Crystal popped against the calf of her leather boot. "Welcome to Mistress Crystal's Dungeon. I do hope you're not foolish enough to be late." Crystal turned a chilling smile to the camera.

"I am the Grand Inquisitor, Bishop Stuart. As you should remember, our prisoner, Mr. Scott, has confessed to heinous and foul acts of sexual perversion. Unfortunately for him, Mr. Scott has not yet revealed the identities of his accomplices. Mistress Ani, please secure the prisoner to the rack."

Ricky risked raising his head enough to see what was going on. In a weird déjà vu, Ani led the masked but otherwise naked Mr. Scott to a large wooden cross shaped like an X in brackets and set in a pivoting suspension base. Devious piece of furniture. The way it pivoted through the reinforced center it would offer full access to the prisoner's ass or pussy as well as his or her head once it was flipped horizontal. Or you could flip it till he hung upside down, or any other angle... like a spider's victim, caught in a swaying web.

Ani secured the prisoner by his ankles, then unlocked the frame and lowered the head end so she could reach his wrists, stretching him out spread eagle. Pivoting him flat, she locked the frame in place again. She circled the cross, inspecting her work. When she was sure he passed inspection, Ani took a moment to lick the prisoner's left nipple, sucking it until it poked out in a hard peak. With no warning she snapped a small butterfly clamp over the protruding bud. Charlie bucked so hard the cross shook in its frame. She draped the chain attached to the clamp low across his belly. With a slow, deliberate stride, designed, he was sure, to drive the poor victim mad with anticipation, Ani circled the rack. She threaded the chain through the ring in Charlie's cock cage and measured it for a close fit before she approached the other nipple. It was ready for her, stabbing out as far as the first one had, despite her lack of attention. Still, Ani took a moment to suck the delicate flesh, making a show of her teeth on his skin for the camera.

Despite the show designed to draw his attention upward, Ricky found his gaze drawn to the prisoner's prick. Chastity device indeed. The poor man's cock was stuffed in an acrylic cage, held in place by an acrylic ring that snapped shut behind his balls and secured at the tip by a Prince Albert piercing.

Not only was there absolutely no way he could masturbate, but Ricky wasn't even sure the man could pee. At least not standing up. A small plastic security tag held it shut. Even without a lock it would have been hard to remove. Locked, the thing wasn't going anywhere. And the tag, though possibly breakable, was printed with a visible serial number.

That ought to teach the bastard to keep his dick in his pants. Any man who was stupid enough to screw around on his Mistress deserved whatever punishment she could think up.

On the other hand, maybe Charlie was into punishment. Maybe he wanted to get caught. But even if he was into pain and punishment, he couldn't have known Mistress Molly would turn him over to Crystal to be featured on Internet pay-per-view.

Charlie screeched in agony. Ricky glanced back in time to see Ani twisting the nipple clamp. Oh God. That had to hurt like hell. His cock leaped to full attention.

Signaling Ricky to stay where he was, Bishop Stuart circled the cross, inspecting Ani's work. "Who were your accomplices, Mr. Scott?" She carried a single taper candle in a pewter bowl with a handle on one side. Ricky eyed the thing suspiciously, but for the moment, at least, it appeared she meant only to use it as a period prop.

"I acted alone, Mistress," Charlie answered. "Bishop. I regret my transgressions, and wish to atone for my actions."

Ricky snorted. Dumb bastard. He had yet to learn the meaning of regret. "What is the prisoner's sentence, Bishop?" Ani asked.

"The prisoner is to be tested by the trial of three. Start with the cane. Ten lashes."

Ten lashes? He'd gotten three times that last session. His ass still stung when the rough leather chaps rubbed him the wrong way. And what was the trial of three?

Ani retrieved a length of bamboo about three feet long from the seemingly limitless collection of toys and implements on the wall. "I don't believe you're at all repentant, Mr. Scott. I think if we let you go you would continue your perversions unchecked. I intend to see to it that you'll remember this punishment, and learn from your transgressions." She cracked her cane over the sole of the prisoner's right foot.

Ricky could see him biting his lip, trying to hold in the pain. "Count the strokes," Crystal ordered, and Ricky grinned, surprised to find he felt more than a little malice toward the man.

"Yes, Bishop. One, Mistress. Thank you, Mistress, may I have --"

Ani struck again before he'd finished his request, this time to the left.

Charlie screamed. Ani waited patiently. Ricky felt his cock getting so hard he wondered if he might come just from watching a man get beaten. Damn. He must be some kind of sick pervert.

Charlie's tortured little prick was so hard inside its plastic cage that the bars made deep dents in his swollen flesh. And each time it jumped, it pulled on the nipple clamps. "Two, Mistress. Thank you, Mistress, may I have another."

Crack!

Charlie's hips bucked up off of the table. "Three, Mistress…"

Richard tuned them out to watch Mistress Crystal. She stood just out of the camera shot now. Her black barrister's robes had fallen open and her finger stroked over her clit. He could see her nipples calling out for attention.

"Mistress?" he whispered.

Crystal reached out a hand to him, pulling him gently to his feet. Moving to stand behind her, Richard reached around with both hands to stroke her breasts, pulling her back against his chest. She spread her legs slightly, riding his cock without letting him penetrate her. "Please, Mistress," he whispered, too low for the mike to pick up, "may I have another."

She ground her ass against the root of his cock, moaning softly when he pinched her nipples. "You like watching as much as he likes the pain, don't you, Mistress."

Crystal laughed. "Maybe."

Ani applied the final swat with her cane. The soles of Charlie's feet had turned a bright, blistering red. Stalking back on set, Crystal stopped next to Ani and pulled her in for a kiss, hard and heavy and directly in the prisoner's line of sight. "Your penance has just begun," she announced. She nodded her head to Ricky. "The second trial will be ice."

Ricky hurried to bring her the ice bucket Ani had had him fill and carry down. He'd wondered if Crystal was planning to serve champagne, but now he suspected she was up to something far more devious. Crystal took the antique ice bucket and tapped the floor with her toe. "Assume the position."

Ricky dropped to his knees, his ass exposed as he lowered his forehead, hands clasped behind his back. His cock was so hard he had to spread his knees more than he should have, but Mistress didn't seem to mind.

The chunks were half moon shaped, long and thin, ideal for... exactly what Ani must have envisioned them for -- rimming the prisoner's tight little asshole with the tip. As the first drops of frigid water started to drip down Charlie's cheeks, Crystal pushed the thin chunk through the tight hole until it disappeared. The prisoner's hips jerked wildly in a parody of what might have been a fight for sexual release, his cries muffled against Ani's pussy. Crystal took another ice cube in each hand and ran them slowly over his ball sac.

Ricky moaned at the sight, having totally forgotten he was supposed to have his head tucked to the floor. His cock ached so badly it was all he could do not to seek some form of relief.

"Executioner."

Executioner? She meant him. Ricky's gaze jerked from the tortured prisoner to Crystal's face, mortified that he'd been caught watching.

Crystal didn't look pissed. In fact her smile looked so devious he was even more worried than if she'd been angry with him. She handed him a condom. For a moment he thought she was going to let him fuck her. Or even Charlie. But apparently she had something else in mind. "Do you enjoy watching us torture the prisoner?"

"Yes, Mistress," he admitted. Whether he should have been watching or not was not the point. Lying to his Mistress was far worse than watching her work.

"Stand up, Executioner. I want you to show the prisoner what he's missing. What he's going to be missing until his Mistress decides to remove his cage."

Ricky scrambled to his feet. Show… Masturbate? She wanted him to masturbate, on camera? With Charlie watching? Could he?

Ani knelt before Crystal, spread her nether lips wide, and began licking her pussy. Ricky swallowed a groan.

"Please, Mistress," Charlie moaned. "I need relief!"

Ricky smiled, unrolling the condom over his rigid cock. Yeah. He could do this. Especially with Charlie watching.

With slow, measured strokes he pumped his hand over his cock, rocking his hips as the pleasure began to build. This was going to be good. So good. With his free hand he cupped his balls, rolling them slowly, with just the right pressure. Charlie's moan kept time to his rocking hips.

Pushing Ani's head down, Crystal picked up the burning taper from the side table. "Trial by fire." With deliberate care she poured the hot wax from its dish in a thin line from the prisoner's sternum to his crotch.

Charlie twisted madly, testing the strength of his restraints, but they refused to give. Every movement tugged on the nipple chains that now seesawed back and forth across the hot wax. Ricky squeezed his cock hard at the base, trying to delay an orgasm that threatened with every jerk of the prisoner's cock.

"Executioner."

Oh God. If she asked him to stop now…

Ani was lapping Crystal's pussy again. Ricky squeezed harder, trying to maintain control.

"Executioner, you will fuck the prisoner's ass."

Who was he to argue with his Mistress? Crystal's side table provided the necessary lube. Ricky took his time slicking his cock and Charlie's ass, no longer caring about the camera that might or might not really be on. Better if it was. Maybe some other poor bastard would learn to keep his dick in his pants.

"Oh, God," Charlie moaned. "Fuck me! Please, Master!"

And he did. With little ceremony, Ricky sheathed his cock in Charlie's tight ass, pushing in until his cockhead buried itself against the melting ice cubes. Oh, fuck. He'd nearly forgotten the ice. He jerked back out, as if his cock had been burnt, only to ram back in, stroke after stroke, burning heat against icy hot cold, burying himself until his balls slapped against flesh, pistoning his hips madly in an aching need for release.

"Oh God. Harder. Fuck me harder!" Charlie moaned. His hips lifted rhythmically, reaching for a release the cock cage would not allow.

Tight, hot flesh coated with trickling ice water licked his cock. Crystal's cries of release filled the room. Ani's cries soon joined her. With a roar, Ricky emptied his balls into the condom in wave after wave of blazing release.

"Please, help me, I can't come," Charlie sobbed, jerking his hips desperately.

"There are two kinds of pain," Ricky repeated. "Erotic pain, and punishment. Punishment is not for your sexual enjoyment. You will learn to do everything in your power to keep your Mistress from having to punish you."

"Please, Master. I swear never to violate my Mistress's trust again."

"You'd fuck anyone in this room if we let you, wouldn't you, Mr. Scott," Crystal accused. "With or without your Mistress's permission."

"Yes, Mistress," Charlie sobbed. "I am unworthy. I deserve to be punished."

Crystal eyed the blubbering fool with a sneer of disgust. "You have failed your test, Mr. Scott. I shall remand you to Mistress Molly's custody, to deal with as she sees fit."

The curtain around the corner booth opened, and a woman who looked a great deal like Crystal, a bit shorter, perhaps, with man-cropped sable hair, stepped out, popping a leather bat against her boot. "Thank you, Bishop. I assure you, the prisoner will repent."

Pieces fell together. Starting with the pile of cash Crystal had passed to the limo driver that first night. Molly's share of the revenue, or a sister's way of helping out, it really didn't matter. Molly was family.

Which meant Charlie was, too.

Molly had probably had a hand in orchestrating the entire scene.

"Mistress," Charlie sobbed. "Forgive me, Mistress. I will not disobey you again."

Molly's smile was not a pretty thing to behold. "You are so right, Mr. Scott."

Her back to the camera, Crystal wiggled the

remote. Molly shook her head slightly, no more than a twitch of her chin. "I'm sure our audience will enjoy watching Mr. Scott suffer." She unlocked the cross and flipped him upside down. "Your punishment has only just begun, Mr. Scott."

Crystal slipped Molly the remote and led her merry band to the door.

A loud thwack sounded behind them. Charlie's voice faded away as they left the dungeon. "One, Mistress. Thank you, Mistress. May I have another?"

3:50 PM, Wednesday, 30 May 2007
Brasden-Marten Agency
Midtown Manhattan
Four Months Later

Richard looked up as Ani stuck her head in the office door. She was dressed in a finely tailored man-cut suit, and looking as hot as ever. His breath caught at the sight of her, remembering her naked and spread before him like a human buffet. He swallowed the wave of lust she always called forth, keeping his tone professional, businesslike. "Yes, Ani?"

She smiled, just a little, as if reading his mind. "Crystal just called. We're having a cookout on the roof tomorrow night. Gave me a shopping list. I called for the limo to pick us up at 4:30."

Oh God. He had such a hard time keeping a straight face around Charlie. "Thank you," Richard managed aloud.

"Dinner for nine. We're having company."

Nine? Oh shit. Richard shifted his legs a little, making room for the erection that hit whenever Crystal thought of a new adventure.

"Don't get too excited. Her sister Molly's coming over, with Charlie, of course, and their parents."

"That's seven. Who…"

Shit. He knew who. So much for enjoyment. Torture time.

"Your parents," Ani confirmed, doing her best to hide her smirk. "Crystal says you get to give them the tour of the condo."

Shit, piss, fuck. He'd known this was coming, ever since they'd moved in. How on earth was he going to explain that locked door?

That room? Oh, I don't go in there. That's Crystal's…

office. She works out of the house. Computer stuff. I don't know all that much about it. But apparently it pays well…

Shelby Morgen

Shelby Morgen loves writing offbeat tales that defy as many rules as possible.

She likes chocolate with her peanut butter, suspense with her romance, and kink with her sex, and she's always had a hard time keeping murder, motorcycles, science fiction, fantasy and paranormal from mixing with her kink.

Shelby shares her belief in electronic publishing with her longtime friend and partner, Bill, her husband of more than four decades.

Shelby at Changeling: changelingpress.com/shelby-morgen-a-21

Changeling Press LLC

Contemporary Action Adventure, Sci-Fi, Steampunk, Dark Fantasy, Urban Fantasy, Paranormal, and BDSM Romance available in e-book, audio, and print format at ChangelingPress.com – MC Romance, Werewolves, Vampires, Dragons, Shapeshifters and Horror -- Tales from the edge of your imagination.

Where can I get Changeling Press Books?

Changeling Press e-books are available at ChangelingPress.com, Amazon, Apple Books, Barnes & Noble, Kobo, Smashwords, and other online retailers, including Everand Subscription and Kobo Subscription Services. Print books are available at Amazon, Barnes and Noble, and by ISBN special order through your local bookstores.

ChangelingPress.com